Selected Reader Comments

"Temple Grandin gave us the poignant metaphor – *'an anthropologist on Mars.'* In this book, Robert Sanders brings us to the archeological dig!"
Diane Twachtman-Cullen, Ph.D.(executive director, ADDCON Center)
Higganum, Connecticut, October 2003

"Robert Sanders is a gentleman with remarkable intelligence and insight. He uses these abilities to explain the world from his perspective, and his experiences and wisdom will be of benefit to parents, professionals, and people with Asperger's syndrome."
Tony Attwood, Ph.D.
Author of *Asperger's Syndrome: A Guide for Parents and Professionals*
Brisbane, Queensland, Australia, July 2004

"Through this unusually fascinating and insightful look into how a person with Asperger's syndrome perceives his interactions with others, Robert shows – piece by hard-earned piece – how he continues to expand into, and make greater sense of the world around him. Anyone interested in learning more about life on the autism spectrum should read this book."
Stephen Shore
Board president of the Asperger's Association of New England
Author of: *Beyond the Wall: Personal Experiences with Autism and Asperger Syndrome*
Editor of: *Ask and Tell: Self-advocacy and Disclosure for People on the Autism Spectrum*
Boston, Massachusetts, August 2004

"Every now and then you may be lucky to come across a work such as this. It's a very honest, sometimes painfully honest account of one man's struggle to live in a world that is almost too alien to bear. The insights into the journey of overcoming Asperger's syndrome, sometimes sublime into the spiritual – to the very ordinary, are an inspiration. This is a must read! Whether your interest is professional or just understanding the human condition. You really do feel that you are walking with him every step of the way."
Martin A. Enticknap, (good friend and literary contact)
Isle of Sanday, Orkney Islands, Scotland, January 2003

On My Own Terms: My Journey with Asperger's
is also available in **Spanish**. (disponible en **español**)
con el título:
En Mis Propios Términos: Mi Jornada con Asperger's

Este libro importante es una historia autobiográfica que retrata de la vida de una persona con el síndrome de Asperger's, el tipo suave de autismo de alto funcionamiento. Roberto Sanders, quien tenía rasgos autísticos cuando era niño, ha sobretriunfado muchos obstáculos para vivir una vida razonable normal. Él tiene un título en ingeniero eléctrico, y se ha ocupado con proyectos de construcción, carpintería y pintura. También es un autor y ha escrito varios libros, entre ellos tres novelas de ciencia ficción y una novela de un americano en México. Viaja extensamente y disfruta irse de paseo en bicicleta, caminar, y tomar fotos. Sus luchas, pero también sus éxitos, están presentados, acompañados de anécdotas, experiencias personales, discernimientos, ideas únicas, y soluciones. Este libro fue escrito para dar esperanza y estímulo a todos lectores, que los con el síndrome de Asperger's también pueden sobretriunfar sus obstáculos.

ON MY OWN TERMS:
My Journey with Asperger's

written by
Robert S. Sanders, Jr.
© 2004

with Forewords by
Diane Twachtman-Cullen, Ph.D.
and
Murphy M. Thomas, Ph.D.

Publisher's note:

This important book, with the intent of helping others, is an anecdotal overview portraying the life of a person with Asperger's syndrome, a high functioning and mild form of autism. The author, who had autistic traits as a child, has successfully overcome numerous obstacles to lead a reasonably normal life. He holds a degree in Electrical Engineering, and he has occupied himself with construction projects, carpentry and painting. He is now an author and has written several books, among them three science fiction novels, and a novel about an American in Mexico. He travels extensively and enjoys bicycling and hiking.

Various experiences of his life are presented from childhood to the present, and most of them bear certain qualities and characteristics of Asperger's syndrome. Other important topics and difficulties related to autism are discussed, such as: childhood idiosyncrasies, obsessions and worries, dwelling on subjects, strong convictions, expecting friendships to continue, collecting things, plus other subjects and ideas. There are several anecdotes that point out some bizarre incidents in his life, along with stories that reveal some of the unique and important projects he has accomplished.

Also discussed are possible causes of autism, whether they be from genetic inheritance, out of balance brain chemistries, or even from heavy metals. Some unique and original solutions including insights are also covered. The author feels that triumph is a process that we go through as we begin the journey to explore new ideas and concepts.

Forewords by
Diane Twachtman-Cullen, Ph.D.
and
Murphy M. Thomas, Ph.D.

proofing and editorial assistance by
Diane Twachtman-Cullen, Ph.D.

disclaimer:
Some names of people and/or places have been changed and/or deleted to
protect identities.

color cover photo taken by
Robert S. Sanders, Jr.
copyright © July 1997 by Robert S. Sanders, Jr.

color cover illustration for *Overcoming Asperger's* created by
Martin A. Enticknap
copyright © May 2002 by Martin A. Enticknap

Library of Congress Control Number: 2004095767

ISBN: 1-928798-06-3

type: psychology/autism

Armstrong Valley Publishing Co.
P.O. Box 1275
Murfreesboro, TN 37133-1275

printed in the United States of America

TABLE OF CONTENTS

Reincarnation? Inexperienced Souls?
Alternate Realities, Parallel Universes
Coincidences in General
Mind Is All One

cover photo: taken by Robert S. Sanders, Jr., July 1997
View looking north along the ridge of Sierra Bustamante and of the Lion's
Head Mountain, elev. 1,860 meters (6,100 feet), near Bustamante, Nuevo
León, Mexico.
photo copyright © 1997 by Robert S. Sanders, Jr.

symbolism behind the photo:

The deep drop-off on the lower left represents the fear and dark void
that Asperger's syndrome gives to so many people. It is a constant
reminder to those of us with Asperger's. The journey north along the ridge
to the peak of the Lion's Head Mountain is symbolic of the journey
through life. The scenery in the photograph is spectacular and is symbolic
to how life appears beautiful and breathtaking at a glance. However, life
has its ups and downs along the way, as the ridge clearly shows. It's an
arduous trek, treacherous in many places, as one has to pick his way
around thick undergrowth, constantly dodging the spikes and thorns of
Lechuguilla, Nopal, and Maguey plants. There are difficult rock ledges
and gaps to cross along the way, as well. All of these symbolize obstacles
and struggles as we live our lives, as we make friends which isn't always
easy, and as we achieve our goals. Reaching the Lion's Head Mountain is
symbolic of reaching triumph.

Acknowledgments

Acknowledgment goes to my parents who raised me and who have inspired me to write this book about Asperger's syndrome and autism. They have cared about me and my well being, and I appreciate their support in various ways, including their resources of knowledge for use in this compilation. Thanks to their love and support, I have had the time and inspiration to write several novels and now this book.

Acknowledgment goes to Murphy M. Thomas, Ph.D. for the excellent and impressive Foreword that he wrote for this book. I am also grateful to him for his psychological counseling and advice to my parents and me during my early childhood.

Acknowledgment goes to the people of Starfish Specialty Press for their belief in this project and for their help in bringing this new version of my book into reality. I particularly want to thank Diane Twachtman-Cullen, Ph.D. for her editing and organizational assistance, for her professional input in many steps along the way, and for her excellent Foreword.

Acknowledgment also goes to Martin A. Enticknap for his computer generated cover image artwork for the 2002 original edition of this book, for his numerous conversations with me pertaining to philosophy and human characteristics, and for his proofreading the manuscript of that original edition, including his ideas and input, some of which I have included in this epistle. Martin is the author of two books: *EXODUS: the Dolph/in Saga* and *Arc of the Ancients and Other Poetry*.

FOREWORD BY:
Diane Twachtman-Cullen, Ph.D.

I never thought that I would find myself in this particular place – writing a foreword for *On My Own Terms: My Journey with Asperger's*. It is not because I do not believe in this book, for surely I do. It is simply that the publishing company that I share with my two children was slated to publish this book, and under that circumstance, a foreword by me would have been inappropriate, if not self-serving. I had mixed emotions about not being able to write about this book because there was much that I wanted to say about its metamorphosis from an earlier version to its present expanded and revised form. All of that has changed, however, because as the "fates" would have it, both Robert and I are free agents, so to speak – he, free to publish his book on his own terms, and I, free to share my thoughts with its readers. And lest you wonder, our free agency status was arrived at mutually and amicably. Hence, the very good news is that I am now able to extol the virtues of this gem of a book, without fear of conflict of interest.

To say that I know this book from the inside out is no understatement, for I have read it countless times at all of its various stages. Temple Grandin gave us the poignant and revealing metaphor, *an anthropologist on Mars*. In the pages of this simple but profoundly important book, Robert takes us to the archeological dig. The reader will share with him his personal struggle to carve out a place for himself in a world that is often inhospitable to his way of thinking and being. You will feel the pain of his rejections, the triumph of his successes, and most of all, you will come to appreciate the strength of his convictions.

Make no mistake about it. Robert's convictions are rock solid. For example, in his book he states, "I knew from age six that I would never smoke, drink, or do drugs." Those of us who have the dubious distinction of being neurotypical (NT) have undoubtedly made several such declarations, only to modify our views with age and circumstances. Not Robert. Indeed, he declares – and in my opinion rightfully so in this case – that, "If my strong convictions, and my refusal to revise them, have anything to do with my being an Aspergers, then I am grateful for that aspect of the condition." That's another thing that comes through loud and clear in this book: Remarkably perhaps in the eyes of NTs, Robert has no desire to be cured of being an Aspergers, for he knows that that would mean that he would have to be "cured" of being himself, for the Asperger's is very much a part of who Robert is.

This book is replete with fascinating glimpses into Robert's thinking. In the section entitled *Anecdotes and Bizarre Stories*, he invites the reader to step into his shoes as he deals with incident after incident that most NTs would trivialize, but that loom large in Robert's mind. More importantly, he helps us to look behind the behavior exhibited to the underlying thought processes that motivated it. You will also see on display throughout this book the embodiment of two of

Robert's rules – that certain words are to be spelled in certain ways, regardless of the *preferred* spelling cited in *Webster's* (e.g., dialling, travelling), and that the names of all trees must be capitalized, in deference to Robert's reverence for nature.

It is on the subject of interpersonal relationships, however, that Robert's book really soars, for it is here that he shares with the reader his struggles to form lasting friendships. He begins his quest from the unlikely premise that ideal friendships can and do exist. He describes these as relationships in which there is "100% peace, love, trust, and honest friendship." Most NTs would likely consider Robert's standard to be unrealistic and unattainable, and as such, in need of modification. Robert, however, is uncompromising in his adherence to the standard he has set, even in the face of disappointment and frustration. Interestingly, when viewed from Robert's perspective as an individual with Asperger's syndrome, the reader will be hard-pressed not to realize that his standard is one that is more likely to be actualized in the Asperger community, where deception, deceit, and lying are virtual strangers, than it is in the world-at-large.

In a particularly poignant and deeply moving passage, Robert encapsulates his quest for friends and the elusiveness and uncomprehending nature of his pursuit in heartbreakingly palpable terms. He states:

"So many times I've seen fellow friends hiking together down a trail, camping together, enjoying their friendship, so easily, so smoothly. How do they do that so easily? How do they go hiking and traveling together so easily? What they do so easily has been seemingly nearly impossible for me." (p.82)

This passage gives one the rarest of glimpses into just how difficult it is for some individuals with Asperger's syndrome to understand and negotiate the world of interpersonal relationships which so many NTs take for granted. It also gives insight into the Asperger individual's desire for friends, a yearning that often goes unrecognized and unrequited in the neurotypical community. That Robert continually returns to the subject of friendships is testimony to the degree of importance it holds for him.

This book has much to offer its readers. The ASD community will find Robert's affirmation of the positive side of Asperger's most welcome. Parents and other family members will not only gain understanding into the condition, but also find hopeful the promise of independence and fulfillment that the example of Robert's life demonstrates. Professionals will gain understanding and valuable insight into Asperger's syndrome, from the inside out. I have gained all of these things from this book, and one thing more – deep respect for a man who has indeed carved out a meaningful, productive, and well-lived life for himself.

Suffice it to say, if you thought *On My Own Terms: My Journey with Asperger's* was just another book about one man's personal odyssey that you would bear witness to as a bystander, fasten your seat belt. You're in for a great ride on a most enlightening journey into the fascinating inner world of Asperger's syndrome.

FOREWORD BY:
Murphy M. Thomas, Ph.D.

I feel greatly honored to write this Foreword for Robert Sanders' book: *On My Own Terms: My Journey with Asperger's*. Back a generation ago in the early 1970s, Robert's parents brought him to me several times for consultation. They were very concerned for him because he was nonverbal in Kindergarten and displayed a variety of aberrant behavior patterns. His first attempt at first grade was a disaster. At the time, I was working with the county guidance center. Robert was transferred to a different school, and thanks to the cooperation of his new teachers who allowed us to monitor his behavior, things greatly improved, and he became much better adjusted. In consideration of Robert's behavior and characteristics during his childhood, he would have been diagnosed (in today's terminology) with Asperger's syndrome.

This non-fiction book, like Robert Sanders' books of fiction, is about a journey, a trip or a saga. While his novels are about his treks to Mexico, Australia, the British Isles, to points in the American landscape, or even to outer space, *On My Own Terms* is a book that recounts Robert's journey to *inner* space. He describes a phenomenological geography, the valleys of hurt, rejection, despair, and the peeks of hope. This is a book about courage, about single-minded determination and persistence. It is about blazing personal paths, while being guided only by a clear sense of right and wrong. This is a book about integrity.

The term "Asperger's" in the title may deceive one to believe that this journey will take us to strange places, to a foreign land of autistic preoccupations. Instead, this narrative is about the commonplace, yet it describes a heroic figure on a quest to connect and communicate, to become fully human. Robert's struggles are our struggles. We all seek to understand ourselves and connect with others. We all seek to be understood and to be valued. We all strive to live a productive, meaningful and moral life. Through the lens of Asperger's, Robert seems to have a sharper focus on what is essential, and a keener sense of what is right and wrong. He is guided, or compelled, to follow an impeccable path. We pay psychotherapists thousands of dollars to gain such vision and courage. Yet, Robert's exquisite sensitivities cut both ways; and he reminds us of the pain, disappointment and tragedy that exist in all of our lives.

On My Own Terms is a <u>must read</u> for mental health and teaching "professionals." You will laugh, you will cry. If you are honest, you will see yourself, and the limitations (even dangers) of what we do. You will see our personal and professional foibles, and what we need to learn. You will be humbled, brought back to earth, less arrogant. You will no longer be able to smugly diagnose, medicate, educate or modify symptoms. You will be inspired to listen with more respect, to trust in and join with others (our clients, their families, and the caring community), and to appreciate the complexity and paradoxical nature of the human condition.

Also, this is a <u>must read</u> for family, friends, neighbors, even bus drivers, shop keepers – for all of us who are perplexed by or fear diversity. In a simple but elegant way, Robert opens a window for us to appreciate what is so difficult to understand. In his stories, we will recognize our prejudices, how we define people in terms of their differences rather than their strengths, how we hurt others, how ignorance breeds fear and estrangement; yet his accounts reveal how *similar* we are to those whom we distance as being different, and how those with unusual perspectives and standards can challenge and enrich our lives. In a poignant but non-judgmental way, Robert helps us see the best and the worst qualities of the human spirit. In the process, Robert reminds us of the value of community, the importance of acceptance, and the power of love.

This is an inspiring and delightful book. It is filled with hope and good cheer. It is naively straightforward and honest. It cuts to the heart. This book is primarily a testament to the power of parental love, the value of friendships, the importance of community, and to the innate strength and wisdom of those who we have labeled as handicapped.

Murphy M. Thomas, Ph.D.
clinical and consulting psychologist
Murfreesboro, Tennessee
August 2002

A NOTE FROM MY FATHER

Robert was a healthy, pleasant, responsive, affectionate toddler until, at age two and a half, he drifted away from us, into the shell of apparent autism. He regressed into being essentially nonverbal, moderately unresponsive, and untouchable. He was a head banger, cried at certain noises (jet airplanes, big trucks, his one and only barber shop haircut). We were puzzled and alarmed. His growth and development seemed otherwise normal. He was curious, tirelessly worked jigsaw puzzles, and he rode his rocking horse for long periods, while looking straight through you.

Evaluations by audiologists and my colleagues in pediatrics, psychology, and psychiatry suggested he was "too bright and too well coordinated" to be autistic. His disorder was labeled "adjustment reaction to childhood." This was twenty-five years before the high functioning section of the autism spectrum (Asperger's syndrome) was a recognized entity.

We were indeed fortunate that a new psychologist, Murphy M. Thomas, Ph.D., moved to Murfreesboro. He and the county guidance center, along with a behavior modification team from a local university, intervened during Robert's second year of kindergarten. Dr. Thomas guided him in and out of an initial and difficult first grade and structured his transfer into another public school with a special education program and kind, caring teachers who were helpful, patient and cooperative.

Robert made great strides in the third grade, thanks to the expertise of another kind and very competent teacher. He became an excellent student, graduating from high school as salutatorian, with awards in Spanish, electronics, geometry, advanced math, and the 4.0 Science award. He received a presidential work scholarship to Tennessee Technological University, and he graduated with a degree in electrical engineering.

In this book, Robert graphically describes his life, his accomplishments, and his struggles with negotiations, interpersonal relationships, and with making friends.

Robert lives in a separate house on our farm in middle Tennessee. He is a writer, carpenter, painter, and an intrepid traveller. He is a collector of rocks, fossils, books, telephones, station wagons, and a variety of trees and wildflowers. His journals and splendid photographs attest to his reverence for nature and the wilderness.

In more recent years, he has collected (as gifts) bicycles, used appliances, kitchen sinks, computers, and lumber to take to Mexico. We sometimes call him the "Gringo Santa."

Despite his many strengths, the norms of socialization, conformity, and empathy have continued to be difficult for him and puzzling for us. He has ongoing episodes of sensory overload, and at times he has been obsessed with the compulsion of completing projects. The latter has been as asset, especially in compiling genealogies and four family photo albums, each over 100 pages, copies of which were distributed to and greatly appreciated by all members of the family. Some fetishes persist, such as using only rotary dial phones in his home, and driving cars only with manual transmissions.

It was not until Robert was twenty-eight that Dr. Oliver Sacks' remarkable article "An Anthropologist on Mars" appeared in *The New Yorker Magazine* (December 1993/January 1994). The similarities to Temple Grandin were striking – a jolt of enlightenment and a reassuring relief to finally better understand Robert's life of feeling "different."

My wife, Pat, and I are very proud of our son. He has indeed overcome so much. We are also obliged to the community of wonderful teachers and counselors who shepherded his school years, and to family and friends who were supportive along the way. We especially appreciate Dr. Murphy M. Thomas for his continuing guidance and for his Foreword in this book.

Robert S. Sanders, MD, FAAP
August 2002

INTRODUCTION

Asperger's syndrome is considered an autism spectrum disorder. I consider it to be a mild form of autism. Asperger's syndrome affects brain functioning, and occurs in a significant percentage of the human population. Until recently, it received little or no attention or consideration. There is no single cause for it. Autism can affect the ability to develop normal emotional stability and coordination when associating with others. Many autistics also have abnormal behavior patterns, and some of them are aloof. Some individuals with autism are very structured in their routines and mannerisms, while others have high levels of awareness and perceptions. One could say that people with autism operate by a different set of codes. It is sometimes difficult for autistics and those with Asperger's to recognize certain social cues, especially subtle ones, such as eye movements and body language, most of which are taken for granted by people without autism. Difficulty with these things leads to having problems with communication and establishing and maintaining relationships in life. People with autism can be helped through training and therapy. There are solutions that can really help them along and bring them out of their world and more into ours.

Sometimes autism is inherited genetically. Other times, it may be caused by out-of-balance brain chemistries, food allergies, or yeast buildup. These cases may be treated by monitoring food intake and/or vitamins, minerals, and other supplements or medications. There are those who feel that heavy metal poisoning from elements such as lead, mercury, aluminum, arsenic, cadmium, and thallium, may also cause autism. Intravenous and oral types of chelation therapy have been used for removing heavy metal toxins in some individuals. However this approach is very controversial.

My autistic traits began during my early childhood. As I grew up, many of my more obvious autistic traits fell by the wayside. However, some residual characteristics stayed with me, such as my sensitivities to sounds, perfumes, camera flashes, and smoke, and my sometimes being naïve.

Making friends was never all that difficult for me, but sometimes keeping those friendships was seemingly a feat beyond my capabilities. While easy for people without autism, it has been difficult at times, for me to know how to read and recognize a true friendship. This is due to the fact that many autistics and Aspergers don't always understand the social expectations of the other person. It is difficult for us to perceive when the other person is tiring of the friendship or becoming bored, or even that the friendship is wearing out or deteriorating.

I also think that making and keeping friends is made more difficult because autism and Asperger's syndrome are conditions that are not very well understood. To most people, autism is like a void or vacuum, and people's worst fears – rather than their understanding and compassion – tend to fill that void. Because of my traits, some people are afraid to associate with me. Maybe they perceive me as a person of extremely high expectations and standards, and they are scared off. People shy away from autistics and Aspergers because they don't understand them. They are afraid of them and can't figure them out. This book helps to give a human face or, you might say, a frame of reference to the characteristics of autistics and Aspergers, in hopes that those who are fearful of people with these conditions might become more understanding and accepting. Even in face of this, there are some friends with whom I have gotten along fine. They have stayed my friends, bless their souls, and I appreciate them. My friendships with those people are success stories.

During my adolescence, I never saw myself as handicapped, and I believe that was to my benefit. Asperger's syndrome is not an illness. It is merely a different template for living. Those who have Asperger's also have a different set of codes to work with as they adapt themselves to life's situations. They have a different way of approaching things, and one might say they take a different and sometimes more difficult road to arrive at the same destination. When you have Asperger's syndrome, arriving at your destination is not as easy as it would be for a person who is "normal."

Many people with Asperger's syndrome think literally, linearly, and in a "one-track" manner. They have to learn social cues manually, step by step. They have to round off the rougher edges of their sometimes intense, stubborn characteristics to be more acceptable in society. Many have adapted very well and are very successful. People with Asperger's are not to be loathed or avoided, even though they might not have the best social skills and behavior. Most of them are good, decent people with a lot to offer. Many are very thorough and exacting, and they have phenomenal memories. Aspergers can be very persistent and meticulous and display other good traits, which are advantageous for accomplishing tasks.

I feel that I have overcome many of my Asperger's traits and many of the challenges that the condition presents. I do, however, still have some lingering autistic traits to this day. It's really easy for me to remember phone numbers. That trait is a welcome convenience to my life. I resist change. I still have the first car I ever bought, and the subsequent ones, as well. I am persistent, and I am thorough, which I consider to be advantages rather than disadvantages, because with these traits, my stubbornness has caused me to get projects completed, make good grades in school, solve problems, and accomplish many tasks that other people have admitted they wouldn't have even considered taking on.

Granted this is not true for all Aspergers. There are some who cannot get things organized, and they don't have the motivation to solve problems and accomplish projects, even though they're highly intelligent. There are many types of Aspergers, and each person is unique in his or her own way. Fortunately, in my case, the autism is mild enough that I still have a sense of competence to lead a mostly normal life. Even though I sometimes take things more literally than others might, I am clear headed and understand many concepts.

There is one thing that needs to be considered before moving on – the suitability of seeking an official "Asperger's syndrome" diagnosis. While writing this book, my parents have worried that if I didn't seek an official diagnosis, experts might challenge the validity of this book. I was not diagnosed with Asperger's syndrome because it was not a label that was used at the time I was a child. Even so, I was indeed diagnosed at three different times during my childhood, with the terminology available to clinicians and psychological assessment teams at that time. In 1968, I was diagnosed with "elective mutism." In 1972, Dr. Murphy Thomas and his colleague diagnosed me with problems of adjustment, noting that I "displayed a variety of aberrant behavior patterns." Finally, in 1976 my problem was labeled "adjustment reaction to childhood" and later "adjustment reaction to adolescence."

The childhood traits that I displayed clearly fit the Asperger's profile, and if I were a child today with the same traits, I believe that I would be diagnosed with Asperger's syndrome, as does Dr. Murphy Thomas. People who read this book will think what they like, but there is no need for me to seek an official diagnosis of Asperger's syndrome today, since the label would serve no purpose in my life.

It would be more productive to go back and take a look at the traits that I displayed in my childhood, and to redefine the diagnoses made then, using present-day terminology. I have photocopies of some fifty pages of literature dealing with the diagnoses of my childhood, including copies of the letters and Weekly Progress Reports done by the psychological assessment team when I was in first and second grades that clearly document the traits that clinicians today would call Asperger's syndrome. So, I have my evidence. Besides, it seems that any clinician who understands the syndrome would clearly see that, based on the traits I had as a child, and reading my anecdotes throughout this book, the name Asperger's syndrome is an appropriate one.

While on the subject of diagnosis, I need to mention that while most people with some form of autism are diagnosed during preschool childhood, this is not necessarily the case in Aspergers. Indeed those with Asperger's syndrome are often diagnosed later. While doctors, clinicians, and physicians go about the processes of diagnosing thousands of people per year, they need to keep an open mind to alternative possibilities to explain autistic traits, even if some of them exist outside their realm of beliefs. People act the way they do for a variety of reasons, and a multitude of factors. Misdiagnoses will be kept to a minimum if those doing the diagnosing would keep open minds and consider various possibilities and causes for the symptoms they are seeing.

In addition, it is important not to overuse the clinical diagnoses of Asperger's syndrome by applying the label too freely. In my own case, the childhood traits that I had clearly constituted what clinicians would today call Asperger's syndrome. I sometimes have the feeling that the Asperger's syndrome label has become, or is becoming a quick and easy catchall term, or a convenient excuse to explain adult idiosyncrasies or childlike behavior in highly intelligent, otherwise normal adults.

(As a quick side note, it is very important to mention that those diagnosed with ADD and/or ADHD are labeled for life, considered impaired, and are subsequently denied access to many types of jobs, security clearance jobs, piloting, military, policeman, etc. I therefore recommend *not* diagnosing in this particular way unless the case is very severe.)

More and more children are being diagnosed with autism or Asperger's syndrome each year, partly due to better testing and awareness, and knowing more about how to recognize the condition. The number of cases is also rising. I personally believe that there may be other reasons for this. In Part 6: *Miscellaneous Concepts & Insights*, I have two topics that go into this.

I consider this book an important addition to the personal libraries of psychologists, psychiatrists, teachers in training, teachers, and of course parents, since it presents a picture of how Asperger's traits can affect one's life. Some of the material in this book expresses my personal viewpoints and may be considered my opinion about how I interpret certain situations. What is most important is that, yes, it is possible to overcome many of the challenges of mild autism and Asperger's syndrome and to enjoy a reasonably normal life.

As you read through my book, you will likely realize that I am a single person who has never been married. I have never pursued marriage, as it is not an interest of mine. The high divorce rate that exists in society makes me even less interested in marriage. I am neither hetero nor homo, and I have no partner either. I consider myself asexual, in other words neutral, because I don't have a preference in terms of associating with humans.

For those of you who like to read and wish to do a more in-depth study of some of my life's experiences, you may obtain and read my novel, *Walking Between Worlds*, a novel of an American in Mexico, written by Robert Alquzok (my pen name), length 436 pages, ISBN 1-928798-02-0. The hero of the novel is Roland Jocelyn, a young American fellow who makes repeated trips to a small quaint town called Bustamante, Nuevo León. He enjoys adventures, experiences some good friendships, but he also experiences conflicts, misunderstandings, and scandals. Roland's experiences are a take off on me and my different adventures in Mexico during a ten-year period. *Walking Between Worlds* is on print-on-demand status with Ingram Book Company and is always available for order from any bookstore. Plus I also have on hand copies for sale.

It is my hope that you will enjoy the following topics, anecdotes, and personal experiences throughout this book and that they will help you gain insights and a better understanding of the life of a high-functioning Aspergers.

Robert Sanders, his parents and grandparents, December 1965

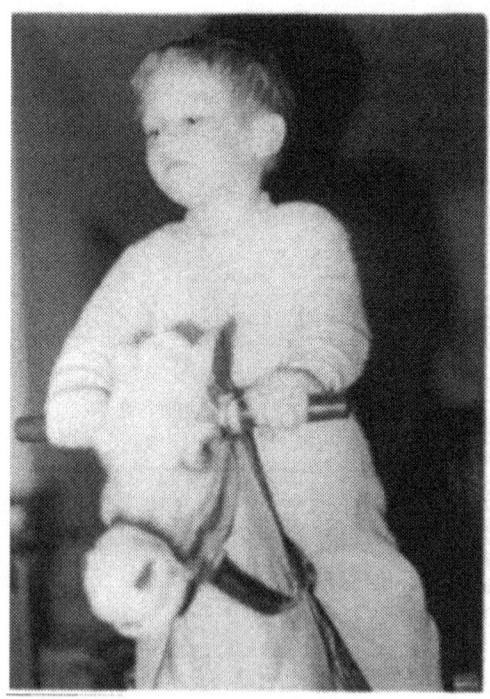

Robert riding his rocking horse, 1968

PART 1
CHILDHOOD & ADOLESCENT DEVELOPMENT

Preschool Childhood

I only have a handful of memories before age four and a few more from ages four to five. I have my first memories of being at my grandparents' house in Crossville, one of being inside at the dining room table, and another of playing in the yard with a woman named Marjorie. We played around a Spruce tree.

Mother used to give me puzzles to work with and solve. Those were very helpful in increasing my intelligence, mental capacity, and mental clarity. Brain development is very important, especially during the first few years of life. I remember the playpen outside where I used to play and run around. I also spent some of my time rocking on a rocking horse called Clip Clop.

I remember my first feelings of sensitivity when I was three. Back in those days – the late 1960s – nearby Smyrna's Sewart Air Force Base was in use, and jets used to fly overhead at times, either on their way to Arnold Engineering Development Center in Tullahoma, Tennessee, or to Huntsville, Alabama and the multitude of military bases there. They sometimes flew closely overhead. One time when I was in the back garden, one of them roared overhead with its shrill sounds, which scared me. I ran back into the house crying. (Perhaps that would have scared any child of three!)

During my early childhood, I had significant autistic traits. I had only a twenty-five word verbal vocabulary at age three, and most of that was baby talk. I didn't talk much, and my parents realized that I was having developmental delays. They were concerned about me and thought perhaps I had hearing problems. They took me to a lady doctor at a medical center in Nashville to have my hearing tested. I actually remember waiting in the waiting room and undergoing the test. My hearing tested excellent. She estimated that I had a 1,500 word receptive vocabulary, of words that I understood, even though I was not speaking them.

My parents asked the doctor if I might be autistic, and she commented that she didn't think so. Autistic people were supposed to be retarded and severely impaired. She told them that my problems were psychological and that I was quiet because of "elective mutism," which basically meant that I was quiet because I elected not to speak. That is how I was first diagnosed, since there was a general lack of information about autism in those days.

Even though I was diagnosed with "elective mutism," I had a yearning desire to communicate. The photo of me at age three with telephones in my hands portrays this. (See page 13.) I don't believe I was "elective mutism" (which I believe is a type of anxiety disorder). It's just that I wasn't yet sure of how to piece the words together at such a young age.

By the time I was four, I finally started talking in complete sentences. Years later, I found out that the same had been true for my father's father, in that one day he surprised his mother with complete sentences at the same age. He was good at math like I am, and we had other similar traits, as well; however, he had one trait that I don't have. He had a photographic memory and could memorize page after page of text, something I can't do. On the other hand, I am good at remembering events during my life, and especially at remembering numbers and names.

When I was nearly four, my parents added a back porch to the house. It was a major change that frustrated me, and I began head banging to release frustration. Sometimes, my head got bruised, and sometimes I broke windowpanes with it. One day when I was five, I broke a windowpane and cut my forehead. That ended my head banging episodes.

In my early childhood, I felt really alien to the culture here, like maybe I was from a faraway star system. I realized that I didn't like it here on Earth, because this world felt so different, hostile at times. I wasn't used to that, and at times I was in anguish. I felt like I had made a mistake by having been born on *this* planet, and I felt trapped and frustrated here. I felt like I wanted out; that is, I wanted to go back home . . . to my "planet of origin." I believe that somewhere during my kindergarten years, ages five and six, I must have decided to stay here. I was becoming a little more accustomed to life here by then. Maybe it wasn't so bad after all. Still, it would take several more years to become better adjusted.

For those who believe in reincarnation, maybe this is my very first lifetime on Earth, while other humans alive here today may be living their tenth, hundredth, or even higher-number lifetime. If so, they've had plenty of experience, but since I am living my first human lifetime here, I've had no prior experience. Maybe that's why I behaved very strangely in early childhood, but through accumulated experience, finally got the hang of it by age nine or ten, the time at which I became at least somewhat more normal. In other words, I would say that I overcame many of my autistic traits by learning step by step, detail by detail the things that others seem to know almost by instinct: the mannerisms of how to be a person and how to grow up during childhood.

I speculate about my feelings regarding reincarnation to point out that there is a lot out there in the universe that we humans don't know. Did my abnormalities in early childhood stem solely from autism? Or could it be that perhaps they also stemmed from living my first life here on Earth? Maybe it was a little bit of both.

As for reincarnation, I had a few strange experiences in early childhood that made me believe that we humans have a life force – a spirit or soul that keeps us animated. I also believe that the spirit is detachable, and that each spirit has its own essence for each human alive on Earth. So, why couldn't that same spirit return to Earth for another lifetime after its body's death, and keep returning to Earth for additional lifetimes?

Robert Sanders playing with the telephones, 1968

Kindergarten

I remember my first day of kindergarten in 1970. In those days there were no public kindergartens, and I was placed at one of the church kindergarten programs with a lady teacher. My father took me to school each day, and he worked diagonally across the street. He would walk me to the door of the classroom. I didn't like the idea of being left alone with strangers, or away from my home and family. Two years earlier, I had

13

been to a Sunday school session in that same room, and I cried the whole period by the door, wanting to leave.

Kindergarten class seemed so alien to me. I didn't know what to make of it. It was a change from my normal routine. I immediately lay down on the floor. As far as talking, I suddenly didn't feel right. I felt that there was some type of barrier – a mental block preventing me from speaking – and although I wanted to talk, I just couldn't bring myself to do it. It was too difficult and embarrassing. What was I going to do? I felt trapped and in despair.

Eventually I got somewhat used to being there, but in subtle protest, there were a couple of things I just refused to do. One of them was talk. I would not talk in the class, or anywhere else in the building – and not even on the playground. It was as if it was prohibited for me to talk while attending school. I forgot my prohibition rule and slipped up only two times, briefly saying something to two different classmates.

My other significant idiosyncrasy in kindergarten was that I refused to swallow my saliva, and every day it would build up in my mouth. Several times a day, when it got to an annoying level, I would enter the classroom bathroom, pull a paper towel out of the dispenser, and release the whole mouthful of spit and saliva into it, simultaneously dropping it into the trash can. As I look back on it, those were embarrassing traits, especially the latter, as back then I reasoned that since I didn't talk, I therefore didn't have to swallow. One of my classmates, Tommy, and his family would pray for me each night in their home. Even still, the talking barrier and saliva problem were not overcome for another year.

Now, mind you, there were a few of those classmates who came out to play with me on the farm. Of course, my parents were the ones who set all that up. Weren't those classmates surprised when I suddenly talked to them as soon as we left the church/school and got in the car! I talked to them at home, as well. One of them, Ricky, later played with me and talked to me at school, but I wouldn't talk to him there. Another classmate who came out to the farm to play was Michael.

Anyway, the year went by, and they never got me to talk. So, guess what? I flunked kindergarten! Or, as we would say, I was "held back."

My second year of kindergarten was at the same church, and that year, I had a good teacher who cared about us, motivated us, and saw it as important that we always completed whatever projects we started. She is likely part of the reason why I have the drive to succeed and that I take on and complete projects, even to this day.

I liked the classmates better in my second year of kindergarten than I did the year before. They weren't quite as big, but then I was a year older and therefore bigger myself. Still, I wouldn't talk, but at least I learned how to swallow. I abolished that restriction myself. Many children with Asperger's syndrome make rules for themselves, and sometimes the only thing that prompts their behavior change is *their* decision to revise their own rules.

There was one classmate I became good friends with. His name was Jody, and we played on the playground. Jody repeatedly came out to visit me on the farm, and even spent the night during some weekends. He, of course, noticed that I talked at home and persistently asked, "Why can't you also talk at school?" Finally, in February, well into the school year, my kindergarten teacher and the whole class gathered around me and repeatedly urged me to talk. Finally I did, but in a "wrong" voice. I wasn't able to use the right one. But I did talk – an improvement indeed.

Now, to add to the complexity, I would not talk in my "right" voice while I had my school clothes on, even though they were not dress clothes or uniforms. Each day when I got out of school and Mother picked me up, I would change into a shirt with a number on it. Only then would I be able to use my right voice. It was as if, during my early school years, I was living a dual existence or a dual personality. One might say that there was possibly an "extra entity" in my psyche that finally exited (along with my wrong voice) when I got to third grade.

I remember much of my childhood very well, and I enjoyed making a few friends during my two years of kindergarten. Jody and I were good friends right through ninth grade, and I still call and talk with him on occasion.

One can realize that I had significant trouble adjusting to change and going to school. I had very stubborn traits, and I purposefully placed excruciating restrictions upon myself, which I wanted to get out of, but once I placed them, I couldn't. I am grateful to my second year kindergarten teacher and to my classmates for caring enough about me and working with me to finally get me to talk.

10,023

Between kindergarten and first grade, I became interested in numbers. Perhaps seeing *Sesame Street* on TV nearly every afternoon was the thing that got me interested. I knew a little bit about numbers, and I knew how to count to 199. One morning I asked my father what number came after 199.

He told me "two hundred." *Oh, of course!* I realized. The next number was 201, and it wasn't long before I realized that 100 numbers after 200 was 300, then 400, 500, 600, 700, and so on. He explained that 10 hundred is exactly one thousand, but I stayed with the "hundred" label, up through 99 hundred. My father also explained that the number after 9,999 was 10 thousand (10,000). The next digit was 100 thousand, then 1 million, then 1 billion, 1 trillion, 1 quadrillion, and so on.

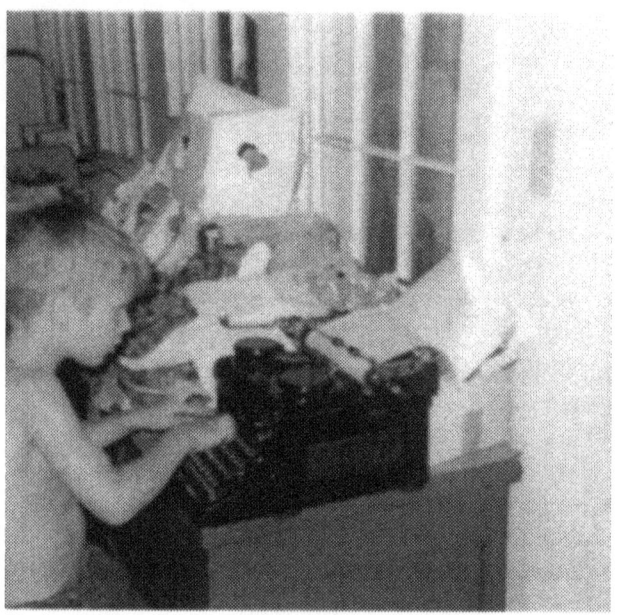

Robert Sanders typing to 10,000, summer of 1972

Mother took me to a summer program one day in Nashville, and I remember counting out loud and silently to as much as 5,000. I was so enthralled with numbers that I took on a major project when I was six years and eleven months. I used my mother's Royal manual typewriter and typed every number from 1 to 10,000. Each day I would put in time on it, in addition to riding my new bike around the farm and playing with Jody when he would come to visit. It took about three weeks for me to do it, but I had the stubbornness and persistence to stay with the task, and I finally reached 10,000. It amounted to around twenty-five pages full of numbers. I certainly had a clear understanding of numbers after that, and also how many of them there were! When I reached 10,000, I was so into it that I didn't exactly stop. I went on just a little bit further, stopping at 10,023. I had those pages of text for several months, perhaps a year, and then they were never seen again – mysteriously lost. The reader must realize that it is very rare for a six or seven year old to type clear to 10,000, well, that is 10,023.

Speedometers and Odometers

While on the subject of numbers, I will mention that I always used to keep up with the mileage on my parents' cars. Our 1970 Volvo had a speedometer/odometer that went to 1,000,000. It also had a smaller odometer that could be punched to zero whenever one liked. It went to 1,000. By the summer of 1974, our car had already reached 100,000, and since its odometer didn't register tenths of a mile, but the smaller one did, I decided to punch it to zero exactly when the car reached 100,000. Several times afterwards, my parents forgot and punched it to zero, and I got upset at that because it was no longer synchronized with the main odometer, and I would have to wait until it would reach another thousand, and then be lucky enough to be present and *remember* to press it at the exact moment! After numerous thousands of miles, I finally got it right and convinced my parents that I wanted the smaller odometer left alone. My parents were never as exacting, like I was and still am now to some degree.

I kept speedometers/odometers on all my earlier bicycles, and by the time the year 2000 came, I finally had to break away from the tradition, because they weren't being made anymore! Plus, I only wanted analog speedometers driven by a cable – nothing electronic. In the early 1990s I had bought several analog speedometers/odometers to keep in stock for the future. When I put one of them on my Schwinn five-speed at the time it reached 10,000 (0000), the replacement speedometer/odometer only reached 279 and stopped turning! So, I put another one on, only to discover that the new cables were defective in size! (By the way, bicycle speedometers/odometers only go up to 10,000 before turning over to 0000.)

Right into my thirties, I was very picky about the mileage on my bicycles. I wanted to be the one to put *all* the miles on my speedometer/ odometer, and no one else. One time, only a few years ago while in Mexico, I loaned my bicycle to someone for thirty minutes. He put a mile on it. I forgot to disconnect the speedometer cable before letting him ride it. When he returned, right in front of him and the others who were with us, I turned my bicycle upside down, turned the front wheel backward, and took that mile off the speedometer/odometer. There! That made that right.

One fellow whose family I was staying with rode my bicycle seventeen or eighteen miles, and when I got home, I took a bike ride just that length, with the cable drive mechanism turned around backward. Made that right again!

I know most people would think that this is very strange behavior, but it's my right to be exacting about who puts *all* the 10,000 miles on my own Schwinn bicycle. That was my goal and I achieved it! The speedometer/odometer lasted the whole way through. It was made in the early 1980s, the days when they were still made right.

I refuse to advance (refuse to succumb) to the digital speedometers/odometers, and I therefore no longer clock my miles on my bicycles. The problem I have with digital speedometers/odometers is that as soon as the battery is removed, all the miles are erased, and any battery is going to discharge after a maximum of ten or fifteen years.

My Accurate Perception of Speed, Time, and Distance

Before 1974, when I was an early child, I remember that the speed limit on the two-lane highway to town was 65 miles per hour. I remember several trips to town with Mother driving the speed limit, and I used to count the dotted lines on the highway. I soon realized that by simply observing the lines go by, I could accurately judge how fast we were going, to within 1 mile per hour. I used to verify it with the speedometer. Not only was that true when I was a child, it is still true now. I don't have to look at the speedometer to know how fast I'm going down the road. I have come to realize that I am pretty accurate on judging speed, distance, time, and even temperature. For example, I can go outside, feel the air, and accurately judge the temperature, to within a degree.

When I was a child, and also during my adolescence, I used to listen to the radio, and also to the short-wave radio stations, including those that were solely dedicated to giving the time. I soon realized exactly how long a second was by hearing the constant second-long beeps.

In my childhood, I used to play records on my record player, listening to 33s, 45s, and 78s. In my mind, I soon realized the rate of rotation of each, and I could accurately repeat it. I still can today. Knowing those numbers, I can feel my pulse or heart beat and know how many beats per minute there are. Seems like everyone else has to check their pulse with their watch and count the number of pulses during an interval of, say, fifteen seconds.

I've always been a good judge of distance and height. I can look at a person and tell how tall he/she is. When driving down a road, I can tell how wide it is, whether it's eighteen feet, twenty feet, or wider. The same is true for bridges.

While I do know some people who are as accurate as I am on these things, I have come to realize that most people are not able to judge speed, distance, time and temperature with the degree of accuracy that I can.

First Grade, (Problems and Solutions)

It was the fall of 1972 when I entered first grade at a school that I shall refer to as "the elite county school," (for reasons that will soon become obvious). While the school was not actually a magnet school in today's terminology, it was a special school in the county school system, and it was commonly known that the most elite people in the town would sign their children up years ahead of time so that they could go to elementary school there. It was "the thing to do." The school even had a precious *waiting list*. In those days the school was a branch of one of the local universities, so it was set up as a special school for training student teachers.

My parents were led to believe that this school would be the ideal school for me. Following my troubles in kindergarten, they were told that it was a fine laboratory school that would have good student teachers and behavior modification teams to benefit students like me. I had already been in a summer enrichment program at the same school two months earlier, and I recognized some of the classmates from there.

My teacher was a middle aged woman who, prior to becoming a teacher, had served in some prestigious positions in town. We had some math and reading sessions together. I was seven and still couldn't read, except of course, for numbers. We had workbooks in which we wrote answers, and things went fine for a few weeks, until I didn't fill out a question well enough, and the teacher told me, "You don't get a hundred for that!"

One day while walking down the hall in line formation, she suddenly came up behind me and spanked me while I was walking. That made me quite angry! At lunch, I stuck my tongue out at her several times, and she declared, "Don't you dare stick your tongue out at me!" Things deteriorated rapidly after that, and she gave spankings in addition to slaps on the thigh and other abuses, such as shaking me when I played with the toys! I became more frustrated! I was all over the classroom. I would crawl under desks and tables, and I threw things out the window. As a result, my teacher became more abominable! The way she treated me was appalling! She moved my desk out of the classroom and into the hall. I became even more frustrated during my last few days in her class. I squeezed classmates on the back of the neck and got into fights. The mother of one of the students whose neck I had squeezed came to the school and complained.

One day in early November, two months into the school year, my teacher called my parents and asked if she could give me a great big paddling! How horrible of her to even think of doing such a thing to me! She had been abominable enough already! My parents quickly told her, "Absolutely not!" Mother was quite irritated at my teacher for the way she had treated me, and she expressed her dissatisfaction about this to her, for which she became quite defensive. Her methods stemmed from an old-fashioned way of thinking, and she wouldn't admit to her incompetency and that she didn't know how to deal with me.

My parents went to the school and were shocked when the school's principal claimed, "We have *no* children with problems in this school," meaning that the school didn't have to deal with special-case children, because they "didn't have any." That was a total lie, what with all the problems that I was undergoing, not to mention the mother of one of the students with a sore neck coming to the school and complaining about me! My parents found out the truth – that the school would *not* under any circumstances allow behavior modification teams to enter the school to work with their students. After all, this was an elitist school, don't you know. My parents took me out of that school.

From the start, my parents had specifically requested a different first-grade teacher. The school's principal was unyielding, however, and perhaps as a means of trying to prove that she knew what was best for each student, she assigned me to the other teacher on purpose. (As a side note, that principal was so unyielding that when various teachers had requested air-conditioning, she had put her foot down and declared no!)

Now don't get me totally wrong. That different first-grade teacher that my parents had requested wasn't exactly an angel either. One of my friends had her for first grade, and on the first day of class, she had every student write the name of the street he or she lived on. Evidently, she expected everyone to spell it right because when my friend, who barely knew how to read at the time, spelled it wrong, she "bit his head off," took him to the front of the class, and yelled at him the correct way to spell it!

To add to the mouth of the lions that I was rescued from, second grade would have been a living nightmare if I had stayed at that school, because that teacher's best friend was the paddle! Another friend of mine told me much later that the teacher paddled him every day in second grade; that is, until his parents went to the school irate with the teacher and firmly told her that if she paddled their son again, they were going to sue the school! Good for them! I'm glad they threatened that schoolteacher. They put her in her place. That school ought to be ashamed of itself for all the paddling and abuse it allowed! Even with all of this, that school has stayed open and still serves an elitist population, complete with its fancy *waiting lists*.

One more thing I will add about my memories of first grade at that school is that I found one of the classmates there to be cute. I wanted to be friends with him, but I didn't know how to go about doing it. In frustration caused by my teacher, and in efforts to be friends with him, I squeezed him on the neck several times during the two and a half months I was there. I felt badly and was sorry about having done that to him. I totally failed on my friendship efforts with that classmate. At least I did know him while I was in high school, and of course, we behaved reasonably with each other. I thought about apologizing to him for the neck squeezing in first grade, but I decided not to remind him that I was the one who had done it. In other words, I didn't want to open up that can of worms.

As for the elite county school, thank goodness my parents took me out of that place! They moved me over to another elementary school, one of the city schools in the same town, where I was well received by the kind principal. My mother met with my new teachers. One of them could tell that my mother was quite upset about my previous school experience and the incompetent way in which I was handled.

There was a psychological assessment team that consisted of several special education officials with the county guidance center. Among the psychologists were Dr. Murphy Thomas and his colleague. They were the ones who communicated with the city schools office and helped get me placed at one of their schools, a superior school with resources available that the elite county school did not have. On the Request for Pupil Personnel Services form, it said: "child kicked out of the elite county school." [actual school name mentioned in report] Dr. Thomas observed that I had problems of adjustment and "displayed a variety of aberrant behavior patterns." That is, my behavior deviated from normal. He kindly wrote a letter to the school superintendent, explaining the situation and recommending me for placement at the city school. He also offered his and colleague's continued interest and willingness to work with the school to aid me in my adjustment to the school environment. For the next year and a half, they did a behind-the-scenes monitoring of my behavior and progress. Periodically, members of the team came to the city school posing as "teachers in training" to observe the classroom that I was in; however, the real reason they were there was to observe me. In addition to that, there were Weekly Progress Reports that were filled out by certain officials. Handwritten comments were made in three different sections of those reports: "Problem," "Treatment," and "Progress & Status." They did a fine job and are to be commended for their efforts and their thoroughness, and I am grateful that such services existed back in the early 1970s.

Though I never knew it until I wrote and compiled this book, my parents also had a meeting with both Dr. Thomas and his colleague about my disaster at the elite county school. They were very worried about me and asked the psychologists if I should be on some sort of medicine to get me back on track. Dr. Thomas was very reassuring to my parents that the city school was a much better place for me and that he and the other psychologists would be monitoring my behavior behind the scenes. He reckoned that my continued association with other students and making new friends would eventually normalize things. He explained to my parents that he was opposed to the use of anti-psychotic drugs because they were known to exacerbate problems, most of the time, rather than solve them. I am very grateful to Dr. Thomas. That was a very important decision and a turning point in my life. Who knows what might have happened if it weren't for his wise decision!

Now that I was in a new school, I had a clean slate. I made the conscious decision that I was never going to be spanked . . . never! I didn't squeeze any more necks, didn't misbehave excessively, and I made some good friends, the normal way. Never ever was I spanked nor paddled for the rest of my whole school career. It's as if I had protection from "upstairs" from November 1972 forward.

One of my new teachers was a special education teacher. Her classroom was in a portable double classroom building set apart from the rest of the school. One might say, in my special case, that she was actually my homeroom teacher, because I spent most of the time in the regular classes with two other teachers. All of them were fine teachers who cared about me. One of my regular classroom teachers taught me how to read and write, and I had a different teacher for math. PE class was taught by a kind and caring man who also had quite a memory for names. I ran all over the place, and I enjoyed that class. For part of the year, my PE teacher had a student teacher.

22

I made some good friends in first grade and was glad to be away from that elite county school! I made sure and behaved myself better, and with more self-control, so my new friends wouldn't turn against me. I will mention a success story pertaining to making friends. Again I picked out someone who I thought was cute, but this time I made sure I didn't squeeze any necks! I talked to him. He responded, and we quickly became friends. He came to my house to play, and I went to his house several times. We had a great friendship. I really felt a sense of accomplishment on making friends, and I knew him through the rest of elementary school. I've talked with him a few times in recent years, as well.

(As a side note, twenty-two years later, 1994, I looked up my first-grade teacher from the elite county school, and I met with her. I told her what she had done to me back when I had her in first grade. She didn't remember much of it, but she was genuinely upset with herself for what she had done, and she said, "Robert, for all those things I did to you, I'm sorry." I accepted her apology, and she asked me, "Friends?" We shook hands. It was nice to work that out while still alive here on Earth.)

In order to monitor my behavior, my special education teacher sent me to PE class with a half sheet of paper so that the teacher could rate my condition: Excellent, Very Good, Good, Fair, and Poor. I usually got Goods or Very Goods, but never got Excellents. One day, I decided to hide in the bleachers instead of forming in line with my classmates. A few minutes later the PE student teacher walked over and found me. I thought it was funny. I wasn't punished, but at the end of the PE period, he gave me a rating of Poor. My special education teacher asked me why I got that rating, and I told her that I had hidden in the bleachers. While she said that wasn't the right thing to do, I could tell that she was somewhat relieved because it would have been worse for me to have picked on the other kids. I later asked my PE student teacher why he never gave me an Excellent, and he said that he would give me that rating if I would talk with the other classmates. So, one day I made sure and behaved very well, and I also talked with the other classmates. I achieved an Excellent, and I felt a great sense of accomplishment!

No one knew about my right and wrong voices, and I didn't want my teachers to find out either. One day, Mother took me over to my special education teacher's house. While they talked and visited, discussing my progress, I said nothing. After an hour, we left, and the next day at school, my teacher asked me why I didn't talk. I didn't have an answer. A week or two later, Mother visited her again, and I went along. Still, I was quiet, but as we drove away, I decided to wave good-bye and decided to use my right voice to call out, "Good-bye." She heard the difference, and first thing the next morning, she asked me what voice I was going to use from now on. I answered, "Right voice," using my normal voice. I was thrilled I could do it, and I ran swiftly to the main building where I had one of my regular classes.

Saying that in my right voice was a major breakthrough, or so I thought, because I still couldn't bring myself to use my right voice once I got to my class a minute later. Even still, I talked very little to my classmates. Mother met with my first-grade teachers, and they devised a plan to encourage me to talk. Mother rewarded me a penny a word every time I talked to my classmates. At first, it was just a few words per day, and each afternoon, Mother would go by the bank and get pennies from the teller. As a result, I became interested in coin collecting, and I found lots of wheat pennies. In 1973, wheat pennies were commonplace. I also liked half dollars, and as the days passed by, I started collecting them. After a month, I had $74 worth of half dollars saved up.

Meanwhile, I talked more and more, and the "pay" was good. One day, I racked up 125 words, and my regular teacher sent the reported amount to my special education teacher, who complimented me. My parents were pleased and they informed me that I was on my own now – that I would no longer be paid to talk. Of course, they were concerned that I might clam up, but I didn't. I continued to talk to my classmates, and I enjoyed knowing them. Still, I used my wrong voice.

As for learning, it was hard for me to learn to read, but my regular classroom teacher knew what to do, and she was able to cause the students to learn – something my previous teacher at the elite county school was unsuccessful in doing with me. I used to look away a lot during reading sessions, and my teacher was concerned that I wasn't grasping the concepts. Well, she soon got her answer, because thanks to her, I did learn to read by the end of the year. However, I was at the bottom of the group.

Now, math was a different story. It was easy doing addition and subtraction, counting how many objects there were, plus other simple problems. No numbers ever went above 99, and it annoyed me why the makers of the first-grade workbooks thought first graders wouldn't be able to comprehend three-digit numbers! Anyway, I spent one early afternoon of my free time in the special education class and answered the whole rest of the workbook. There! That took care of that boring nuisance! I was very pleased with myself, and my special education teacher was impressed,

24

followed by my regular classroom teachers, and my parents! With that, I proved my intelligence, and when the end of the school year came, I certainly passed and went on to second grade, even though I was slow in reading.

To me, first grade seemed as if it went on for more than a year, since I attended two different schools. I am grateful to my parents for taking me out of the elite county school, placing me in the city school, and for encouraging me to talk. A lot of students had parents who couldn't have cared less about helping their children. They never even came to the school, nor met their children's teachers. Mother always got involved and met all of the teachers. She had been a schoolteacher before she married and saw it as important to know the people who taught her children.

Robert Sanders looking at the world, 1972

Second Grade, Achievement Tests

In second grade, I had a teacher who was very strict and much less enjoyed than my first-grade teachers at the city school. I did not advance in my social skills that whole year. I talked very little in second grade, because the teacher would send anyone who talked to the corner or to the cloakroom. For me, that was counterproductive because I needed to talk more. I remember on the way to lunch one day, a fellow student told me,

"Say something Robert." Many times when I raised my hand to ask the teacher a question, she snapped, "Put your hand down Robert!" Sometimes I would walk up to her desk to ask her a question, and she almost always barked, "Sit down!" in a rude manner! She was just too strict, very old fashioned in her ways, and most of the time she lacked compassion! Several times during the year, she would put us down by telling us that we were the worst class she ever had. At that time, I believed her because I interpreted things literally. Several subsequent teachers told us the same thing, and years later I began to realize that it wasn't really true, that it was just a put-down tactic to humiliate us. I lament that I wasn't able to pursue any friendships in class that year, because the teacher was just too strict!

Let me tell you an incident when, "Put your hand down Robert!" was not convenient to her. One morning an extra lunch card turned up in my teacher's hands, and she read the name Donald Chanford to all of us, asking if we knew who he was. Indeed I knew. He was over in the portable in special education class. So, I raised my hand, and the teacher snapped, "Put your hand down Robert!" She sent another student to the classroom next door where there was another Donald. Of course I knew that was the wrong one, and I knew that she would soon realize that, but then she didn't give me a chance to tell her, did she! It took her more than half an hour of searching to finally find out who that Donald was.

One morning, the principal gave her announcements over the loud speaker, and she gave a certain set of instructions that I didn't exactly understand. So, I asked my teacher why the principal said what she said, so I could get a better explanation. My teacher explained it to me, but then when parent conferences came up, my parents told me that she said I had been questioning authority! That had never crossed my mind. Maybe that's why so many people don't speak up in their adulthood, because they learn in school that they're *not* supposed to question authority. I think that questioning authority is a *good* thing. After all, there is the motto, "Government; for the people, by the people."

For the final hour of each class day, I used to go to the portable classroom with my special education teacher, as a means of continued monitoring of my behavior. That was a relief to me, to be away from that strict atmosphere! At least third grade was going to be a lot better.

I want to make a comment about my second-grade teacher's regular practice of shouting, "Put your hand down, Robert!" When I arrived at the city school the year before, my special education teacher told me that if I needed to say something, to raise my hand. My former first-grade teacher at the elite county school had never taught me that. Sometimes I wondered if my second-grade teacher didn't know why I was raising my hand so much. Of course it goes without saying that she was aware that I had been a problem child in first grade. It could be that she therefore thought less of me than of the other students. After all, she sent that other student to the class next door to search for Donald. One must observe that she refused to call on me when I raised my hand in attempts to answer her question to all of us, about who that Donald was. Perhaps she viewed me as incompetent and that therefore I didn't count as much as the other students. I thought about blurting out the answer to her, but then she would have punished me by sending me to the cloakroom!

I do recall one time when my second-grade teacher was more compassionate. There was an incident during PE class when one of my classmates broke off one of his permanent front teeth while playing. Back in the classroom, our teacher talked to all of us for some ten minutes, lamenting that he had broken his tooth and that no one had been able to find the tooth fragment on the gym floor. Even though dentists would be able to glue something onto it in attempts to restore it, it would never be the same as the original.

There were a few of us that had speech problems, and we had our sessions once a week in a Ford Econoline van with a teacher who drove to the five different city schools. The letters I had trouble pronouncing were the "s" and the "th" sounds, which I corrected without much trouble.

My reading improved greatly in second grade, and I went from the bottom to the top reading group. Where I really did well, however, was in math. I remember when the achievement tests were given that I even answered several multiplication problems that were *extra* problems that weren't expected of second graders. While taking the test, I figured out a multiplication trick. Instead of performing the normal multiplication procedure, I solved the problem by using long addition. For example, if a 3-digit number was multiplied by 4, I wrote out the 3-digit number 4 times and did long addition. When the time was up, my teacher saw that I had answered those extra problems, and she marveled over them, staring in disbelief. She said to another teacher who happened to be in the room, "But look at these. He *answered* them." She was very much impressed. Needless to say, my percentile rank was very high in the math section of that achievement test. Keep in mind, in those days, in the state where I lived, you didn't fill in circles on the test form. You manually answered the questions. In our area, computers weren't used to grade students' achievement tests until the next year, 1975.

I used to draw during my kindergarten and primary school years. Below is one of my better drawings that I did during second grade. It is titled, "Abraham Lincoln on Skis."

Robert Sanders' drawing of "Abraham Lincoln on Skis"

Third Grade

The next year was a much better year for me. I had a marvelous and young teacher who knew how to communicate with her students. My parents knew about her, and they were very pleased that I had been placed in her classroom. As far as social development is concerned, I really soared that year. I felt so much more welcome in that classroom than I had the previous year that I got rid of my wrong voice. I felt more relaxed. I was able to pursue friendships again, and I made several more friends. Plus, I talked normally with my classmates; that is, in my *right* voice. Several friends came out to my house to play, and I went to their houses, as well. I did very well in reading and math, and my social development normalized to the point that the psychological assessment team terminated their monitoring and recognized that I belonged in the classroom just like everyone else.

My third-grade teacher taught us a very important topic called

Communication. I have a picture of her at her desk, and beside the desk was a bulletin board with communication topics pasted on it. She took us on various field trips, one to see the telephone exchange, which at that time was an electro-mechanical crossbar exchange and would remain so for another ten years until 1985. That was quite a place with all the electro-mechanical switches and relays. We also went to WSM TV and toured the studio where we were on *Teddy Bart's Noon Show*. I sincerely appreciate her for having taken us on such original and interesting field trips, something a lot of my teachers didn't do.

Robert Sanders and friends taking a field trip in third grade,1975

I feel very fortunate to have had such an extraordinary woman for my third-grade teacher, and she was one of my favorites throughout my whole school career. She was very efficient, and she motivated us to finish our assignments on time, so that we would have some free time, as well. She used to read us children's books, such as *Eddie and Gardenia*, and *Charlotte's Web*. She used to play us records and show us interesting movies, and at times she rewarded us with cartoon shows. There were certain days when we had show-and-tell, and I remember Mother bringing my dog one day, so I could show it to the class.

My third-grade teacher was very considerate and never humiliated any of us. Never once did she put us down by saying that we were the worst class she ever had. If she needed to call down a student, she usually took him or her out into the hall, so as not to embarrass him or her in front of the rest of us. I am grateful to my third-grade teacher for helping to bring me out of my world and more into everyone else's.

Fourth Grade, Listening Problems

After having a wonderful teacher for third grade, I entered fourth grade. My new teacher was tall at five 5'10½". She was a temperamental type and was *not* one of my best teachers. She thought I had listening problems. I remember her calling me up to the side of her desk one day where she quietly lectured me, telling me that if I didn't improve my listening skills, I would be punished. She also rudely added with trembling anger in her voice, "Ohhh . . . sometimes I feel like shaking you!" That made me quite angry, and when I went home that afternoon, I told my parents what my teacher felt like doing to me! My parents got right to it and had a serious talk with her, resulting in another lecture from her, this time in private in the bookstore closet of the front office! I told her it would take me about a month for me to become perfect, and she then told me, "I don't *want* you to be perfect." Yes, she did! After all, she was a perfectionist, and if she hadn't wanted me to be perfect, she wouldn't have gone to all the fuss! The problem lay in the fact that she would give instructions, and I would get right on the assignment. As I was working on it, she had a bad habit of adding, "Oh, by the way, do it this way, etc. . . ." I was already well into the assignment, concentrating on it, and tuning out everything else.

The same day that my teacher made that uncalled-for comment about shaking me, I had just one hour earlier thoughtfully brought from home and given her a Chinese air plant seedling, and still she had the audacity to tell me how she would like to shake me! Well, the first opportunity I had, I took that plant off her desk and took it back to mine. She soon discovered it missing, and never realizing why I took it back, she accused me of "Indian giving." She asked me to give it back to her. I wouldn't do it. I hope it dawned on her later that I took it back to get the message across to her that I don't approve of being shaken, not even for teachers to contemplate it!

One morning our teacher was trying to teach us some grammar lessons, and we weren't understanding them well enough. She became extremely impatient and inexcusably frustrated with us, and she counted out loud to ten to avoid blowing her top! Even still, she was throwing a tantrum, and she scared all of us. As I look back on it, I should have walked out of the classroom, marched right into the principal's office, and requested that they send the woman home for the day! Of course, at age ten, that didn't occur to me. Plus, children are afraid to do that. Temperamental people with emotional problems should not be teachers!

For our not having been good enough for her that morning, she punished us by not letting us eat lunch in the cafeteria that day. She made us eat lunch in the classroom, eating with one hand and writing with the other. First, I ate my lunch, and *then* I did the writing. I refused to do both simultaneously. I didn't care what she said! When I eat a meal, my work gets put to the side.

Even though she never actually paddled anyone, she made threats such as, "If you don't bla bla bla, I'm going to paddle you so hard, you won't be able to sit down for a week!" Now that is a horrible thing to say to anybody, especially to a child! Teachers should have been taught in their university training programs *not* to say things like that to their students – not to even think that!

Despite not being the best teacher, she was nice to us at times. I did make some more friends, and several of them came out to the farm to play. There were some good moments that year in school. We did take some field trips, and we did a lot of activities pertinent to 1776 and the Bicentennial. One day, we went over to the nearby house of one of my classmates. His mother was good friends with the teacher. The whole day was colonial style, and we made crafts, cut things out of construction paper, and cooked food like they did it 200 years ago. I learned a lot about the Bicentennial and the colonial days of early America.

At the end of the year, we all had a day at my house on the farm. I enjoyed having all my classmates visit. We played around the house and swung on some ropes that I had hung from one of the trees. We played in the tree house, and went down to the barns and haylofts where we played some more. We also went up in the woods. That was a treat as far as I was concerned, and it was a great day for all of us.

Fifth Grade

My fourth-grade teacher did do one thing the next year that made things somewhat right, and compensated for her previous year's bad behavior. She came along at the right moment, and right there in the hallway, she talked my fifth-grade teacher out of paddling several of us, over a matter of throwing peanuts in the lunchroom. She suggested that he have his students write letters and take them home to their parents – a good suggestion. Though he had paddled students on a regular basis and was a person who never knew how to apologize, he miraculously took her suggestion. That was the closest I ever came to being paddled, and thanks to her I was spared. I preserved my perfect record (of never being paddled) throughout my whole school career.

To explain to the reader why I wrote that my fifth-grade teacher was a man who never knew how to apologize, there was an incident one afternoon after school, when I was still in fourth grade. As I was walking down the hall to the parking lot to be picked up by my mother, a patrol boy was treating me very rudely and was being bossy. So, I told him off. My future fifth-grade teacher happened to be walking down the hall and heard the ruckus. Instead of rightfully calling down the patrol boy, like he should have done, he immediately shouted at me, "Hey! Shut up! Get on!" That made me angry and hurt my feelings! In anguish and frustration, I ran out of the hall to the parking lot, got into Mother's car, and began crying. I told her what had just happened.

That night, my parents called my special education teacher, and they told her how upset I was. The next day, she came to my fourth grade class, and she took me down the hall to my fifth-grade teacher's class, where he was called into the hallway. There we talked some ten minutes about the incident, and I requested an apology. He explained that I was the one who had been wrong, to have "smarted off" to that patrol boy, and he saw no need for an apology. Even though my special education teacher was mediating, and even though I reiterated that the patrol boy had been rude and bossy, he would not apologize. So, we finished the talk, and I returned to my class.

No matter what, my fifth-grade teacher should have had enough compassion to try and make me feel better, that is, to *apologize* to me. Plus, they should have brought that patrol boy to me to apologize, as well. Instead, I was left feeling frustrated and very dissatisfied!

In general, for those who *apologize*, it is much *easier* for me to forgive them.

Although I had that problem with my fifth-grade teacher when I was still in fourth grade, he still became my fifth-grade teacher, and for the most part, the year went well. Even though he never apologized, I think he learned something that day because he was never that harsh to me again. We learned Tennessee history under him, and I was one of the few students who got a Plus (same as an A) in that subject.

I finish this topic with an important note to teachers and teachers-in-training. If I were a teacher, I wouldn't want to be remembered by my students, a quarter century later, as a person who didn't know how to apologize. I wouldn't want that kind of reputation in my students' minds. Teachers need to realize that some of their students are very sensitive. They need to humble themselves enough to apologize to their students when they're rude to them. After all, students have feelings, and they and their feelings count too.

Robert Sanders and his friend Jody playing in the creek, April 1977

Sixth Grade

My last year at the city school was sixth grade. My teacher was an extraordinary woman who cared about her students. She was fair, and she diligently prepared us for seventh grade. At the city school, we had never been on the letter grading system. Letter grading was the standard for grades seven through twelve. So, with that in mind, and with her willingness to prepare us better, she had her own letter grading system that went alongside the city school's plus/check/dot system. I then learned what letter grades meant, and I am grateful that she prepared us ahead of time.

33

The elite county school always took *their* sixth graders on a trip to Huntsville, Alabama to see the rocket and space center. None of the five city schools ever made the Huntsville trip. Well, my sixth-grade teacher decided to change that, and she got the other three sixth-grade teachers together and talked the principal into approving the trip. I remember her returning to our classroom half an hour later. She had a smile of triumph on her face, and she declared, "We got it!"

A few weeks later, we all took a Trailways bus down to Huntsville. What an interesting trip it was! I saw the actual first Space Shuttle craft, and that was in the days before it ever lifted off. We saw plenty of other sights and some big rockets, as well.

In April of that year, we took a wonderful trip to Land Between the Lakes in Kentucky and stayed a whole week. All sixth graders went there as part of the school's curriculum. We took hikes and saw many different sights each day. That was a great week, and I enjoyed the trail hikes. Since we stayed in cabins near the lakeshore, I collected 100 Crinoid Stem fossils from the lakeside.

All in all, I learned a lot in sixth grade. We studied various and different subjects. Also I became better accepted by my classmates and made more friends. What's more? They appreciated me for my intelligence.

At the end of the school year, our teacher took all of us out to my house, and we enjoyed a day on the farm, much like what had occurred two years earlier at the end of fourth grade.

Before I move on to the next topic, I want to express my appreciation to several more teachers at the city school, for encouraging me to be a writer and for their support. I had written some short stories in fifth grade, and one of them kindly ran off some ditto copies of my manuscript to send to different publishers. Although my stories were never published, those teachers' encouragement sparked my interest in becoming a writer.

Childhood Idiosyncrasies

There were several childhood idiosyncrasies that I had. One of the main ones already mentioned was that I didn't talk during my first year of kindergarten and then later only in my wrong voice until third grade. Another one was my sensitivity to being touched by others. I didn't like to be touched, as it was not comfortable for me. This is a common trait among autistics and some Aspergers children. I was ten years old before I would even shake hands with other people, and only then at my parents' urging. Hugging and kissing are things I did even less.

Now, there were a few childhood friends to whom I gave exemptions about not being touched, and we used to play like normal children. By the time I was a teenager, there were more and more friends that I gave exemptions to, without telling them. For the most part, I outgrew that idiosyncrasy. However, if a person who I don't like touches me, I still "rub it off."

Between the ages of five and eight years, I could not relate to certain situations, and I had a lack of understanding of social skills. I was very straightforward and literal, and I couldn't relate to nor understand figurative expressions. Little by little, I learned the meaning of many of these types of expressions, as well as plenty of abstract concepts.

As an example of my trouble with certain expressions, when I was around seven years old, I was in a grocery store with Mother, and she was talking with a friend of hers about a young man who accidentally fell down a silo and was miraculously only slightly injured. Falling that distance is usually deadly or can result in serious injuries. Mother told her friend that the young man had a *close call*. I thought, *Close call . . . What?* I had no idea why Mother referred to it as a "close call," – a common expression that I would later learn. What went through my mind was a telephone call occurring in the silo and/or a nearby phone call, and it made no sense to me. Well, maybe the barn had a telephone, for all I knew. The above example points out how literal I was at that age, and how hard it was to understand expressions that can't be taken literally. I'm not as gullible as I used to be, but I do have a tendency to believe a person literally when he or she tells me something.

For example, say a "friend" doesn't want you coming around, but he's too polite to outright tell you. You ask him if it's okay to continue coming over to visit or chat, and out of his wanting to be polite, he says "yes." That's an answer I still take literally, but the truth of the situation is that the person doesn't want me coming over but can't bring himself to tell me. I would view that person's answer of "yes" as a lie, but others, as I have learned over the years, might consider the person to be simply "wishy washy", or not straightforward. So, based on *their* viewpoint, the person isn't actually lying, even though he isn't actually telling the truth.

At times in childhood, I had nervous twitches such as looking up every so often or to the side a lot, or sometimes a certain number of times before doing something. It was a tight feeling and a compelling urge that was quite annoying to me, and something I wanted to get rid of. Some of these compulsions occurred due to feelings of competition with others, sometimes jealousy, and also general anxiety. I haven't had any nervous twitches since childhood.

Another idiosyncrasy of mine was that I used the same white wooden high chair that I had used when I was a toddler all the way up to the age of twelve, at which time I physically outgrew it. It was the chair I was used to, and I didn't want to change to a new and different chair. Of course, I had to when I outgrew it. Now, don't misinterpret how I used the high chair. After I was about three or four, the tray that clamped across the front of the high chair was removed, and I sat in the chair in a more normal fashion, almost like a swivel high stool used in bars or at lunch counters.

Other things I had to learn during childhood were how to say "Hi" and "Good-bye" and "See you later" to people. I had to be taught how to answer the telephone. Those things were not natural for me. They were learned responses. Perhaps having to be taught those courtesies is normal for everyone, but I have observed even four and five year olds who seemed to have been *born* with that kind of knowledge and are a natural at it.

I had other idiosyncrasies pertaining to clothing. For example, I did not like belts and never wore them on any pants. I hate ties and I refuse to wear them to this day. I think society is really absurd in terms of how picky some people can be, and how some places of business, and even restaurants require them! What's it going to hurt to live your life without a tie and without a belt?! I'm just fine without them. They're useless anyway, especially the tie. It appalls me how many people wear ties on a regular basis!

When I was in kindergarten, I wore Farah jeans that had an elastic waistband, not a belt, and I liked them. By second grade, they were already out of style and were hard to find. I resisted change. Mother managed to find a couple more pairs of larger Farah jeans, and that got me through third grade. Of course, as I continued growing, I was forced to adapt, as Farah jeans became obsolete. I advanced to the Levi's type of jeans with a zipper, but I still refused the belt, and to this day, I wear pants without a belt. The only belt I wear is a seatbelt when I'm driving my car or truck or when I'm riding as a passenger.

Feelings, Psychiatric Assessment

Even though I did make vast improvements in the social area during my elementary school years, and even though the psychological assessment team recognized that I belonged in a regular classroom, I still had some social problems due to having Asperger's. My parents were concerned for

36

me, and they sought the help of a psychiatrist in Nashville named Dr. Caruthers. A Dr. Lavine administered a psychiatric assessment test consisting of a bunch of questions that I answered very well – except for feelings – which I didn't understand too well. Granted I had feelings, but I didn't know what to say in terms of talking about them. They were so complex for me at the time. How can a ten-year-old child be expected to fully understand feelings? That comes later on with maturity and becoming an adult.

On the same day Dr. Lavine evaluated me, I also had a meeting with Dr. Caruthers, the psychiatrist. He came across to me as a nice man who showed compassion and concern. I could relate to him, and I liked him well enough to invite him to come visit us on the farm and see my woods. He was honored by my invitation and realized that I trusted him.

While I was never formally diagnosed with autism or Asperger's syndrome, I was indeed diagnosed with psychological problems that, according to Dr. Lavine, needed serious attention *right away*. My diagnosis at the time (in the days before there was any recognition of Asperger's syndrome) was "adjustment reaction to childhood" and later "adjustment reaction to adolescence." That was in 1976 when I was in fourth grade. As one can see, my psychological state was labeled in accordance with the terminology of the time.

It wasn't until December 1993 that *The New Yorker* magazine printed Oliver Sacks' article, "An Anthropologist on Mars," which was an in-depth story and interview about the struggles and accomplishments of a famous high-functioning autistic named Temple Grandin. The next year, Oliver Sacks published his book with the same title, which helped to focus attention on the works and discoveries of Dr. Hans Asperger, an Austrian physician in the 1940s. For fifty years prior to the 1990s, Dr. Asperger's works were confined primarily to Europe. It wasn't until 1991 that Hans Asperger's descriptions were translated into English. Finally, and for the first time in 1994, Asperger's syndrome was included in the *Diagnostic and Statistical Manual of Mental Disorders, Fourth Edition (DSM-IV)* as an official diagnostic category by the American Psychiatric Association. This helped to broaden the view of autism, as well as the scope of diagnosis.

As an aside, Dr. Leo Kanner of Baltimore, Maryland had "discovered" autism only one year before Hans Asperger talked about the syndrome bearing his name. Even so, recognition of Asperger's syndrome as an acceptable diagnostic label here in the United States would not come for many years – not until after Hans Asperger's works were translated into English. If the terminology had been in existence in the 1970s, when I was a child, I would likely have been diagnosed as being a high-functioning autistic, and by that I mean Asperger's syndrome.

A week later when the test results were ready, I met again with Dr. Caruthers. I remember he commented that while I did very well on the test that Dr. Lavine had administered, the feelings section was deficient and needed some attention right away. I had an above-average vocabulary, and my only weak verbal area was in social comprehension and my ability to plan and interpret social situations. I felt better and more at peace in the woods and up in a tall tree than I did associating with certain people (those with whom I was incompatible, and those who humiliated me). I had told Dr. Lavine, "I don't work much with feelings," and "I don't think about feelings." Even though I had friends, the doctors determined that my fears about the pain involved in relationships, and also my feelings of inadequacy in social situations, were what led me to isolate myself. Well, that was partly true, but some of it also had to do with living and growing up on a farm. No matter what, the fact remains that I did indeed have friends come out to play, and I also played and socialized with others at school.

I will admit that Dr. Lavine was indeed right about my fears of pain involved in relationships. I didn't want my feelings hurt, nor did I want to be rejected. I had feelings, no doubt about that. It's just that they were personal and private, and I didn't want to share my feelings with others.

They honed in on the feelings deficiencies, and Dr. Caruthers and my parents decided that it would be best if I went to *weekly* consultations with a psychiatrist! While it was true that I was deficient in the feelings area, I thought the psychiatrist sector was overdoing it, that is, they were making a mountain out of a molehill. Monthly consultation sessions would have been enough. As it turned out, Dr. Caruthers was just leaving to go work in Colorado, so they assigned me to a new psychiatrist from Lebanon (the country) named Dr. Jezzini.

I resented weekly visits, and I was angry at my parents for that! Monthly consultation sessions, I reiterate, would have been enough. We had to go all the way to Nashville, some forty miles away. I wanted to be home playing in the woods, riding my bicycle, or playing with my friends instead of occupying (losing) a whole afternoon after school per week with a nonproductive and non-helpful psychiatric session. I didn't know what to tell the psychiatrist, and his favorite comment was, "What do *you* think?"

We never talked about feelings, anyway. I used to talk to him about what I did at home, what I did in the woods, where I took bike rides, and who I played with. I can add that Dr. Jezzini was a good man, calm mannered, and easy going, and I appreciate that he never pressured me nor coerced me.

There was one thing I didn't realize until recently, and that was that Dr. Lavine's test results and recommendations had stated: "This boy very quickly needs to be involved in an intensive treatment program, including psychotherapy and possibly a residential therapeutic milieu program." *Milieu* means environment or surroundings, and in that case would have meant a hospital environment surrounded by overwhelming treatment programs and therapists! For all I knew, that could have entailed electro-shock therapy, plus a round of shots and sedatives, not excluding Thorazine (*chlorpromazine*)! Treatments like that were commonly used back in the 1970s. Based on Dr. Lavine's test results, and without my ever knowing it, that is, behind my back, Dr. Caruthers strongly suggested to my parents that such dramatic steps be taken! That would have meant taking me out of school, separating me from my routine, and institutionalizing me for weeks or even months! Plus, it would have been an embarrassment for me upon returning to school, when I would have had to explain to my peers and classmates why I disappeared for a while.

When I began writing this book, my parents came forth and only recently informed me of this shocking possibility! They have assured me – well that is, they have told me – that the shock therapy, shots and sedatives would *not* have been administered. That was not a common practice in Nashville, even though many other hospitals across the nation relied on those procedures. Besides, that type of therapy was not administered to children. It was more commonly used with adults. What they would have done is talk with me and get me (well, coerce me) to more openly express my feelings.

They told me that Dr. Caruthers had recommended a residential therapy program, since he was concerned about me because, as I enter puberty, I would have more hormones flowing through me and would therefore go into rages as a result. With that can of worms opened, I am now thankful to my parents that they said NO to that type of treatment!

The truth is, I never became violent. It never even crossed my mind to become that way. Why were those psychiatrists so concerned about me? Even though I was never placed under the treatment they recommended, I still never became violent, which proves that my parents made the correct decision, and that I never needed such dramatic therapy.

My parents, especially my father, were people who worried a lot, and while in one sense I can appreciate their concern, they were obsessed with it. Sometimes, being overly worried and obsessed with something can lead to serious complications and hinder a situation instead of help it. While they think the psychiatric sessions were helpful to me and that I was improving, the truth is that I improved because I was learning on my own through social interactions at school and playing with my friends.

Now, don't misunderstand me. Psychiatrists have their purpose, and they are a great help to certain people with serious psychiatric problems. I admit there are some people with serious mental health problems and mental illnesses who need those types of doctors, but my mental health was not that much out of kilter to warrant that type of treatment, especially what Dr. Caruthers had suggested! As a ten-year-old child, I had my ways of thinking and interpreting life. In all honesty, I believe some of my better teachers and certain friends I played with, were much better "psychiatrists" for me than the official ones in Nashville. Instead of a "residential therapeutic milieu program," a much better treatment for me would have been to go to a summer camp and enjoy activities and social interactions with kids my age.

In the summer of 1975 when I was out of third grade, my parents actually tried to place me in a camp over in eastern Tennessee, but the camp owner realized my quirks, shied away, and made up an excuse by saying, "I think he's too young." We had visited the place and I had liked it. I was very disappointed when he turned me down.

Someone later told us how he found out about my quirks, and it is a classic example of small-town gossip. One day, his wife was at a grocery store where she happened to see a friend of my parents. They got to talking about me, and that friend of ours leaned over to her and quietly informed her that I didn't talk in kindergarten. *Oh, my lord!* She subsequently took the news home and warned her husband. That was it when he found out about that! He didn't want any problem children, as if I were going to be a problem. I mean really, I had greatly overcome many of my quirks since kindergarten.

At age twelve, I joined the Boy Scouts, and there I did make some friends. We had camp-outs every season, and plenty of other activities. We hiked the Appalachian Trail for a week one summer. I also went to a summer camp for a week at one of the designated Boy Scout camps. I earned merit badges and I achieved. I became an Eagle Scout by age fifteen, and I enjoyed the National Scout Jamboree the following summer at Fort A.P. Hill, Virginia. Boy Scouts was an enriching experience for me, and I will always be glad I joined it and stayed with it for my adolescent years.

I continued to visit Dr. Jezzini right through my senior year in high school, but *not* once a week! After the first year, I convinced my parents to reduce those visits to once a month or even less. I talked to Dr. Jezzini about feelings when I entered puberty, as it was then that I began to develop feelings for girls.

Seventh Grade, Overwhelming Feelings

In seventh grade, I entered a new school, one of the middle schools in the county system. I had some good teachers who cared for us and prepared us well for high school. There were lots more students at this new school, and I met plenty of classmates who came from the other city schools. I made some more friends. A few of them were those who I remembered from my two and a half months of first grade at the elite county school. For my two years in middle school, things went very well.

I entered puberty during my seventh grade year. My feelings developed, and some of the feelings were quite strong, such as crushes on several girls, for example. Sometimes the feelings were overwhelming and embarrassing, making it hard to concentrate on whatever I was doing, and sometimes making it difficult to talk to that certain girl that I had special feelings for. This was a pertinent matter that I did indeed talk over with the psychiatrist, Dr. Jezzini, since I was seeing him anyway. He had thankfully quit saying, "What do *you* think?" so much. While he was calm mannered and easy going and did have some comments for me on the subject, there was nothing novel or outstanding that he told me.

My feelings persisted. I wanted to continue with just normal feelings, as those overwhelming crush feelings were quite bothersome. Indeed they were just too much for me. I didn't want them. So, I squelched them. It was one of the hardest things I ever did. I have understood from seventh grade forward, what the phrase, "Cupid's arrow flew" means. Now yes, I still have feelings for people even today, but the level is no longer intense and is much more normal and manageable.

During seventh grade, some of the teachers organized a trip to New York City, Philadelphia, Washington DC, and Williamsburg. It was a great trip that I signed up for right away, and it was the first time I travelled outside the supervision of my parents. We all boarded a Trailways bus (with a 4-speed standard shift) and pulled away from the school campus on March 16, 1979. It was an all-night trip, our first stop being Thomas Jefferson's home, Monticello, near Charlottesville, Virginia. This was followed by several days of seeing the sights in Washington DC. After that, we went on up to New York City and did many activities, including going up into the Statue of Liberty and up to the top of the World Trade Center, elev. 1,377 feet. What views indeed! Then we went to Independence Hall in Philadelphia, followed by seeing Williamsburg, Virginia. We then made an all-night bus ride back to Murfreesboro, arriving March 25. It was a packed trip, and I enjoyed the trip very much.

In addition to enjoying the trip, there was something else I remember very well, something I wanted to accomplish but didn't know how and/or felt uncomfortable. One young girl that I really had a crush on was also along on the trip, and one night in New York City, there was a Broadway presentation called *Sweeney Todd, the Demon Barber of Fleet Street* that we all went to. Well, the thing to do was to take a date, and all the guys on the trip were making their choices. One night we all went to a movie, and I attempted to ask her out by talking to her, but I somehow didn't make it to the question of actually inviting her. The next night, I went to the hotel room to ask her out, and when I asked the others if I could speak to her, she came out into the hall and asked, "What?!" in an exasperated manner. The sharp pain that I felt was too much for me, and instead of asking her for the date, I replied that it was nothing. When the Broadway presentation took place the following night, I noticed that she went with another guy – and he also escorted three other dates, a total of four to that show! What a hog! I felt sad that I couldn't take her. I didn't want to take somebody else, so I took no one. The show was loud, so I put my earplugs in. As it turned out, I fell asleep shortly after the show began, and in short order, the three-hour show was over. I had enjoyed the sleep and felt well rested!

So much for dates. I have to admit that the pain I feared in relationships was certainly brought to the forefront when that young girl responded to me with, "What?!" I just didn't want anything to do with dates after that, and I have done very little dating since. Of course, I realize there are plenty of other girls I could have enjoyed some fine dates with, but I simply lost interest in that type of social activity. I had more interesting things to do, namely travelling and enjoying adventures. Now don't get me totally wrong. I have had friendships with girl classmates throughout high school and college, but only with those that I felt comfortable being around – no *special* feelings. There were even some girls that I really liked. It's just that I never made the commitment of "going with them" or taking them out on dates.

Strong Convictions

In early childhood, I had strong convictions, and sometimes I placed unnecessary restrictions on myself – for example, my speaking prohibition in kindergarten. Perhaps this gave me good practice in having strong convictions even now, which is why I have never fallen prey to drugs, alcohol, smoking, premarital sex, or even using foul language.

As an example, before I was age ten, I used to eat chocolate like all kids do. However, I discovered that it made me feel hyper, agitated, and irritable. One day in September 1975, when I was in fourth grade, I began to eat a chocolate chip cookie. I put it back in the lunch box. I haven't eaten any chocolate since. There were several tempting moments since then, but I told myself that I no longer eat chocolate. I didn't break my conviction nor revise it.

As I now look back on that strong decision I made at age ten, I now realize that it was an excellent practice run for learning to refuse to smoke, drink, or do drugs. Early in life, I made a decision I was never going to do those things, and my conscience is so strong that I could never have crossed those lines that I set.

When I was a child, I made some decisions about what I would do or not do in my life. I knew from age six that I would never smoke, drink, or do drugs. I remember my parents saying that when I would be older, say age twelve, they would let me try alcoholic beverages. Well, when I was age eight, we were visiting some friends in Birmingham, Alabama. I reached for what I thought was a Sprite or Ginger Ale. It was a beer, and what an awful taste it had! I spat it out and washed my mouth out with water. If that's what beer tastes like, why does anyone want it? That became my philosophy, and I saw no need to modify or revise it when I reached adolescence. As for whiskey, champagne, wine and the rest, one whiff of each immediately told me they taste as bad as they smelled!

When I reached age twelve, I knew that since I wasn't ever going to smoke, drink, or do drugs, I saw no need to sample those things. What for? I had already made my decision. I have watched so many teenagers take up smoking, drinking, and other bad habits. What is really sad is that some of them had actually told me, when they were eleven or twelve, that they would never take up those bad habits. Here's how I see it. Where's their memory?! What happened to their convictions? When I was eleven and twelve, I told other people I would never smoke, drink, or do drugs. I kept to my word and my convictions. Why haven't those other teenagers kept to theirs? I guess they don't care. They're not as literal as I am, and they don't actually mean what they say.

I remember when I went to my ten-year high school class reunion. I was surprised at how many of them were drinking and smoking. What surprised me even more was that one fellow with a beer in his hand had told me back when we were in high school that he didn't drink. He actually said he was proud that he didn't drink.

So, I asked him in a puzzled manner, "You're drinking, too? I thought you didn't drink."

He answered by saying, "Well, I went to college."

I reminded him of what he had told me back when we were sophomores in high school. I even mentioned the details of where we were when he told me, and who else was with us. He didn't remember telling me. I was surprised he didn't remember.

From that moment on, I have come to realize that I do indeed have a phenomenal memory for details and conversation. I used to think that others remembered events as well as I do, but surprisingly most people don't.

At a family reunion when I was age twelve, I remember surprising my aunt and uncle by declaring, "Never!" pertaining to drinking champagne. My uncle was so surprised that he mentioned it three or four times to everyone else at the family reunion. I made sure I stayed true to my word as far as drinking, smoking, and doing drugs are concerned. *Never!*

For all those teenagers who break their word, it seems like their faces change, and they take on a different look. The look in their eyes also changes. Some other-level influencing factor like peer pressure somehow overrides their previous convictions. I think that happens because their convictions aren't as strong as mine. If my strong convictions, and my refusal to revise them, have anything to do with my being an Aspergers, then I am grateful for that aspect of the condition.

How I Think and Remember

This is as good a place as any to explain to the reader how I think and remember. I consider it unique, compared to most people and the way they think. Some autistics – for example Temple Grandin – think in pictures. They have a visual memory or a photographic memory. I have a good memory for numbers, events, and long-ago conversations, but my memory is not photographic. Granted, I see plenty of images in my mind while I'm dreaming, and I dream in color, but while I'm awake, I cannot see visual images in my mind, not even while my eyes are closed. Even so, I have the ability to recognize a person's face, and in my mind, I know what he or she would look like, but it's a memory, not a visual image. I can remember quite a lot of shapes and designs – for example, types of trees, cars, and telephone styles – but I cannot see those images in my mind.

As an analogy, my memory could best be described or compared to Microsoft DOS® on a computer, in other words, pure text, while those with photographic memories could be compared to Microsoft Windows®, in other words, images on a computer monitor. I can't even see images of text in my mind, but somehow I'm a good speller, and I know in my mind how a word should look, with correct spelling and lettering.

I don't even see phone numbers in my mind, but I have quite a lot of them (hundreds, in fact) memorized. I remember the phone numbers of many friends and relatives, even including the phone numbers of a few friends I had back in kindergarten and first grade.

My memory for events and how they happened is pretty accurate, and as far as I know, my memory doesn't change over time. People tell me I have a good memory. For various reasons, a lot of people's memories change, and some get repressed or even forgotten. Emotional factors could have something to do with this. For me, I remember almost everything regardless of emotional factors.

High School and College Years

I attended high school and did very well, making nearly straight A's. I was second in the class of 320 students. My IQ was measured at 130. Most of the people liked me, and I fit in pretty well. I had plenty of friends. Several times, I enjoyed doing activities with them, playing in sports with some of them, and marching in the high school band during one of those years. I ran track for two years, doing the mile and the 880. I was even rushed to join a fraternity and was accepted, except I turned it down because they drank and had keg parties. In high school, I had more freedoms, especially pertaining to where I could eat my lunch, and I could visit with *anyone* in the lunchroom, not just those from my homeroom.

I need to mention, however, that there were times, especially during my first year of high school, when I experienced exclusion from my friends. I remember several incidents during group activities, say when we gathered in the auditorium. I walked in with those classmates who I thought of as my better friends. As we took our seats, all too often they did it in such a way that they perfectly occupied *all* of the seats in that row! There was no seat left for me. As a result, I had to go sit somewhere else, and I felt a little bit excluded.

I experienced less of that after my freshman year, and things improved. I made a good number of friends in high school. Some of them became great friends. We did things together, and they would come out to my house and camp up in the woods with me. I still know some of them today.

In my senior year, I was voted the Most Intellectual, an honor indeed. I also received several awards for being first in the class. One was the Spanish award, and another was the Geometry award, plus the Advanced Math award. I even topped out the valedictorian in those areas. Being second in my graduating class, I was the salutatorian, and I had understood that not only does the valedictorian speak at graduation, so does the salutatorian.

However, in the spring of my senior year, I received the surprising news that it was decided (new policy) that only the valedictorian would speak at graduation. How strange! As I look back on it, maybe I should have contested it, but I just didn't. I believe, to this day, that when they realized I was going to be the salutatorian, they purposefully fabricated a new policy to prevent me from speaking. Very clever! I will also mention that there were certain clubs that met every two weeks during alternate schedule that I felt excluded me. One was called the Key Club, and all of the better students were invited to be members. I had never been invited. I don't think it had to do so much with my having been an Aspergers as much as the probable fact that a few of the faculty – those who happened to be in charge of that decision – just didn't like me. I have seen them several times since then, by chance, and they are always cold-shouldered to me. No matter what, most of my teachers genuinely liked me, and that even included the principal and some of his assistants.

Once I graduated, I was glad to be through with high school. Even though I enjoyed many things about it, the curriculum and work load were intense. Even still, I knew I would miss my friends.

The following autumn, I entered Tennessee Technological University in Cookeville. I had been awarded a university academic work scholarship, where I worked forty-four hours a quarter. I stayed in the dorms. It was quite an adjustment – having a roommate who was a total stranger. Things didn't go too well for the first two weeks, and one night he had his girlfriend in bed with him and denied me access to my room! I objected, and boy did he get defensive! I moved out the next day and became quite angry when I suddenly discovered that he had urinated in my water canteen! Well, in his little refrigerator, he had a bottle of Gatorade, the perfect drink to mask the taste. You can imagine what I did. I really enjoyed doing it, and I never told him either!

I had just become friends with a fellow from Kentucky, and he let me move in. The rest of the year went great. I made plenty of friends, and we did activities together. Some of them even took me home with them on some weekends. Some also came to my house and farm to visit. One of them even travelled with me to Cumberland Island in Georgia. I succeeded! I had actually made a good number of friends, and though we've all drifted apart since then, I look several of them up from time to time. At the end of the first year, my roommate paid me a high compliment by saying, "God could not have created a more considerate, friendly roommate." He also told me that it was nice to not have to worry about what shape his room would be in each time he walked in.

Cookeville was a somewhat small town, and I used to take regular bike rides out of town. I kept a map on the wall and marked all the roads I explored by bicycle. The countryside was scenic, but it was hilly. There were times when friends of mine took bike rides with me.

The school curriculum of electrical engineering (EE) was tough, and I made plenty of B's and C's, to go along with many A's. Even through my last final exam, I felt like they were trying to weed us out! My quality point average (QPA), when I graduated, was barely over a 3.0, out of a 4.0 maximum, which was still quite good for an EE. I had to study a lot, and at times, I felt mental blocks with the vague theories and abstract concepts. Calculus, differential equations and complex variables were not straight-forward like the math I had previously studied in high school, and they were much harder for me to understand. Of all the math courses I took, I made only one A (calculus III).

Nevertheless, I enjoyed making friends, and even though I refused to join fraternities, I enjoyed the social side of college more than the curriculum. Several classmates used to study and do homework with me, especially during the last year. When I graduated, I felt sad because I knew I would miss my friends.

Since that time, not being in school, it's not been as easy to make friends.

*   *   *

Robert Sanders beside his igloo, January 1979

PART 2

My Sister

The original self-published edition of this book makes no mention whatsoever of the fact that I have a sister. Her name is Priscilla. I had made a conscious decision not to include her in that book, since my sister and I had been distant with each other since 1994, and I thought she might be touchy on the subject. She had been working through a lot of things and had wanted little to do with me. Plus, she was sensitive about some matters and usually didn't want things in writing because it might hold people more accountable. So, I therefore reasoned that I would simply not write about her in my book.

To my surprise, upon the self-publication of that previous edition, my sister wondered why she wondered why she hadn't been mentioned. She told me she wanted to be discussed in my book. Actually, she insisted on it, because she thought by including this important dynamic, it would help people to understand the anguish and the difficulties that siblings go through by living with an Aspergers. Very well then. I added this new section to this new edition of my book.

In June of 1967, when I was nearly age two, I had a sister born into the family. My parents brought her home. I didn't know what to make of having a new addition to the household. To me it was a surprise. I went to my parents and whimpered. After all, she was getting attention, too. It was a significant change in routine, and I realized that there was competition. I don't remember my reactions in those days. This is what my parents told me.

For most of our childhood, my sister and I didn't get along very well. We were incompatible in many ways. That's not to say that we didn't do some things together, but many times when we tried to play together, it resulted in squabbling and bickering. I do, however, remember a few times in our early childhood when we did play together peacefully in the yard.

It was difficult for our parents to raise us. Mother was agitated and frustrated, and she became flustered too easily. Some of that made me angry – our parents not knowing very well how to raise us. As I look back on all this, I realize now that because of my Asperger's syndrome traits, I was likely a difficult brother to live with. I'm sorry things didn't go better, and I'm sorry I wasn't a better brother to Priscilla, especially in our childhood.

My sister Priscilla, who presently lives in the Los Angeles area, came

49

to visit my parents and me during Christmas of 2002, and she wrote out a page of notes, mostly of things she remembers from our childhood. I have referred to that list in writing this part. At the bottom of the page, she titled the list, "Behaviors of Robert that made me . . ." and she listed several types of feelings of discomfort. She also wrote, "Thank you for being open to hearing my interpretation of these memories. I'm proud of you for facing all this and wanting to write about it. I'm sure I frustrated you too, etc. – Remembering I've let this stuff go, but it took a lot of work! It's the past."

After reading through her list, I realized that she was right about most of what she wrote, but I also realized that there were some other incidents and bothersome idiosyncrasies and characteristics of mine which she actually forgot about. In a way, I can be proud of her for forgetting those details.

I remember one incident when I was eight. A friend of mine and I took her up the driveway on our bicycles to the entrance by the road. We rode back without her, leaving her there to walk back home on foot. We have a long driveway, and she was crying when she got home.

I remember another incident a year or two later when I pulled her in the toy wagon, and I suddenly tilted it upward, dumping her on the ground. She got up angry and chased me into the house with a board. That was a violent reaction for which my mother scolded her. There was another incident that occurred that resulted in her storming into the house, slamming the door, and shouting, "I hate him!"

As I have already stated, I realize now that I was likely a difficult brother to live with. Even though we had separate bedrooms, there were several things I did that really bothered her and even violated her space. One thing I did several times was to enter her bedroom through the inside hall window instead of her door, since it was locked. I did so because she was playing the stereo while I was in my room trying to study for various tests back in high school. The stereo bothered me and broke (well, violated) my concentration. I would ask her to turn it down, and sometimes she did, but there were several times when she wouldn't accommodate my requests. On those occasions I entered forcefully to turn it down myself. She told me that no matter how low she turned down the stereo, it was never low enough for me. I didn't ever consider that she would be holding grudges for that for years on end.

Over the years, my sister observed that I had heightened sensitivities, and she used to wonder, *What is wrong with him?! Other people aren't so picky like my brother is.* I would complain and get upset about smells, such as hair spray, or the use of her electric curlers or her hair dryer, and the putrid smell they would make from cooking the hair! Nauseating! Even though, in those days, all of the boys used hair dryers, I was never able to use one because of the putrid smell and the loud shrill noise!

My sister said that in general, she felt like she couldn't even put her toe in my room or touch any of my stuff, but that I could mess with any of her stuff and barge into her room whenever I wanted to. Yes, that was unfair.

We had a two-door coupe for several years, and the seats would go forward to let people into the back seat. I remember several incidents when my sister was going through early adolescence, ages twelve and thirteen, a time when many people become more sarcastic and somewhat rebellious. They are sometimes cocky and they smirk, including rolling their eyes upward in reaction to being scolded by an adult. My sister had some of those traits, and that made her more difficult to get along with. Several times I would ask her to either turn down the radio, change the station because I didn't like the song that was playing, or roll down the window before closing the door. In defiance, she wouldn't accommodate me, and she would mutter several sarcastic words under her breath, which made me angry. I would kick the seat forward, which I know was mean of me, but I'm trying to explain why I did it – because I didn't appreciate her sarcasm.

There were some other things that also bothered my sister, though not as much as the above-mentioned incident. One thing was that my sister felt offended because I would say "my parents" or "my grandparents" while speaking to her instead of saying "our parents" or "our grandparents." I didn't do it on purpose, and certainly not with any intent to offend or frustrate her. Looking at the situation logically, my sister is the only person in the world where the word *our* applies to my parents. To everyone else, I say *my*, and I kept forgetting to say the word *our* when talking specifically to Priscilla. I would expect that situation to exist within many families with siblings. It's difficult even now to remember to say *our* when talking with my sister. I recently wrote her a note and in referring to our parents, I instinctively wrote *my*, realized it, marked through it, and wrote *our* above it.

There were things that bothered me about my sister, too. Since I was born first and my sister second, I always thought that we should be referred to as *Robert and Priscilla*. So many times, my parents and other friends and relatives of the family always said, *Priscilla and Robert*, and I almost never heard anyone say it right: *Robert and Priscilla.* During my early childhood, this became annoying to me – always mentioning my sister first, as if she were the first born and more important than I was. It made me feel quite frustrated and second rate, which is why it was so annoying to me! So, I began correcting everybody that said it by saying, "No, it's *Robert* and Priscilla. I was born first." Of course, now I realize that my sister and I are equally important, but still I agree with how I wanted my name listed first, since I was the first child in the family.

One detail my sister left out of her list was that many times during our childhood, we had friends (playmates) come and visit. As for competition, throughout our whole childhood I used to keep track of the hours of playmate time for each of us, and I became very jealous if she ever got one up on me by having more playmate time than I did. It was very important that our parents be fair to us, by making sure that she never got more than I did in that aspect. Now, of course, in my child's mind at the time, it was perfectly all right if I got more playmate time than she did. It made me feel blessed and richer. Since age fifteen or so, I have matured in that aspect, because from that age on I understood that my attitude about playmate time was not very considerate – even selfish.

My sister told me that she felt like I used to get angry because she had friends, or that she had successes in school, and so on. Perhaps she felt that for what I explained above. I'm sorry that she interpreted it that way. It was just a childhood sense of competition to do with playmate time. As far as I can remember, I was fine with my sister having successes in school.

One of the things that really surprised me on the list that my sister wrote out is that she felt uncomfortable that I would not dress appropriately for special occasions, such as weddings. As you will remember, I never wore a tie. I wore tennis or running shoes, not those uncomfortable dress shoes! It never crossed my mind that the way I dressed would bother my sister, or be embarrassing to her. After all, ties are something I hate. They are like a hangman's noose around the neck.

I remember going to a cousin's wedding when I was seventeen. Needless to say, I wasn't wearing a tie. My grandfather was very condescending and expressed extreme disapproval of me, which I did not like! After all, I had presentable attire – just no tie. If I had arrived at that wedding, say drunk, wearing a ragged t-shirt, soiled blue jeans, and without having bathed, then my grandfather's extreme disapproval would have been justified!

It amazes me how some people are so intolerant, especially about small things, like whether or not a person is wearing a tie. In the scheme of things, it just doesn't matter, which I am out to prove. I live my life without wearing a tie, no matter what the occasion, even if I were to be invited to a special banquet with the president of the United States!

I regret that my sister felt oppressed during our childhood, that most of the time she felt unwanted as a sister and that she felt like I was angry at her a lot of the time – perhaps that I even hated her. She felt like I didn't want to play with her, and had other negative feelings, which I'm sure was difficult for her.

When Priscilla and I reached college age, we got along better and had some conversations in a friendly sibling manner. I was glad that we were through our childhood and that those unpleasant incidents were in the past. My sister and I had a smooth road ahead of us. Yeah, famous last words!

My sister moved to Boston, Massachusetts in 1990, and she returned in December of 1993. I drove up there with my pickup truck and moved all of her stuff back home to Tennessee. Several weeks later, she found a house for rent in Nashville. We had some more conversations, which I enjoyed. Again I was glad the rough road of our childhood was behind us.

Once in Nashville, Priscilla located a therapist who did family counseling. She asked if my parents and I would attend. We went to several sessions and discussed our childhood. Let's just say some cats got let out of the bag. In the next several weeks, I talked with my sister about some of the things that she had mentioned in counseling, and was trying to work through in order to resolve them. I noticed that she had resentment building up in her. Ice started getting between us, and she was becoming more detached. In March of 1994, she angrily told me that I could tell her any information I wanted to, but that she didn't have to tell me anything! I didn't like that, and I told her that I didn't agree with that. I considered it very unfair and one sided! If I was going to be open with her, I expected her to be open with me. And then a bomb dropped! The demon was let loose! My sister became hysterical, screaming various vulgarities and telling me how awful I was to her during our whole childhood! I was appalled, to say the least!

We did go to one more family counseling session after that, and she was crying, accusing me of having hit her during our childhood, among other monstrosities! Yes, I did hit her a few times during our childhood. Such is the norm with sibling rivalry, but we never had knock-down drag-out fights or anything that serious. I don't think I was all that bad a brother. I was appalled at my sister's after-the-fact turn against me in

1994! Really, I thought we had resolved all our childhood difficulties, forgiven each other and all that by the time we were in our college years in the mid 1980s.

My sister decided to start seeing some other therapists and that sort of thing. I don't believe it was such a good idea; that is, dragging garbage out of the trash can from at least nine years earlier, resurrecting it, and rehashing it. As far as Priscilla was concerned, there were mountains of grudges! I'm sure the therapists must have comforted her by telling her, "There, there, it's not your fault."

My sister put excruciating demands on herself in counseling to overcome her rancor against me, all of which in my view was unnecessary and overly extreme. After all, I was not *that* bad a brother. There are some friends of mine who have told me horrible stories (horror stories!) about how they were treated by their older brothers or sisters. I won't mention specifically what those awful details are, except to say that if I had done things that awful to my sister, I would feel so guilty I wouldn't be able to live with myself! While I wasn't friendly with my sister, thank goodness I wasn't that abominable.

My sister later explained her viewpoint about why she saw it as all right that I could tell her any information I wanted to, but that she didn't have to tell me anything. She has a belief in what are termed "boundaries," what she also calls her "physical space." In our family, concepts like that didn't occur to us. It never crossed our parents' minds to teach that, at least not in that terminology. After all, we are a family, and therefore we are supposed to be open with each other. That's how my parents and I saw it.

In childhood my sister had felt oppressed by me because she felt that she was usually not able to get her way. She has told me that I was very adamant about getting my way in childhood, and if I didn't get my way, I would get angry. So, she would have to give in. In other words, she considered that a violation of her boundaries and physical space. For example, I used to barge into her bedroom, at times.

There were many things that she considered very private, and she didn't want to talk about them. I on the other hand was more open with people. While I do make efforts to be respectful toward people, I have always been bothered by the concept of boundaries and those who make it such a big issue in their lives. They close themselves off and make themselves inaccessible. I don't like it when people do that. I like to be more open and talk freely with people about things. If they don't want to talk freely about things, then I don't consider them very trusting of me, and that's what bothers me.

During the next eight years, 1994 to 2002, my sister and I were distant. That's not to say that we didn't have conversations and speak to each other, but whenever I talked with her, I could sense the wall of ice and the grudges. I also made numerous attempts, both verbal and written, to try and reconcile with her. She just wasn't coming 'round. She was staying behind the mountain, she was staying!

In December 1998, I became frustrated with her, because it really bothered me how she was giving subtle brush-offs and talking with ice between us. I was so tired of it. Something she did triggered an angry response on my part, and I shouted at her. After that episode, she rejected me even more, and she didn't even come to the farm while I was there, even though I *never* tried to prevent her from coming to her home place. Believe it or not, it was two and a half years before I even saw my sister again!

The last attempt I made to reconcile with her was in June of 2000. I had not seen her in a year and a half. So, I sent her a letter. Three months went by, and she hadn't answered it. So I e-mailed it to her. Still no answer! So, I e-mailed it twice the next day, three times the day after that. With that, she answered me. I had plans to increase the number of mailings per day until she answered me, even if that meant increasing it to 100 times a day!

Her one and only e-mail response to me was very cold indeed! While she thanked me for apologizing for any and all things I ever did to offend her, she told me that she wanted *no* contact with me of any kind, even though I would likely not understand her reasons. She also asked me to please *not* respond to her e-mail, as if my response would cause me bad luck. At least that is what she subtlely implied. Very strange!

My parents were quite displeased that my sister was continuing to be so distant with me and with the fact that she wanted so little to do with me. Our father had been having ill feelings about it for several years. He was constantly worried about it because it meant that there was disharmony within the family. In general, when people worry about things a lot, they tend to become ill.

Well, a "miracle" occurred in the summer of 2001. I put miracle in quotes because it was a false forgiving episode. My sister communicates regularly with my parents by telephone. In May of 2001, our father was feeling quite ill, and he told her that perhaps he was "on his way out." My sister became very concerned – alarmed actually – and she had a vivid dream that our father was on his deathbed. As a result, she cried all night.

She came home quickly, and came 'round. She even told me that she appreciated me for taking care of our parents by living on the farm and helping them with things around the place. I was pleased. Her coming 'round was only temporary, however. She firmed up again when I tried to ask her to answer her e-mails and tried to ask her if I could communicate. She only said a weak "maybe," and I wrote *tried* because she instinctively knew what I was going to bring up, and she squelched me from being able to complete asking her the question!

Anyway, we had another year of little or no communication. My sister was about to come home at Christmas in 2001, and she requested to my parents that I not talk to her nor follow her around. My mother got irritated at her and said, "Robert would like to talk to you, but he knows that you're not interested in talking to him!" While she was home for Christmas, I was there, but I didn't talk to her, because I knew. It felt really strange, being purposefully indifferent to my sister, but then that's what she wanted!

Finally, a *real* miracle occurred in the summer of 2002, and she spoke with me by telephone in an ice-free friendly manner. I was pleasantly surprised, and I could sense that all of the grudges were wiped away. Again, and this time more sincerely, she told me that she appreciated me for taking care of our parents by living on the farm and helping them with things around the place.

In that same year, 2002, she wrote, "Josephine," a song dedicated to our grandmother. It's an amazing piece that did more good for us than we will probably ever realize. When my parents and I first heard it, we were really moved by the piece, and we found it emotionally touching. I wrote my sister a note, commending her on her new song, telling her that her grandmother would be more than pleased – that she would be speechless – and I wished her good luck on getting the song published and produced. My sister was very pleasantly surprised at my note of praise, and she thanked me for that.

She came home in December 2002 and greeted me in a friendly manner. I was pleasantly surprised, and after several days went by, I coughed up her cold e-mail letter to me of September 2000, and I asked her to nullify it, please. I wanted assurance that I could communicate with her, without that thorn in my side. It was then that she requested to be discussed in this book, and she wrote the following note on the e-mail printout. "I forgive you, Robert. Let's move on from here in friendship, okay? Letting these terms go & remembering mutual respect. All the best, Priscilla." *Well, Halleluyah!* Miracles do occur.

It is important to mention that from December 2002 forward, my father has been very pleased about my sister's and my reconciliation. Harmony in the family is very important to him. He feels more uplifted in spirit now, for which I am glad.

In recent years, I was quite bothered that my sister was holding such grudges against me for what happened so long ago, but I can now be thankful for the miracle that occurred in 2002 that brought her around to do what was most important – to *forgive*.

*   *   *

Robert Sanders and Priscilla Sanders at home, 1972

Priscilla Sanders and Robert Sanders, 1977

The Sanders family, summer of 1981

PART 3

PROJECTS & INTERESTS

Travelling

Since I was a child, I have liked to travel. When I became sixteen and could drive, I began to travel on my own. When I was eighteen, I travelled up to Canada and visited some friends in Toronto. In the summer of 1985, between my first and second year of college, I drove my 1970 Ford Fairlane station wagon out West for seven weeks. I took my bicycle and backpack and enjoyed the trip very much. I was nineteen, and I had to take the whole trip alone, which wasn't exactly my choice. I had sincerely searched – even advertised – for a travelling companion to take the trip with me, but I had no takers. I backpacked and camped in several parks and wilderness areas, and I climbed several mountains. I must admit that I felt lonely at times during my first trip out there, but I got used to it. Since then, I have made several more trips out West and to other areas of this country, as well. I have also visited Canada and Mexico.

I had saved money through high school, and I took a year off from college to work and travel. I flew to Australia and New Zealand and was there for several months during *their* summer of 1985-1986. Again, I took my bicycle and backpack. In Australia, I did some wilderness back-packing, using topographical maps and a compass. Australia is such a big country that I also bought a car to use there, and I sold it back at the end of my trip. Having a car was convenient for the road trip I took and for sleeping in at night. In New Zealand, I travelled much of the time on my bicycle, and I enjoyed the scenery there, as well. I made several friends in both countries, and I still know some of them today.

From 1986 forward, I took on a project of hiking sections of the Pacific Crest Trail each time I went out West. Though I didn't hike the whole trail all in one season like some do, I have enjoyed numerous sections, and I have some great pictures of the excellent scenery in some of the areas. I also wrote detailed daily accounts of my trail hikes, which include descriptions of the terrain and scenery, plus the types of trees and wildflowers I saw along the way. At times, I met people while hiking, but I have only been able to keep up with very few through the years.

Before my final year of college, I took another year off to work and travel. I returned to Australia and New Zealand, and I took my bicycle and backpack with me again. As I did four years earlier, I bought a car and sold it back before I left. It was nice to see and explore more of Australia and New Zealand, and I feel fortunate that I was able to do so. I also enjoyed looking up friends who I had known four years earlier. I made some new friends, as well.

In more recent years, I have taken my bicycle and backpack over to England and Scotland where I have gone walking and camping on some of their trails and rights-of-way. The countryside is great for bicycling, and I have bicycled for days – even weeks – through the English countryside, camping each night in farmland or in woods.

Travelling has been one of my favorite things to do in life, and I have also enjoyed meeting and associating with people along the way.

Robert Sanders petting a Bennetts Wallaby, January 1990

The Bicycle Rides Project

At age ten, I began to bicycle on the local back roads in the county where I still live to this day. I enjoyed the rides through the farmland. At age eleven, I decided to begin a project of riding on *every* back road and highway in the southwest portion of the county. My strong desire to explore and my thoroughness drove me to accomplish the task. On selected weekends, I chose certain roads and made various bicycle rides.

In those days, the late 1970s, more than half of the roads in the county were gravel. Since 1990, all but a very few of those roads have been paved. I had a map of the county on my bedroom wall, and I used to mark with a red felt tip pen the roads on which I had bicycled.

I remember one favorite country store I used to visit called Versailles Grocery, run by a nice lady named Mrs. Carlton. She used to cook lunch for several locals each day. It was set in a beautiful hilly area of the county, and occasionally friends used to ride with me to that store.

One day, I rode to a community called Newtown, and I got caught in a downpour of rain. As a result, I had to call my parents to come and get me. Since I had to be picked up instead of riding home myself, those roads didn't count, and I had to bicycle there again on a better day to make that right.

By the time I was thirteen, I had completed my project, even reaching and covering all of the back roads on the west side of Eagleville. So, next I expanded my project to include all of the back roads to the east of the southwest portion; that is, the entire southeast portion of the county. Now I would cover every back road within a fifteen to twenty-two mile radius of my home, depending on the direction. I was fifteen and a half when I made my final ride to complete the coverage of the furthest roads from me – some of them as much as twenty-two miles from my house at a community called Readyville. A couple of those bicycle rides had been ninety miles long! I also covered some of the roads in the northwest portion of the county, those that were nearest me.

In addition to that major project, I decided to ride my bicycle to and from my grandparents' house in Crossville, 100 miles away. I succeeded, riding there in eight hours and twenty-five minutes, after I left home. My grandparents were sitting in the front yard at the time I arrived, and my grandmother upon seeing me commented, "Well, I'll declare!" They were both impressed, and my grandfather complimented me by telling me I sure was smart to have been able to ride all that way. I rested there on the second day and returned home on my bicycle on the third day. It was quite a trip, and I remembered how several people had earlier told me it would not be possible – that my legs would just not handle such a long ride. I was glad to have proven them wrong on that one! To add to the amazement, I did all of that bicycle riding on a regular one-speed bicycle. I finally bought a multi-speed bicycle at the age of eighteen.

Robert Sanders and Lewis Collins on their bicycles, September 1979

Radio DXing

When I was age nine, I started listening to the radio. It is important to mention that while I like it quiet a lot of the time, there were also times that I listened to the radio, especially the AM band. I used to enjoy picking up stations from faraway cities, and I kept a detailed log book of all the stations I was able to receive. In other words, I was a DXer. DXing is a hobby of seeing how many stations you can receive and keeping detailed records of those receptions. The furthest station I ever received on AM was KSL from Salt Lake City, Utah. I never ever picked up any from California.

My favorite radio station in those days was Musicradio WLS 890 from Chicago, Illinois. They played mostly pop songs, and I liked a lot of those songs, especially from the 1970s and 1980s. I have a record collection from those days. Of course, I was forced to change over to CDs when vinyl records stopped being made on a grand scale around 1990. I liked listening to two disc jockeys: John Landecker and Larry Lujack. John did a "WLS Boogie Check" every night around 9:30 PM when people would call in, and he occasionally did "Can I Get a Witness News," where he would ask famous people questions, and for their answers he would play excerpts of recordings of their speeches. It was hilarious! Larry Lujack did a funny "Show Biz Report" every morning around 7:30 AM.

I began DXing in third grade, and I did more of it in fifth grade. My parents bought me a General Electric 10-band radio, which I still have in good condition. With that, I added quite a bit to my log book. When summer came, I got away from it and then returned to DXing in seventh grade. Again, I entered into my log book a lot more first time receptions for more stations. I had quite a list. Since seventh grade, I have pretty much gotten away from DXing.

By the mid 1980s a lot of stations like WLS went off clear channel, and a lot more radio stations were added by permission of the FCC. I am disappointed by the overloading of the AM band! Back in 1979, when I first visited California, I actually picked up WLS out there, and also WWL from New Orleans, but that sort of phenomenon is no longer possible. One can see the traits of a high functioning Aspergers, considering all of the detailed records of DXing that I used to keep. In a way, my listening to the radio was a portrayal of my desire to communicate.

There was one really positive benefit that came from my radio DXing. When I was in fifth grade, I wrote letters to some fifty radio stations across the country, asking them how they got their call letters and what was the furthest place they had received a reception letter from? Most of them replied. WLIJ, a 1,000-watt station from nearby Shelbyville, Tennessee, actually sent me a copy of their furthest reception letter, a long and detailed letter from Toronto, Ontario. I wrote the fellow, and we became DXing pen pals, and later just pen pals when the DXing interests went by the wayside. He and his family are the friends I went to visit after high school, when I was eighteen. Some of his cousins were also visiting, and we went hiking in one of the provincial parks. I still know him and his family to this day, and they are nice people.

The Log Cabin Project

Ever since I was age ten, I had wanted to build a log cabin in the ninety-acre woods on our farm. I was spending time in the woods on many afternoons, and I used to run around up there with my dog "Puppy," whom I had found at my grandparents' house when I was in second grade. My dog and I used to run around a lot together when I was growing up. On occasion, we even camped up in the woods. I had my dog for fifteen years.

Robert Sanders, the day he found his dog, 1974

I cleared several trails in the woods, while thinking about the cabin and studying ways to build it. One day when scouting out a place for my cabin I came upon a rise that looked perfect for it. Two years later when I was twelve, I had a few Hickory tree saplings removed that were growing exactly where I would build it. (I was still too young to use the chain saw myself.) I left all the other trees in place, and they are great shade trees.

Finally, during my second year in high school, I decided to begin my project. My parents said I wouldn't be capable of doing it, but I proved them wrong on that one, and I began to build the cabin. I cut seventy-seven Cedar logs, some twelve feet long, and others seventeen feet, and I dragged each log up the trail to the site using ropes and roller logs. Using a chain saw, I notched the logs, and I assembled them. My father came up the trail to see my progress, and he was pleasantly surprised at how quickly the cabin was taking shape. I even put a loft in the cabin, and I completed it with a tin roof. I was very pleased with the finished product – a log cabin for me to enjoy. It was a nice get-away place that was secluded in the woods, and I'm glad that I built it.

Later that year, friends of mine came to visit, and other friends of my parents and relatives visited and saw the cabin also. Many of them were impressed. Several times, high school friends would come out on a

Saturday, and we would sleep in the cabin. Even a few friends from college came and slept a night up there with me.

I even installed phone service in the cabin, by running army phone wire underground and along the forest floor to reach the cabin nearly half a mile from the main house. My parents had two army crank phones, and my friends and I would call home with them. Plus, we still had the first original telephone from the farmhouse, a wooden wall crank phone. I bought some 1.5 volt dry cell batteries and connected that telephone to the system also. That is actually when my interest in telephones began, and one can see that in a sense, I was displaying a desire to communicate. The cabin still stands today, over twenty years later, and I still go up there and enjoy it at times. My trails are also still in place, and I maintain them every year.

Robert Sanders, his parents, and his sister, at his log cabin, 1982

Keeping Detailed Records

There were many ways through my life that I kept detailed records – for example during the radio DXing period. Keeping detailed records is something that I still do. I already mentioned how I kept detailed daily accounts of my trail hikes. These not only include my hikes along the Pacific Crest Trail, but also the other major hiking that I have done, such as the Alpine Walking Track in the mountains of southeast Australia, the Cradle Mountain-Lake St. Clair walk in Tasmania, and also the Pennine

Way walk in northern England.

During my travels I have taken lots of great pictures of nature scenery, and I have my trip pictures in photo albums. Some of my best pictures are enlarged, and I have them hanging on the walls inside my house. In my earlier travels, I was using a Voigtländer camera, but now I mostly use an Olympus OM-1. Both of them take clear, sharp pictures.

When I first started backpacking, I didn't have any supply list to refer to, and I almost always forgot something on a hike. Well, in the summer of 1986, I remembered everything, and when I finished that hike, I decided to inventory *every* item in the backpack, including the food I took with me. That list was very useful to me in the future and saved me time in having to remember every detail.

When I was a child and later a teenager, I kept a written log of my dreams for several years. Then I got away from it. In 1992, I began writing down my dreams again, and I have been keeping a log of them ever since. Having a written record of my dreams helps me analyze life better. Plus, dreams are useful for ideas that I include in my novels.

Later on I will talk about *The Family Photo Albums Project* where you'll realize how I have kept detailed genealogical records. I also keep a complete list of the addresses and phone numbers of my friends and relatives, with backup copies of all that data in another building, so that it won't get lost. To me, having friends and relatives is important. Pertaining to friendships, I have written detailed overviews about my friendships with some of my better friends. Part of the reason I did that was to help me gain a better understanding of friendships and how they work. However, since 1997, I have gotten away from that because it was becoming too time consuming.

Starting in 1983, when I bought my first car, my 1970 Ford Fairlane station wagon, I became more aware of station wagons with a 3-speed standard shift on the column. It was rare that I saw one on the road. So, I started keeping a list on which I recorded each sighting, including the type of car and approximate year. Some types of station wagons equipped with a 3-speed on the column really surprised me. Some of the more surprising ones were a 1974 Ford Country Sedan station wagon, and a mid 1970s AMC Matador station wagon. The reason I found this surprising was that it was my understanding that standard shift was no longer available in full-size cars after 1970. By the early 1990s, I had a list of some thirty sightings. 3-speed station wagons were pretty rare in the United States, but in Australia and New Zealand, they were pretty common.

While in Australia and also in Great Britain, I took pictures of all of the types of cars commonly seen on the road, took more than 100 pictures, and I compiled photo albums of those cars. Some friends who have looked at my albums were intrigued by how meticulous and thorough I was in compiling them.

When I was in Australia, I kept a detailed log book of my expenses, so I would know exactly how much a long trip like that cost me. Though I rarely consult the log book, it's nice to have the record in case anyone ever asks me how much a trip like that costs. I keep up with my business expenses the same way, and I have a thorough record when I report my income each year for tax purposes.

Pertaining to school, I kept all my homework and written assignments. I even made photo copies (for myself only) of all the music we played while I was in the band, both in middle school and high school. Two footlockers in the attic contain all the homework I did, one for high school and one for university. I collected all my textbooks, as well. I didn't sell them back, like a lot of students did. After all, I might have needed them for future reference while in school, or perhaps at my job after graduating.

In high school, it was a tradition for classmates to get yearbook signatures from each other. I made a point to get signatures and notes from all my friends and everyone I knew. When I got to college, I was told that it was not the norm to collect yearbook signatures. People didn't do that in college. I explained that I wanted to remember who my friends were, and I collected lots of signatures and notes. All but one person accommodated my request. It's nice to look back at those yearbooks and reminisce about my friends then. You know, I was the *only* one who ignored the norm and made a point to get yearbook signatures from all my friends.

Also, during my first year of college, there was almost no one there who had gone to high school with me. So, to help me learn the names of all my new friends, I kept a detailed list of names of everyone I met, including when and where for each person.

In a book called *Diagnosing Jefferson*, written by Norm Ledgin, I realized how Thomas Jefferson had many Asperger's traits. He kept exact and thorough records of his spending, right down to the penny. He liked sameness; that is, he resisted change. He was also obsessed with finishing all of the details of his house, Monticello, among other traits. In many ways, Jefferson was a genius.

There are other ways that I also keep detailed records, as the reader will realize while reading the topics of this book.

The Ford LTD Station Wagon Project

For several years, while I was still in school, I had an obsession to put a manual transmission into a later model full-size station wagon, a Ford LTD Crown Victoria. It had annoyed me for quite some time that nearly all of America's mid-size cars, and all full-size cars since 1971, contained mandatory automatic transmissions, except for pickup trucks, vans, and some suburbans. One couldn't even special order a big station wagon with a standard shift.

Well, when I got out of school, I made that situation right, at least for my use! I bought a 1980 Ford LTD Crown Victoria station wagon and installed an in-line 6-cylinder 240 motor and a 3-speed w/OD (4-speed) manual transmission out of a pickup truck. The project became quite involved, especially pertaining to installing the clutch and brake pedal assembly, having to fabricate the clutch linkage and motor mounts, and the need to take careful precise measurements. Even some welding had to be done. The project was a success. I have driven that car on long trips, totaling more than 100,000 miles.

That was a major project that required tenacity and patience, and it was another triumph. It shows how I begin a project and see it through to completion. One can observe that in one sense, I was obsessed with having a standard shift in a car that never carried that option. The fact that I got that 6-cylinder motor to fit in there was another triumph in and of itself. No Ford LTD Crown Victoria ever had an in-line 6, nor a standard shift!

My first car, which I still have, is a 1970 Ford Fairlane station wagon, with factory standard shift. While keeping it and still using it at times, I accepted enough change to get a newer car for long trips, but I don't like automatics. I didn't even drive the LTD Crown Victoria until I had converted it to a standard shift. I didn't want to start out on the wrong foot, so to speak, by driving it for the very first time with the wrong trans-mission. In other words, I wanted to do it right – that is, before I drove it, it needed to have the options that I preferred and in fact brought into reality. A friend of mine drove the LTD Crown Victoria for me when I bought it, so that I wouldn't have to, and he was the one who parked it on the concrete pad where I began the converting process.

After I finished the project, I compiled all of my receipts, and I wrote out a detailed list of my expenses, so I would know exactly what the project cost me. Plus, I wrote a complete account of all the procedures that were done to convert the car to standard shift.

It's a good feeling to know that I have a unique car, with a simpler engine and normal carburetor, not fuel injection, and no computer. My car is easier to work on, for which I feel better on long trips.

Collecting Things

Many people like to collect things, such as coins, teaspoons, rocks and fossils. I like to collect most of those things too. I even used to collect my own hair for several years after each haircut. I still like to collect things to this day, and rocks and fossils are some of those. However, there are some unique things I collect. Among them are old telephones, newspaper comics, and even trees and tree seeds.

From the time I was eight, I became interested in fossils, and I used to collect black fossilized shark's teeth from the beach in South Carolina. My family used to take me to Pawley's Island for a week every summer, and in addition to swimming in the ocean and walking and running up and down the beach, I spent part of each day hunting for shark's teeth in broken up shell deposits. I became very good at it, and I found and collected other types of fossils also. I used to keep count of how many teeth I found each day, and each year. Some years I didn't find very many, and other years, I found more than 1,000. It all depended on whether the previous year's weather had been calm or rough. The rougher it was, the more shark's teeth that got washed up for people like me to find. Ranging from the years 1974 through 1992, I have found over 5,000 shark's teeth, and I have them stored in ex-medicine bottles, each labeled with the year I found them and how many per year that I found.

I also got started hunting for and collecting fossils out of the creek bed on our farm in Tennessee. There weren't any shark's teeth there, but there were other types of fossils, including Crinoid Stems (locally called Indian money).

I remember back in sixth grade when my classmates and I were at Land Between the Lakes in Kentucky. Since the cabins were very near the lakeshore, I discovered plenty of Crinoid Stems. So, I began to collect them. I realized I could find as many as 100, and I made it a project to achieve that number before we would return to Murfreesboro. Well, the final morning came up, and I had found ninety-three of them, and I needed to find seven more. So, despite the rules that we were not supposed to be down by the shore early in the morning, I went on down there long enough to find and collect seven more Crinoid Stems, to meet my requirement. I picked up number 100 right when one of the teachers caught me and informed me that I had broken a rule. It was my former fifth-grade teacher, and I made sure I did *not* apologize to him. They didn't punish me, since it was time to go back to Murfreesboro, and also since my father was there with us all week. My father understood my obsession about finding 100 Crinoid Stems, and he explained it to the teacher, who then understood the reason why I had broken the rule.

When I was age nine, I began collecting the Sunday edition of Dagwood comic strips, (*Blondie*). That was my favorite comic strip and still is. I always make a point to read it first. Anyway, I collected every Sunday's edition for fifteen years. At the end of each year, I would staple the fifty-two pages together, but it was too thick for conventional staplers. So, what I did was carefully puncture the left margins with an ice pick and then I bound them with wire. In the autumn of 1986, The *Nashville Tennessean*'s comic styling suddenly changed, and Dagwood was no longer on the front page, which disappointed me! By the later 1980s, it was becoming too much trouble to continue collecting Dagwood comic strips. I was away at university by then and was also travelling at times. So, I decided to finally let it go. The end of 1989 was a good stopping point. No matter what, it's nice to have collected fifteen years of Dagwood (*Blondie*).

I also like to collect old expired license plates that I find in car salvage yards. Some yards give them to me and others sell them. Friends and relatives have also given me their old license plates. I have collected license plates from all fifty states.

As I began travelling on my own at age seventeen, I began to collect rocks from each place of interest that I visited, be it a beach, historic site, wilderness area trail, or a mountaintop. I now have a good collection of rocks from faraway places. Some of my rocks are in boxes in storage, and my better ones are displayed on shelving at home.

Collecting Old Telephones

In addition to rocks and fossils, I also like to collect old telephone instruments, and I have gathered quite a collection of dial phones, along with a few crank phones. Many of my phones are from other countries, and I have many countries represented. While travelling in other countries, I have visited the phone companies and telephone exchanges where I have requested old dial phones, for future use in a museum. Most people have been friendly and accommodating. I appreciate old telephones in a time of such modern technology, and I still use dial phones to make calls. (I do have a touch-tone phone beside my dial phone to answer all those annoying "menu" selections.) It's my intention to create a telephone museum in the future.

To demonstrate one example of how unique I am in the collecting of old telephones, when I was in New Zealand in 1986, I noticed that a lot of the small towns at that time (not anymore) had manual exchanges that required operators to connect all calls. To be specific, Kaikoura with a population of 3,000 people had a manual exchange with nine operators. The telephones were made of black bakelite, and each one had a crank handle. Early the next year, I wrote the New Zealand Post Office (which in those days also included the phone company) and inquired about the possibility of their selling me some of those crank phones. The postmaster wrote me back and said that Kaikoura had converted to an automatic exchange on October 15, 1986, and that they were selling the old instruments for NZ $2 each. I wrote back and sent cash to purchase three of them, which including postage added up to around US $60. Upon receiving my money, the postmaster sent the telephones to me by surface mail.

Several years later, I was travelling in New Zealand again, and when going through Kaikoura, I stopped by the New Zealand Post Office. The postmaster was still there, and I thanked him for accommodating my request by selling and sending me those crank phones. I told him that they were well appreciated. He surprised me by telling me that I was the *only* American who had corresponded with him and ordered crank phones. The only one?! I had a moment of realization about how unique I am in this world. I just assumed that there would have been at least ten or twenty Americans, including phone collectors, who would certainly have ordered crank phones from Kaikoura. Of course, there were plenty of other towns in New Zealand on manual exchange in those days, and some of them might have gotten the odd order from an American. However, as I think about it, I am likely the *only* American who obtained any crank phones from New Zealand at all.

By 1990 New Zealand was selling a lot of old dial telephones as well, some of them the GEC 332, the bakelite English style desk and wall phones. Touch-tone service was the latest rave, and towns were converting over to it as fast as possible. I purchased and surfaced mailed home several great telephones, which are greatly appreciated in my collection. What New Zealand was tossing, I was treasuring.

Telephone collecting has been a great hobby, and I like to compare the styles between different countries. Plus, telephones represent communication, which is something I have always believed in doing. I also keep a complete inventory list of each type of telephone I have.

Not only have I collected telephones, I have also collected part of a step office (step by step electro-mechanical telephone exchange). That was in 1995, when several small towns in Georgia were converting their telephone exchanges to digital. I tried to purchase the equipment from their local phone companies, but the bureaucracy and red tape were so thick that they weren't allowed to sell me the equipment. So, I went around their system and talked to one of the tear-out crews, (the people who dismantle the old and disused exchange equipment) and they kindly accommodated my wishes and sold me enough of each type of Strowger switch (20 of each) plus the additional equipment necessary to make the exchange work. The tear-out crew hired me as one of their employees, which permitted me to enter the exchange and help them remove the equipment. That was brilliant. I was with them two days cutting wires and carefully removing the Strowger switches, racks, and other components. I placed them inside a U-Haul trailer that I had rented for the job. I am glad that I was able to obtain that equipment, which I plan to install in the telephone museum that I want to build.

Collecting Trees

I also like to dig up tree seedlings and collect seeds. Ever since I was a young child, I have been interested in the trees of this world. Since age eight, I have known what tree is what, even with the leaves off in winter. Trees are miracles that represent life. There are thousands of varieties of trees. They grow in many different types of environment here on planet Earth, and they cover much of the land surface. They give life by providing oxygen to all animals and humans, as well. They also purify the air, maintain ground water stability, and provide shade from the Sun. Many trees provide us with food and/or extracts for medicinal purposes.

Trees parallel the life cycles of humans in that they are born, grow to maturity, give their fruits, and eventually die. They give companionship to humans the way they grow throughout the forests and gardens. Trees are not conditional like so many humans are. Trees are also not like humans in that they don't fight, they don't abuse, they don't threaten, they don't reject, they don't attack, and they are not aggressive. With the trees, one doesn't have to worry about complex family dynamics and problems. To be a tree in the forest, such a *peaceful* existence it is.

While not removing any plant life from national park lands, I have dug up trees from roadsides, and I have mailed them home. I have sent home many varieties of trees, and some of them lived, while others died. To this day, I have numerous Western Red Cedars from Washington. They do very well in Tennessee. I have a Douglas Fir which is also from Washington. I have an Incense Cedar from southwest Oregon, and it's the fastest growing conifer I have. I also have a Ponderosa Pine from Idaho.

Trees that only lived a few years have been the Western Hemlock, Western White Pine, Giant Sequoia, and the Larch, or that is, Tamarack. I regret that one tree I had was never very successful, and that is the Giant Sequoia. They don't like the Tennessee climate nor the soil. I do have some Coastal Redwoods in pots so that they can be brought in during the winter.

I have a Balsam Fir from northern Minnesota. It is now fifteen feet tall. I've had it for twenty years, since I brought it home as a tiny seedling in a fishing tackle box from a Boy Scout canoeing trip in 1984. It has done very well. Believe it or not, Fraser Firs from east Tennessee and North Carolina will *not* live here in middle Tennessee, but the Balsam Fir will. In 1984, I also collected a native American Chestnut tree seedling from the slopes of Mt. Mitchell in North Carolina. I was very surprised to find one. You see a lot of growths from stumps, but you see very few seedlings. It lived, and it's now over twenty feet tall. It has a trunk around six inches in diameter, and it's been blooming for the past five years, only the seeds have never been fertile. More recently I brought home a second native American Chestnut tree seedling as a pollinator. I hope they will continue to grow, and maybe one day I'll get some seedlings from them.

I have even collected trees and seeds from as far away as Australia and Tasmania. I grew some Black Cypress-Pines from Victoria, which I have given away to people in California, Mexico, and Florida, since they can't grow outside in winter, here in Tennessee. I have sent home seeds from various places and have grown many different types of trees. Some did very well while others got barely started and died. While in Tasmania, I went to various nurseries and bought a King William Pine seedling and a Celery Top Pine seedling, and I successfully mailed them home to Tennessee. The King William Pine died within weeks, and the Celery Top Pine grew slowly for seven or eight months before also giving up.

No matter what, collecting and caring for trees has been one of my favorite past times, and I'm grateful that I live on a farm to have the space to plant them.

*   *   *

Robert Sanders at the base of a Giant Sequoia tree in California,
September 1998

PART 4

FRIENDSHIPS

This next section deals with a very important issue, especially for autistics and Aspergers: the difficulty in making and keeping friends. It includes success stories but also trials and tribulations. I also include my ideas, insights, and speculations in hopes that people without these conditions will better understand the problems that people with autism and Asperger's syndrome have in making and keeping friends. Perhaps the reader will benefit and compare notes, and I also hope that those in the autism spectrum might find solutions for his/her own friendship situations in this section of the book.

My Godparents

I remember one day when I was an early teenager when my parents and I were visiting my godparents, Phemie and Marion Young in Chattanooga. When we finished visiting and were getting in our car, they kindly saw us off. Marion touched the hood of the car with a friendly and sincere gesture, his way of saying goodbye. As we were driving away, Mother commented that that's what real friends are. I learned the truth that day about the meaning of true friendship. In other words, that gave me a frame of reference to know and understand what friendship really is. Phemie and Marion were lifelong friends who never turned me away and never removed their hand of friendship. They represented love and hospitality and I was always welcome in their home. They have passed away in recent years, but I will always be grateful to them for their kindness, and for being my godparents.

Ideals of Friendship

We live in a day and age where most friendships are far from ideal. There are people who are hostile, and there are some people who hold grudges. Peace does not exist in every part of the world, nor does it exist in every family. I suppose that a lot of people have a longing desire for peace and friendship, the ideal kind, what most would call a utopia. While there may be some people who have achieved something close to that in this world, that is not the case for the large majority of the human population. Instead, many people are aggressive and violent. Some nations are even at war with one another! That is atrocious, considering that we are human beings – highly advanced mammals who have reasoning faculties and intelligence well above most mammalian species. Therefore, humans ought to know how to really be at peace with one another.

I have sometimes pondered on what it would be like to have an ideal friendship. With an ideal friend, you can feel 100% at peace and you can feel 100% comfortable in his or her presence. The ideal friend makes you feel good and feel rejuvenated when you're around him/her. An ideal friend is 100% honest and straightforward, invites you to join him/her in activities and enjoys your company. An ideal friend includes you and welcomes you into his/her home. An ideal friend lets you get close, is comforting and reassuring to you, is supportive, and cares for you and your well being. He or she is faithful, appreciates you, and is proud of you and your accomplishments. Most of all, an ideal friend is glad to have your friendship. With an ideal friend, there is no such thing as shrieking or struggling away with abhorrence because true friends don't treat each other that way. Think about it. Ideal friends do not have any emotional upset either. There is no such thing as lying, avoidance, embarrassment, hostility, aggressiveness, fear, violence, and other negative traits. Instead, there is 100% peace, love, trust, and honest friendship.

At times through my life, I have had dreams of being with one or more really good friends. Even though we don't know each other in real life, we do in the dream. We have visited with each other, enjoyed each other's company, and have gone places together. With some of those people I have dreamed about, the sense of peace and closeness of friendship I have felt is incredible. Sometimes I even remember their names after I wake up, and I feel like those friends are so real that surely I must know them in real life, but I don't. I wake up truly missing friends like that, and I wish that I really knew them. Good dreams like that instill a longing desire in me to search for ideal friends and to find that type of peace because I believe that it exists.

Many people who are autistic and/or have Asperger's syndrome have more difficulty in making really good friendships, even though their intentions are usually very good. They usually have a high sense of loyalty to their friends, but they also have quirks about them and idiosyncrasies, and they don't always know what to expect in social situations. Because friendships are so difficult to achieve, I think that many autistics and Aspergers have more of a yearning desire for real friends than most other people. They have suffered more than their fair share of losses and rejections, so it seems logical that they would therefore have more of an urge to compensate for their losses by having an increased desire for real friends.

My idea of an ideal society – a utopia – is that if you see someone who looks attractive or friendly, you ought to be able to walk right up to that person, introduce yourself, and become friends, just like that. Instead, we as a society have pigeonholed ourselves into various and sundry social rules and social cues that inhibit our free ability to make friends. Think about it. How much embarrassment do you feel when walking up to a stranger in an effort to become friends with him or her? Does it feel like there is a barrier? In most cases the answer is likely to be yes. For example, to open the door to a friendship with that person, you would likely try to figure a way in, a clever path or tactic to use, or perhaps a unique subject to talk about, in order to break the ice and open that door. Well, it shouldn't have to be that way. It shouldn't be so difficult. Instead it should be very straightforward. For a truly advanced and ideal society, making friends *is* straightforward, and there are *no* barriers.

Personally, I believe in life on other planets throughout the galaxy and the universe. I even believe there are many worlds with humans or at least human-like beings. Many of them are certainly more advanced than we are on this world, and because of that, I'm sure that their culture is more ideal and more welcoming to friendships than ours.

I must admit that there are many times through my life that I have seen someone with whom I immediately felt a yearning desire to be friends, but because of the social cues and barriers that exist in our human society, I have been unable to walk up to that person. I couldn't figure out a path or tactic, you might say. I couldn't figure out a subject to talk about. I lost the opportunity – the potential friendship lost forever. Granted, in some cases, I was able to think of something fast enough. In those cases I managed to open the door, and we actually did become friends. There were also a few cases where I had lost the opportunity, but I was given a second chance, as you'll read in some of the following topics. For those recoveries, I am grateful.

As our society advances in the generations to come, we need to remove these social barriers and remove the pigeonholes that presently exist. Lost opportunities occur continuously in our world, and I'm sure that some of those opportunities and potential friendships would have been very important to those who have missed out on them. One will never know the difference for the better that those friendships would have made.

Dwelling on Subjects, Repeated Thinking

Many Aspergers have a tendency to dwell on certain subjects. So do I. If I'm thinking about something, I can think about it for quite a while, or numerous times a day. That is known as repetitive thinking. I sometimes ruminate over things and need to hash things out by talking about them several times – what others consider "over and over." Some things are hard to let go of. For example, I might be concerned or worried about a friend for various reasons or for something he/she did.

What I have noticed is that other "normal" people quickly get bored with things, especially in this day and age when nearly everyone wants action and something *new*. People quickly tire of talking about the same thing more than once, and when it happens they sometimes show impatience and anger! It amazes me that many people don't concentrate on a problem long enough to figure out a solution, nor do they even appear to be interested in figuring out why something might be bothering them or why something strange might have happened.

While most clinicians with expertise in Asperger's syndrome would likely say that dwelling on certain subjects counts as a negative, I must disagree. I have the trait of sticking to a project long enough to see it through to completion without getting bored. One example is the Ford LTD station wagon project. The work I did on that LTD was laborious and tedious, and most people wouldn't have even bothered to undertake the task. The same is true with my writing novels. A lot of people like to rush through the reading of a novel, but the truth is that when I *write* a novel, I cannot read it any faster than the rate at which I am writing it or typing it. While it is tedious work, it is necessary. A lot of potentially great writers or would-be writers don't have the patience to stay with a story to its end, because the writing of it would be too slow for them. In this case, my ability to stick with a subject is clearly a positive.

Repetitive thinking has other advantages, as well. Since I can think about subjects repeatedly for long periods of time without getting bored, my mind has greater access to deeper thinking about those subjects. I find that with repeated tenacious thoughts, things that were initially difficult to figure out do eventually get figured out. For example, I even have the perception to figure out scenarios and conversations that go on behind my back, if I think about them long enough. This is helpful in arriving at conclusions or reasons why certain people have behaved strangely toward me, or have wronged me in some way. Mysterious behavior does annoy me, and I can usually resolve the mystery by dwelling on it and thinking about it long enough to figure it out, after which I can release it and move on. For me, it comes down to this. It's perfectly all right to dwell on the same subjects, even if it's annoyingly boring to people without Asperger's. I have found this trait to be a benefit, instead of hindrance.

Attraction Forces, Getting What I Desire

In past years, up until I was twenty-seven or so, I felt that I was able to attract certain situations to me, especially concerning my desires to get to know certain people. Since 1992, this has occurred with much less frequency than it used to. I attribute this phenomenon to the powers of the subconscious mind. In my case the ability to do this has somewhat dissipated in recent years. I can remember back to first grade when I would "choose out" the people I desired to know, and almost invariably those "chosen ones" would become my better friends. What it seems like to me is that I placed a desire in motion mentally, and unconsciously letting the "energy" do its work, my subconscious mind would place those people in my life – like bringing paths to a junction. It was great to know and be friends with the people that I desired to know.

Even during my college years, the same phenomenon worked. I remember noticing one person during my third year in university. Then the next quarter, we were in the same lab class, and lo and behold, to my surprise we were thrown together as lab partners!

During my trip to Australia and New Zealand, when I was at the ticket counter before boarding my flight to New Zealand, I talked to a fellow my age who lived in Dunedin. Immediately, I had the desire to become friends with him, and after our chat, he walked down the hallway to board the plane. I boarded a few minutes later, and when looking for my assigned seat, I was pleasantly surprised that he had been assigned the seat right by mine! He was surprised, as well. We became friends, swapped addresses, and I looked him and his family up while in New Zealand. I still know them. They send me Christmas cards and calendars. I've sent them books and gifts, and I've called them every few years.

When I was travelling over in Great Britain in 1991, I was on a train one afternoon, and I was sitting across from a young fellow who looked a little familiar. After several minutes went by, he pulled out his checkbook and wrote a check to British Rail. I decided to make conversation with him by asking him about the formatting of British checks, as compared to American checks. I actually had a couple of blank checks in my wallet, and I showed him one of them. He remarked with interest, saying, "That's different." That opened the door, and as we talked about other subjects, I realized he was a friendly person indeed. We arrived at Royston, and he stepped off the train, saying, "Have a nice day."

He was already off the train, likely never to be seen again. I really wished to have become friends with him. I felt it was somehow important. I wished we had swapped addresses, but then we were only on the train together for half an hour. Then I suddenly realized that there was one saving grace in all of this. I had noticed and remembered his last name which showed up on his check. It was a rare last name. Well, resourceful as I am, I went to a library several days later, and in Great Britain's libraries, they have a long shelf with every phone book of that country. The United States does not do that. I looked in the Cambridge region, and with the help of my Great Britain road atlas, I pinpointed a listing with that last name I was looking for in a small community near Royston. I wrote down the address and phone number.

Several weeks later, I was bicycling through that region, and I decided to stop by there. It was a Sunday, and he would more than likely be home. I arrived at the residence, and I cautiously knocked on the door. I felt somewhat apprehensive. Sure enough, it was answered by the same fellow I had seen on the train! A look of total surprise came across his face, and after greeting me, he asked, "How did you know where to find me?"

I explained that we had looked at each other's checks, and while doing so, I admitted that I had noticed and remembered his last name, and that the phone book had helped me with the rest. We told each other our names. His name was Andrew. With ease, we started talking, and my apprehension disappeared quickly. He stepped outside where he saw my bicycle and touring gear. I showed him some of my pictures of Tennessee that I carried with me. Soon, his kind father noticed us from the backyard, and he invited me to come on through the gate and visit. We introduced ourselves, and I soon met his wife and Andrew's younger brother.

As it turned out, I stayed for three hours, and I had a really enjoyable visit with a very nice family who seemed to enjoy the pleasant surprise of having the American that Andrew had met on the train turn up! We even watched a TV show, *Bay Watch*, before I left. I had to leave before dark, so I could find a place to camp. They were glad to have met me and saw me off by jokingly reminding me to ride on the left side of the road. As for me, I felt a real sense of accomplishment at making those new friends. I still know them to this day, and I call them every few years to see how they're doing.

A year later in 1992, I saw a fellow at Sears who helped load some air conditioners on my truck. I felt like I wanted to be his friend, and I wondered how it would ever be possible to know him. Well, six years later, when I was looking for an artist for my second science fiction novel, I felt compelled (or instinct told me) to check with somebody I knew that worked at a corner printer. I went and asked that person if he knew of an artist who could do me some drawings. He gave me a name and number. I called the person up, met with him, and hired him. Not only did he do an excellent job on the drawings for my novel, he was the same person I had seen at Sears six years earlier!

In the summer of 1995, I was making copies at an office supply store in Nashville. I noticed a fellow who looked familiar. I suddenly felt a desire to be his friend, but how was I ever going to get to know someone in Nashville? What connection would there ever be? Lo and behold, a year later, I was introduced to him by a long-time friend of mine, Roger Schultz, who turned out to be his next-door neighbor! I was quite surprised! Read the anecdote, *The Frustrating "Friendship" with Chip.*

These kinds of experiences make life an interesting phenomenon – specifically how people are seemingly placed in my life, perhaps by destiny. These types of experiences that I call coincidences and synchronicities have occurred with several people that I've known. Some are similar to those that I have already explained.

What all of this comes down to is that these special phenomena – these attraction forces – which in recent years haven't occurred as frequently, are characteristic of many high functioning Aspergers. I have a good memory for details and events, and some say only I would have the phenomenal memory to notice and realize these types of coincidences that have occurred in my life.

There are likely various reasons why my ability to attract certain situations to me has somewhat dissipated. Among the most likely is that young people are less complex have a clearer mindset. As they live more years, their minds become more cluttered with more issues, grudges, and experiences, including learning experiences, in their lives. They make more decisions in life and they place more conditions on how they go about getting what they want. As a result, the process of attracting certain situations becomes more difficult. All of these things add up and create "clutter" which somewhat interferes with the ability of the mind, including the subconscious, to go about setting up important situations and synchronicities in their lives. This "clutter" can also be compared to vortices in a river. Vortices have remarkable stability. Opinions, beliefs, and conditions, like vortices, are also remarkably stable. These vortices can be detrimental to human spiritual growth, and they can also hinder the abilities of people to attract certain situations to themselves.

There are some people who know how to dump this kind of clutter, to clear the vortices, so that the subconscious mind can work more freely and unhindered. They are the ones who have better luck and are able to bring paths to a junction. They are the ones who have the knack in getting what they want, including the friends they desire.

Some Pursuits and Goals in Friendships

Many times, while backpacking and hiking, I've seen friends hiking together. I remember one time in particular, September 1992, while I was on Mt. Rainier's Wonderland Trail, I saw three college fellows from Phoenix, Arizona. They were great people. I wish I had become friends with them, but we were hiking in opposite directions, and we only knew each other for five minutes.

So many times I've seen fellow friends hiking together down a trail, camping together, enjoying their friendship, so easily, so smoothly. How do they do that so easily? How do they go hiking and travelling together so easily? What they do so easily has been seemingly nearly impossible for me. It's as if all of the conditions to make it happen are wrong for me, as though I were in the wrong place at the wrong time. How do those without Asperger's achieve such a high level of friendship that they reach the point of making plans to travel or go hiking? How do they actually invite each other to do that? No one ever calls me up to invite me travelling or hiking. Never. It is I who has to do that, and it seldom works out, and when it does, it's only after ridiculously excessive efforts on my part, strange as that might seem.

Yes, I have friends, but not for travelling, hiking, and camping, and you can be sure I feel lonely in that aspect. As I briefly mentioned at the beginning of *Projects & Interests*, I sincerely searched, even advertised for a travelling companion to take my first trip out West with me, but I had no takers. Well, there was one taker three years later, but it didn't work out very well. We took the trip, but his heart was back home in Tennessee with his just acquired girlfriend, instead of in the trip, and he was mostly malcontent as a result!

How I've longed for a good fellow friend to travel with me, somebody congenial, somebody who takes me at face value, understands me, and enjoys my company. In a world of some 6 billion people, why is it so difficult? I'm not talking about marriage, nor about gay relationships either, just a good friend with whom to travel – just like those college fellows from Phoenix, Arizona were travelling together.

I've made repeated trips out West, and I've really enjoyed the trips, but apart from that one trip with that malcontent friend, I've had to take all those trips and hikes by myself. In more recent years during my trips to Mexico, I've always gone alone. No friend or relative has ever been interested enough in me or my travels to Mexico, to travel down there with me.

While backpacking and camping, I've met people and made friends, and I've enjoyed that part of it. It's always been a goal of mine to collect addresses for people I meet who live out of state or out of the country. With a few of them I've become good friends. However, by the early 1990s, I began to experience some instances where I felt people were outrunning me to beat me to the parking lot so they could get away from me. Some of these folks would suddenly clear out of camp at the crack of dawn, or give me a false address! In general, it's becoming even more difficult to make and keep friends, since we live in a world of rising suspicion and lack of trust, which really is a shame.

I remember meeting a nice fellow in the mid 1990s, and we hiked north on a trail for several miles. I really enjoyed the afternoon with him. We camped in different places, and we made plans to hike together the next day continuing north, but I never saw him! He had gotten an early start and made tracks. I didn't want to lose the chance at making this friend, so I walked and walked. It was a tough and long day, and it was 10 PM before I finally reached the campsite where he was staying. As it turned out, he hadn't done it in efforts to outrun me. He'd been looking for me all day, too. So, we swapped addresses the next morning and parted ways. However, we haven't communicated since. I look back on it and wonder if it was worth all the pursuit and efforts I made to catch up with him to swap addresses? At the time I felt it was worth it, even though we never saw each other again. Better to have swapped addresses instead of regretting never having made the effort to do so.

There are people I see at places of business around town, for example, and I'd like to become good friends with some of them, too. While we even have great conversations at times, they are no more than acquaintances. There seems to be no way for that to be moved on up to the next level – friendship. That next level would automatically entail finding out where the other person lives, exchanging phone numbers, and inviting each other to do activities together from time to time. How do others do it? I mean, I've even taken my photo albums of, say, Mexico and shown it to some of these people. Hint, hint, hint! But it never crosses their minds to invite me anywhere. Never. Why don't any of these store workers ever take the easy enough step and invite me to do something? I've made more than enough initial steps. I'm waiting for one of them to come forth, although it certainly would surprise me if one of them ever does. Is it just me, or is it just normal for this to occur, or is this only what people with autism and Asperger's syndrome experience?

During the past ten years, I have observed the increasing difficulty at making new friends. I'm not sure if it's just me or if it's occurring with a lot of people, but times have changed. Styles and customs have changed, and it's as if making new friends is becoming a lost art. At least I made a good number of friends in past years, and I'm grateful for that much. I'll keep as many of those friendships as possible.

Friends versus Acquaintances

Some people have asked me to distinguish between *friends* and *acquaintances*. In the previous topic, I explained that people I know who I see at places of business are no more than acquaintances, and in order to move on up to the friendship level, they would have to invite me to do some activities with them and of course swap addresses and phone numbers with me.

I will briefly relate an example of another time I was backpacking and hiking, this time on the Pacific Crest Trail in Washington's Alpine Lakes Wilderness. The year was 1986. On the second day of my hike, I met two young fellows named Jeff and Tim from Seattle, and the three of us visited and chatted with each other at a beautiful spot called Spectacle Lake, where we also camped together that night. Jeff told me that he had hiked the Pacific Crest Trail through Alpine Lakes Wilderness with his father the previous year, and he recommended to me that on my way to Stevens Pass that I camp at a place called Tuck Lake. The next morning, Jeff, Tim and I hiked a few miles along the trail, and then we parted ways, never to see each other again. For the next three days, I hiked alone, and I missed my new friends I had just met. Still, I enjoyed the scenery along the way as the trail went up and down over ridges and mountain passes.

One person to whom I was relating the above story commented, "How can they be friends? You barely knew them, hardly 24 hours!" Well, I'll tell you how. As soon as we met, we struck up a friendship and had some great conversations. They were decent and intelligent people. I felt at ease with them, and I enjoyed the visit. I also felt compatible with them. Yes, the next day we parted ways, but we parted on good terms. We swapped addresses, and Jeff even gave me his correct address, which is certainly better than I've obtained from some other people I've met hiking. They have gained my trust in that aspect, and if either one of them chooses to look me up one day, I'll be glad to hear from them. They'll be welcome to come by and visit. To me, that's friendship, and it ranks above just knowing people at a place of business.

To state it another way, acquaintances and people I've barely known are the three college fellows from Phoenix, Arizona, who I saw for only five minutes on the Mt. Rainier's Wonderland Trail. Yes, I could sense that they were great people, but since we didn't get a chance to visit (like Jeff and Tim and I did) they therefore didn't have a chance to become my friends.

The best way to draw a line between an acquaintance and a friend is to say that once the swapping of the addresses and phone numbers takes place, the friendship level is thereby achieved with whomever that person is, keeping in mind that the addresses must be correct! It requires a level of trust and a sense of compatibility to give an address, and once that's done, they deserve to be on my list of friends.

There are a bunch of people I've met while hiking or travelling, and we've swapped addresses, like Jeff and Tim did with me. Some I've looked up and seen again, and others I haven't, and I'm sure I've lost contact with likely half of them by now. Even still, I consider *all* of them to be on my list of friends.

Looking Up Old Friends, Resourcefulness

Since I've been alive, I have always had the desire to keep up with old friends, a good trait indeed. I have always been resourceful, and knowing how my parents send out some 200 Christmas greetings every year, I naturally picked up the habit of looking up and keeping up with old friends in the same manner. Plus, since I like to travel, I consider it important to keep in touch with people out of state and even out of the country. As I mentioned in *Keeping Detailed Records*, I have a complete list of addresses and phone numbers of people and friends that I know. I even consider keeping in touch with them so important that I have photo copies of all that data in another building, the same way I have genealogical

85

information stored, so that it won't get lost. I also have all the university student directories for the years I went to college. Many of the student listings also give the parents' home address. That has proven very helpful in looking up some friends of mine several years later, especially those that went to that school only for a year or two and are therefore not in the alumni directory.

Of course, I have looked up many old friends, which means they have heard from me out of the clear blue. It would literally take me a thousand years to hear from people out of the clear blue as many times as others combined have heard from me. Many of them are glad to hear from me, but in more recent years, I have discovered that some of them have become a little bit evasive. Some have thought I was strange, and some have even slightly resented my call! Part of the reason for that is the increase in general paranoia in society.

Of course, my looking them up is always with the good intention of enjoying the visit or doing activities with them. As time goes on, I have observed that it is more difficult to keep in touch because nearly 100% of my friends leave it up to me to contact them. Plus, if they move or get an unlisted phone number, I lose contact with them. I like to be able to call them on the telephone because if I write them, I usually don't hear from them. At least on the telephone, we have two-way communication *during* the phone conversation. By mail or e-mail, communication is almost always one way, from me to them. I have to admit that with most of my friends, I feel like we have a one-way bridge.

In order to look up several of my friends, I have to go through their parents. This is necessary especially for the few I know in the military service, and also true for others who have unlisted phone numbers. Not all parents are accommodating, either for lack of trust or simply not knowing me, which adds to the difficulty! For those parents who have accommodated me, I am grateful, but I know that when they die in the future, I will lose contact with their children, who are my friends. I won't have any avenue to reach them anymore, and I know that I will be sorry to lose them. Plus, I doubt it will ever occur to any of them to contact me during the rest of our lives. It's just not that important to them. One mother was so unaccommodating and non-responsive that I marched myself right over to the Register of Deeds and secured the deed information (and therefore his address) for one friend of mine and I found him! Deed information is public, and it's available to anyone. While there are unlisted phone numbers, there are *no* unlisted deeds.

To do with resourcefulness, as a side note, I have observed that other people don't take the time to open and review their bank statements, phone bills, insurance policies, or other important documents. They check it barely long enough to see how much the bill is, and they simply pay it without reviewing it. I've always made a practice of opening up my bills and checking through all the details. It doesn't take but a few minutes. I used to think everyone else did the same. How could they not? That's why a lot of people get ripped off.

I have also observed that most people don't take the time or effort to keep up with others, much less keep a list of the addresses of their friends. They don't seem to be organized enough. This is especially true in Latin America, where I have had great difficulty in keeping up with friends, especially those that live in larger cities, like Monterrey. For example, the mother of one good friend of mine wasn't up-to-date enough to ever give me her son's correct and recent phone number in Texas. Instead she kept giving me the previous expired (disconnected) phone numbers! Well, I later found out that it had to do with the mother's lack of trust in me. That rightfully irritated me enough that I went to the neighbor's house where she had placed her calls, and I secured that number I wanted from their phone bill. It was sneaky of me, but I'm also proud of my resourcefulness and for being able to jump that mother's hurdle!

To state another example from Mexico, a few years ago while staying in Bustamante, N.L., I wanted to look up a friend of mine that had moved up to Texas. Even though I stayed in the Bustamante area for over a month, his mother never did get it together to secure the phone number of her cousins in Texas where her son was living. I was surprised that she never had the number in the first place. After the month went by, I proceeded to ask her the obvious question: *If you all had an emergency here in Mexico, how in the world would you let your son know?* She said she has an aunt in Monterrey who has the number of her cousin. I asked her if she would be willing to call her son through her aunt, because I was only going to be in town a few more days before driving back to Tennessee. She didn't do it. You see, phone calls are very expensive in Mexico, especially when calling the USA. So, that's part of the reason why Mexicans don't always have the phone numbers of their Texas relatives. Emergency calls are worth the expense, but nothing less urgent.

The lack of resourcefulness and the lack of trust that I see in others gets very frustrating at times. It makes me work that much harder – sometimes out of spite – to get the information and find what I want. I mean really, all

I want to do is enjoy knowing my friends. I'm not a threat to them. Plus, it's not that hard to be resourceful, and I always thought that being better organized was a good trait to have. I wish people would see it as more important to keep up with their friends, like I do. People need to trust each other more.

Expecting Friendships to Continue

Several years ago, a friend told me, "You know, Robert, when someone is nice to you, you expect it to continue, but unfortunately that's not always the case." Right he is. He also told me that if a person sees a stranger who looks friendly, then he ought to be able to walk right up to him, tell him he likes him, and become friends with him. My friend thinks that should be an acceptable norm in society and so do I.

From day one, I have always been a person to appreciate friendships and to sincerely appreciate those who are my friends. I have a high sense of loyalty to them. As I live my life, I have noticed that a lot of friends come and go. For some friends of mine, I just don't have enough assurance that they are indeed my friends, and assurance is something that I need. Some people say that for your whole lifetime, you can count your friends on one hand. Well, I won't be so extreme to say that, but I will admit that a lot of friendships are just temporary and your really good friends are just a small percentage of the lot.

As I have the trait of resisting change, I naturally expect things to continue. Friendships are one of those things. I've made a lot of friends in life, and I like to keep up with them. When travelling I swap addresses with people I meet along the way. When I was in university, I made plenty of friends, and after graduating, I have made efforts to keep up with them. Despite my efforts, I have heard (out of the clear blue) from only four of them since graduating in 1991.

Each Christmas, I have been known to send from 50 to 100 Season's Greetings, and I used to have the positive expectation that I would hear from them and swap Christmas greetings with them year after year, like my parents do with their friends. Well, I only heard back from a very few. In more recent years, I have gotten away from sending out so many greetings because I just don't hear back from people. There are, however, a few people who do write back, and subsequently send me a greeting with a thanks for staying in touch. So, out of the lot, I always find a few good ones.

Since I graduated from university in 1991, I have found that it has been more difficult to make new friends. While I have made a few good friends, and I am grateful for that much, I have to admit that I find it appalling how many new friendships were only temporary and have fallen by the wayside. Granted, in many of those cases we just drifted apart, which I consider to be an acceptable norm, but there are also other friendships that have ended because of resentment, anger, or even hatred toward me. I've had falling outs both with some new friends in this country and also in other countries, and yes some of those have occurred in Mexico. A selected few of those rejections have been *worse* than just annoying to me. Now don't misinterpret me. Mexico does have a lot of great people, and I have indeed made some good friends in that country during the past ten years.

It's difficult for people with autism and Asperger's syndrome to discern who is and who isn't a friend. It seems that we have to be taught, and we have to learn to realize that not all people are true friends. Learning how to make this distinction is an art in itself that does not come easily to those of us in the autism spectrum. It is all too easy to be deceived by people, even when we are genuinely paying attention to our inner feelings. It seems to me that the ability to recognize or feel out a friendship is almost instinctive in people without autism and Asperger's syndrome. I believe my instincts lack development in this area. In a few instances, maintaining my friendships with some people was like navigating a mine field without road signs!

Of all the friends I've ever had, I have never done anything with the intent of severing a friendship. It's not my nature to sever friendships. Even though I treat people nicely and I'm considerate, the number of mysterious rejections I have suffered since graduating from university do indeed exceed the number I would have expected. As a result, it's been very difficult for me to depend on who my true friends really are.

I do realize that in a few of the cases where people have rejected me, their reasons likely had something to do with my idiosyncrasies and intolerance of smoke and perfume. I also know that my high standards have been a problem for some people. Others have told me that I'm pushy or intolerant. The way I see it, is that I expect to be treated with respect by my friends.

I believe that I have tolerated quite a bit, particularly when I have stayed with families on my various trips. For example, even though it made me uncomfortable, I have had to tolerate their smoke and their perfume use! I have always tried to explain that because of my sensitivities, smoke and perfume bother me. Some people have accommodated me, but others have been very defensive, even hostile!

I have lifted an excerpt out of my novel: *Walking Between Worlds*, about Roland's sensitivities. Here it is.

*   *   *

Next, Isalia explained to Lavinia and her son Raul that Roland was a very fine person who was honest and straight. She explained that she had known Roland 17 years and was good friends with him and his family. Roland was very intelligent, a genius in some ways, but he had a lack of understanding of some of the cultural traits. Most of all, Roland was very sensitive in his hearing and his smell, a trait of autism, and he stayed away from smoke, perfume, and loud noises.

Raul listened intently, and Roland was very glad he got to hear that. Raul had not believed Roland on those sensitivity traits, but now he had verification from Isalia, and he gained more respect for Roland as a result. Raul had previously interpreted Roland's sensitivity as traits of being gay, but they weren't. They were traits of autism. Isalia went on to say that Roland needs to be wanted and loved as a friend, especially by those who he stays with. Amen.

*   *   *

I have learned over the years that some of my "friends" are only "friends" when it is convenient for them! I have been taken advantage of several times, for my unassuming and unsuspecting nature, and some people have mysteriously avoided saying the words "thank you" or "gracias" to me.

Most of you realize that dogs either like you or dislike you, and almost 100% of the time, it stays that way – once a friend, always a friend. Right? Why can't all humans be as loyal and friendly to each other as dogs are? Granted, there are a few unpredictable dogs out there in the world, but I've found that the percentage of unpredictable humans is much higher!

This is the type of loyal friend that I am. Whenever I make friends with people, I have good feelings, and yes I naturally take it for granted that my friendship will last for a lifetime. That's always my preconception and my positive way of thinking as I enter into new friendships. With some of my friends, it really is this way. I recognize and appreciate those who are my true friends, and I look forward to their happily greeting me each time I look them up.

I have lifted another excerpt out of my novel: *Walking Between Worlds* about coming on too strong. Here it is.

Roland talked with Lorenzo and Glenda about people in general, and they thought Roland was coming on too strong, that he was going over to Leonardo's house too much and might be coming across as pushy. Well, Roland didn't think that was true. Leonardo was repeatedly not at home, and Roland had to go by there more than once to have any chance of finding him at home. Plus, he was just going about the normal maneuvers to succeed in making plans about going up in the mountains with Leonardo and camping. They also said to Roland that he was stubborn. Yes, that was true. When Roland set some goals for himself and possibly with others, he did whatever was necessary to accomplish them. To him, his maneuvers were reasonable in nature, even if others didn't agree with that.

*   *   *

One can see the characteristics of an Aspergers, the way Roland was persistent in "going over there too much," even though he didn't agree with that.

To add a positive note to this topic, about Leonardo, I still know him, and I average seeing him about once a year. That is, I happen to catch him at home. We catch up with each other and what we are doing, and he still shows an interest in being a friend. He even gave me his new address in Monterrey the last time I saw him, telling me to look him up in the future.

While in Mexico, I actually enjoy going around town and visiting people who are my friends. After all, having friends is important, and it's something that I enjoy.

High Expectations of Behavior

I was once told by someone that I expect people to be better than they actually are. That is very true, and it's not something to be ashamed of. I do indeed expect people to be on good behavior. Like I mentioned in the previous topic, I have high standards, and I expect to be treated with respect by my friends. While some people are very good about that, others aren't. Some people behave badly and act according to low standards. When people like this are around me, I think that they are uncomfortable because they feel that they have to behave better around me. As a result, they resent my expectations and high standards. I don't approve of bad behavior, and while my intolerance of it has cost me some friendships, I must admit that it is a relief not to know those abusive people anymore. What is very important to keep in mind is that bad behavior is unacceptable and is not to be tolerated.

Granted, many autistics and Aspergers do throw tantrums and create scenes. While I do not condone such rash behavior, it is important to recognize that tantrums sometimes occur because people with these conditions lack the understanding of expectations or the norms of society, or because they are in an "overload" situation. Instead of punishing them harshly, I believe that they can be taught ways to improve their behavior and meet the norms of society.

To be fair, I must mention that it isn't only autistics and Aspergers who throw tantrums. There are plenty of clinically normal people who are aggressive and throw tantrums, even well into their adulthood. For example, there was one past friend of mine in college who had a bad temper. One day there was an error with his bank account bookkeeping, and as a result he overdrew his account. He didn't realize it until his bank statement arrived in the mail. I happened to be with him when he found out about the overdraft. Talk about being angry! He was like a hornet! One could say he freaked out. He ranted and raved, cussed a blue streak, and talked about how he was going to have it out with the bank president, and so on! My goodness! I know I don't do things like that. I was quite surprised!

There was another incident I remember involving the same person. I was riding with him in his car, and as he was parking, some other driver called out to him about watching where he was going and then drove away. My friend got so angry – inordinately angry – at that man for having called out to him! I was appalled at my friend's excessive and aggressive reaction! As far as I know, this now past friend of mine was clinically normal, but he sure did have a bad temper. Thankfully, he never totally freaked out at me. I naturally prefer to be around people who are calm, reasonable, and easy going. It's more enjoyable for me.

In recent years, there was a fellow who I knew pretty well when he came out to work for us on our farm numerous times. He became good friends with me and also with my parents. Though he seemed sincere, I found out later that he was hiding a lot of "trash" (many problems). He acted like he was a good friend, and he even invited me to travel with him. He also told me that he didn't smoke, which is *very* important for anyone who travels with me. During our whole friendship, he seemed tired and very troubled in his mind, like he wasn't sleeping much. Well, around four months into our friendship, I happened to see him in town, and he had a pack of cigarettes in his shirt pocket! Of course I noticed, and I mentioned it to him. He got really defensive, and without telling me, he knew he'd been caught. Of course, he has the right to be a smoker, but he knew that he'd lied to me and to my parents about not smoking, especially with the travelling invitation at hand. That certainly went out the window, along with our friendship. He knew I felt tricked, and he felt guilty and couldn't face it well enough to admit it and apologize. I was too much for him, and he likely thought that he was unable to meet my high expectations. In other words, he felt like it was too late and that he couldn't backtrack to make it right. I wrote him a letter, but he sent it back without reading it. I also made several attempts to talk with him, but he had closed the door completely, and he steadfastly would not give me a chance to straighten out the misunderstanding with him. His pride got in the way. Later when talking with one of his relatives, my parents and I found out that there was a whole lot we didn't know about him, things he'd done and troubles he had been into, prior to moving to Tennessee.

Derailed Good Intentions

I have observed a very strange and discouraging phenomenon in life concerning some "friends" that I have known. Several times I have kindly and innocently looked forward to looking up a friend, having had the good thoughts and intentions of visiting him/her in my mind for several years before I actually arranged do it. Many of those people live out of state or even out of the country. With several of them, something went wrong. In other words, one could say that "something got in the water."

One example concerns a high school friend who saw me at a ball game and sincerely told me to stop by and visit sometime. I kept that good intention in mind for several years – eight years – but I never actually went by there, even though I wanted to. Well, our ten-year high school reunion came up, and we saw each other there and caught up with each other. I recalled his invitation from eight years ago, and a week after the reunion, I stopped by his house. Well, he was working nights, and so he was asleep. His mother had always been friendly for the eighteen years that I had known her, but on the day I went by to look up her son, she was strangely cold shouldered. She firmly stated that she would *not* wake him! I felt put off! I tried two or three times after that to call him, and his mother – without greeting me – would always answer with, "No he **isn't**," when I would ask if he was home. I never got to see him again, and all I wanted to do was enjoy and continue my friendship with someone I knew back in school. Perhaps she thought I was strange – or perhaps gay – to be looking up her son after the reunion. If that's what she really thought, then that's pathetic! What I do know is that she resented my kindly looking up her son!

I met a fellow named Chris while I was in Australia in 1990. We became good friends on the spot, and during the next four years, he wrote me several letters inviting me to come over and visit him, that we could do some hiking and travelling. Even though he moved to Europe and then to England, he continued to write. In 1993, I invited him to come over to America so that we could go to California and hike the John Muir Trail. He said that he would really like to, but he never actually came. Finally in 1994, I had the chance to fly to England, where I was glad to look him up. Well, he had just gotten a girlfriend who he was totally in love with, and it was a whole different kettle of fish, as a result! It really frustrated me that he was strangely cold shouldered and was always rushing out the door to see his girlfriend. We had a disagreement about taking me to the airport, which severed our friendship! I also believe that he was intimidated by my phenomenal memory, because I was innocently remembering all of our conversations from four years ago. It's now been fourteen years, and I still remember all of those conversations!

Another classic example of a derailed good intention occurred when I went to look up a college friend in Austin, Texas. Back in school he was a good friend, but when I looked him up ten years later, he was cautious. His face kept going cold every few minutes with an expression of, *Who is this guy?! What does he want?* I had wanted to stop through overnight, but he told me he didn't know me that well, and he kept acting like he didn't remember me. Maybe he really didn't, which is hard for me to believe, but something was strangely cold in his eyes. I never looked him up again!

Another case involves my sincere appreciation for some "friends" in Miami, Florida, who I had visited in 1990 and 1995. I wanted to return there to visit my "friends" again, and I looked forward to the time when I would finally do so. In the spring of 2001, I drove to Miami and visited for a three-day weekend. Even though I truly behaved myself very well and was enjoying my time with these people, I was suddenly and surprisingly rejected by two members in that family in less than 48 hours! The "friend" who was my age even had the audacity to tell me, "Robert, your coming down here and asking to stay with my family sets up an excellent chance for rejection." *Whew!* What an awful comment! My "wearing out my welcome" that fast just didn't make any sense. I was appalled, to say the least!

I could go on. There are several more stories. The main point is that many of my innocent and good intentions have, for strange reasons, been frustratingly derailed. I have to admit that because of these incidents, I have somewhat lost my desire to look up old friends. To speculate, this discouraging phenomenon may occur because my good intentions and thoughts of looking forward to visiting with them are likely being unconsciously picked up by those people in their sleep, perhaps resulting in dreams that scare them off. It's like they're receiving a telepathic forewarning from me – as if I'm a threat – which I know I'm not. Are they afraid I might say things that might alter their strong convictions and belief systems? Are they feeling mysteriously bored when talking with me, even though I don't talk about arcane subjects? Are they afraid I might remember too much about them if they let themselves become close friends of mine? Does it have to do with other-level "entities" sending dreams to my friends with the mission of ruining friendships?

No matter what the reasons, this phenomenon of rejection should not occur in society! Rejections do not belong in our lives. Instead of setting up excellent chances for rejection, all of us need to clear out our "clutter" and then set up excellent chances for *acceptance*.

To acknowledge those people who *are* my friends, and to add a more positive note to this topic, I recently looked up a family I hadn't seen for eighteen years. They were glad to see me, and they welcomed me into their house to visit. They even thanked me for stopping by, and it was great to see them. Also, in 1994, I befriended an eighteen-year-old fellow for two days while hiking in Great Britain, and I later received a kind letter from his mother who wrote, "Thank you for your kindnesses to my son."

What is important for the reader to learn from this section of the book is that, as the years have gone on, lasting friendships have become frustratingly difficult to establish! To add to the difficulty, I don't always know which ones are going to remain my friends either. Some of them tell me things like, "I will always be your friend," or, "Your friend always." At times I think I really have it made, but then even some of *those* friends suddenly go strange on me!

I don't know if having the traits of a high-functioning Aspergers has something to do with friendship difficulties, like the above mentioned. I would be inclined to think that it does. If nothing else, experts in autism and Asperger's syndrome need to study and analyze this important area of establishing and maintaining friendships for people with these conditions.

As a commentary, I want to ask the reader, *How many times do you hear from an old friend out of the clear blue?* Likely very rarely. For me, I average hearing from one or two a year. Some years I don't hear from anyone at all. Almost everybody I know leaves it up to me to contact them. I wonder if it's just me or if this happens to most everyone.

It seems to me that people are not used to looking up old friends, and it really bothers me that it is not in our culture to do so. For many people, it feels strangely abnormal to look up old friends, for lack of cultural training! Many of us are never taught as children to look up friends; therefore we never learn the habit and never do so when we are adults. That is something that society needs to add to its agenda, to train people in childhood to *look up* their friends. If that were done, there would be a lot less strange reactions when being looked up by people like me. After all, having friends is very important in life.

In more recent years, there are web sites about Personals and Dating services that flash up their announcements on screen periodically. Some of them offer services of looking up old high school friends, and they offer ways of finding them. Another announcement offers services of placing personal ads, and services of finding people of similar interests and making new friends. These services are encouraging. Maybe after another generation, things will improve and society will become more social in that aspect. I will certainly welcome that.

Normals and Typicals versus Aspergers

To discuss some comparisons between normal and typical people (what some clinicians call neurotypicals) and people on the autism spectrum, specifically Asperger's syndrome, I have lifted and repeated a paragraph from my topic, *Childhood Idiosyncrasies.*

One classic example of literal interpretation is, say a "friend" doesn't want you coming around, but he's too polite to outright tell you. You ask him if it's okay to continue coming over to visit or chat, and out of his wanting to be polite, he says "yes." That's an answer I take literally, but the truth of the situation is the person doesn't want me coming over but can't bring himself to tell me. I would view that person's answer of "yes" as a lie, but others, as I have learned over the years, would consider the person "wishy washy" or not straightforward. So, based on *their* view-point, the person isn't actually lying.

People like in the above example aren't doing me or those with Asperger's syndrome any favors by literally giving me an answer com-pletely opposite of their actual wishes. However in the above particular case, I could sense or feel that he didn't want me coming over, and I have never been there since. I must also say that was in recent times. I managed to take the hint, but then I had been living on Earth for some thirty years by that time. I'm sure there were plenty of earlier situations that I didn't pick up on the hints, and without realizing it, I was visiting and trying to maintain friendships with people who just didn't want me around.

I have wondered so many times why many people who I'm friendly to and look up from time to time, never look me up at all. Is it because I'm a little different and live by a different set of codes? Do I react or gesture in slightly different ways compared to normal typical people? Do my characteristics grate on their nerves? There are even cases of my laughing with them, and to me, I've really enjoyed the visit, but the truth is that some of them, from their perspective, have been enduring and tolerating. They didn't enjoy knowing me, as I later realized.

If I'm doing something that is bothering one or others or grating on their nerves, they likely don't tell me right away. I'm supposed to sense or "read between the lines" that they are bothered, but I usually don't take the hint. Sometimes I don't even realize that they are bothered. What usually results is that they get angry after the third or fourth time I've done something, instead of having told me calmly at a sooner time. As a result, that gets me angry at them, and I see them as being very poor at social relations with their fellow man. They're not doing me any favors by getting angry at me after the third of fourth time, and they ruin our friendship as a result!

Keep in mind that the above example only occurs with *some* people, because there are plenty of nice people who enjoy me and my friendship with them. Also keep in mind that it never occurred to me that I was a person with Asperger's syndrome until 1994 when Oliver Sacks' magazine article about Temple Grandin was published. I just took it for granted that some people simply didn't know very well how to handle a situation and didn't know how to be straightforward in general. It really frustrated me, but after 1994 and my reading that article, at least I have realized a valid reason, that Aspergers don't always take hints. They are not usually adept at picking up subtle and social cues that normal typical people do automatically. As far as I'm concerned, how can anyone be expected know how, and to pick up all those hints?

Lack of Trust and its Jeopardizing Qualities

One of the things that I find very disturbing has to do with trust –

specifically some parents' lack of trust in me. This was particularly obvious when I was a teenager, but it has occurred with less frequency in recent years, now that I am in my thirties and have very few teenage friends. However, there are a few teenagers that I still befriend, like a big brother would.

To state an example, back when I was in my early twenties, I had some teenage friends who lived around 150 miles east of me, and I invited them to come and visit me some weekend. They were ready to come and wanted to come, but their mother cancelled their plans by saying no, even though she knew me and knew that I was a decent person. I guess she didn't trust me enough to let them come here on their own. Well, later on when she turned forty, her sister had some bumper stickers made that stated her age. I proudly put one of those bumper stickers on my station wagon, and wherever I drove, my bumper made that announcement! I kept it on there for several months. That was my subtle protest against that mother and her decision! I also took a picture of the back of my car, and I mailed it to her, along with a note telling her why I did that.

Several years ago, a mother of a good friend of mine had lack of trust in me due to my Asperger's syndrome traits. She was afraid of it and couldn't figure me out. Asperger's syndrome was like a void to her, and she placed her worst fears in it, instead of trying to understand it. I speculated that behind the scenes, she was warning her son of my "dangerous characteristics" and telling him to keep his distance. I felt like she was jeopardizing my friendship with him. She even had the audacity to tell me there was no way her son was doing activities with me, unless her husband came along as a chaperone! Well, that rightfully irritated me! In addition to expressing my disapproval, I'll tell you what else I did. I called my friend on the phone, spot on the day he became eighteen, and I wished him a Happy Birthday. I reminded him that he was no longer under the strict jurisdiction of his parents, and I invited him to travel with me, too. His parents resented my phone call, but then I was angry at his mother for her lack of trust in me, which is why I made sure that I called him on that exact day!

These are just a few of several examples that have frustrated me. Lack of parental trust is something that really annoys me, because I know that I am a decent honest person with good intentions. I don't deserve to be mistrusted. Some people have told me not to worry about what others think of me, that it's not important. Well, I have to disagree. I believe it's *very* important to worry about what other people think of me, especially when it jeopardizes my friendships with their sons, as the above examples point out!

Why can't parents like those I have discussed above approve of my friendship with their sons instead of warning against it? Why are they so wary of someone like me who is a little different, even though I'm harmless? Why are they so uncomfortable when I show an interest in befriending their sons? Let's not be so paranoid!

Diversionary Tactics

Many people with Asperger's syndrome are direct and very straightforward. So am I. I have been known to confront people who have displayed bad feelings or mistrust against me. I cut to the heart of the matter, and I do this with the intent of straightening out misunderstandings, and also with the goal of winning the approval of those who I confront. I am a person who needs reassurance that everything is okay. There have been a few times when I've been successful, but most of the time, the people I confront do not want to talk about the issues I raise, nor do they want to deal with them.

Some people have turned their backs on me and ignored me. Those who actually will talk to me avoid discussing the issue at hand by bringing up *other* issues. In other words, they use diversionary tactics to avoid the pain of talking about the real issue at hand. This is a very clever way to keep it safe and talk about something else. Some people who do this even alter the scenarios of some past issue in order to throw the blame on me! Deep down, I think they know they are guilty of having bad feelings toward me, or for something they've done to me, or that they've turned against me. When I confront them, even though I'm courteous about it, they feel uncomfortable, and some of them even get angry! They don't like to admit it. For some of them, apologizing is a feat seemingly beyond their capabilities.

I must admit that it really frustrates me that there are so many people in society who are not straightforward. A lot of them don't want to talk about pertinent issues, nor straighten out a misunderstanding. Perhaps during their childhood, their parents did not stress the importance of communication, and as a result, they never learned that important skill.

Mexico

During the past ten years, since graduating from university, I have been going to Mexico more frequently. At first I went with the goal of becoming fluent in Spanish – to become bilingual – which I have been since 1996. Over the years, I have made more friends, and now I go to Mexico for other reasons, for example, to enjoy the area, the mountains, and to do things with certain friends there.

My various stays in Mexico have been enriching cultural experiences for me, especially along the lines of how to deal better with people and to learn more about the dynamics of friends and families. While some of my experiences have led to hurtful rejection, others have been very rewarding in that I have made several friends, feel accepted by them, and know that some of them will always be glad to see me whenever I stop by to visit.

In a way, I feel like I've lived two youths, having gone to university where I studied electrical engineering, and then to a very different type of "school" in Mexico. Going to the small quaint town of Bustamante, Nuevo León and other parts of Mexico to study the dynamics of friendship, families, and people has provided me a different type of "schooling" experience.

Mexico has given me a chance to cultivate many friendships, in ways a little different than how I would have done it back home in Tennessee. I have made friends with people outside of my age group. In Mexican culture, people are not usually bothered by age differences. They see you as the individual regardless of age, more so than Americans do. In other words, they take you at face value. As a result, I have felt perfectly all right becoming good friends with people up to twenty years apart from me in age. Most of these people are on the younger side. At times, with some of them, I have "forgotten" all about the age difference, and I have felt as though we were in the same age group. These are cases of good and welcoming feelings that I have felt, regarding some of the people of Mexico.

People may have the preconception that I'm incompetent, having the traits and characteristics of an Aspergers, but the truth is that I am highly competent and capable in many ways, and far less naïve than I was in my childhood and teenage adolescence. Granted, I am unique in several ways, but then remember, people with Asperger's operate on a somewhat different set of codes.

Over the past several years while spending time in Mexico, I have learned not to be so meticulous and precise. As I mentioned earlier, I have a tendency to keep everything documented and in order. I even kept detailed written accounts (stories) of my experiences pertaining to certain friendships that I saw as important at the time. Of course a lot of that is good, but I believe I was a little bit extreme about it. Some of my friends used to tell me that I was *fijado*, which means being too conscious of every detail.

Being an engineer and also an Aspergers, I used to be conscious of very small matters, such as five peso (45¢) loans, for example. I used to raise a fuss over small amounts of money that I loaned my friends in Mexico when they didn't pay me back. I learned from those experiences that Mexicans loan each other small amounts of money on regular basis, and then they just forget about it. Most of the time, they don't charge each other, and they don't pay each other back either. I have learned to be more generous and helpful to them, and now if they need something, say a small loan or something reasonable, I just give it to them without expecting to be paid back. In other words, I don't charge them down to the detail anymore. This is one of the more important ways that I have "gone to school" in Mexico, and it has helped me to overcome a characteristic Asperger's trait – being overly conscious of details.

All in all, Mexico has been an excellent place to learn more about culture, and Bustamante has become like a home away from home. I like most of the people there, and over various trips, I have taken over fifty bicycles to give to people who need them. Other items I have taken and charged them at cost only. Some of those items include Cedar sawmill lumber for one of the carpentry businesses.

Obsessions and Worries

This is one trait I only recently outgrew in my thirties: obsessions and being overly worried about things – from what people would do, to whether or not friendships would continue. Mexico and its culture have also helped me overcome my gnawing obsessions about things. I used to worry about my new friends, especially some who were still teenagers. Would they remain straight? Would they stay away from liquor and tobacco? Would they remain true and faithful friends? I kept needing that type of reassurance.

Back home in Tennessee, I also used to worry about some of my friends and what they would do. I remember one past friend, who I felt I was meant to meet. He was trying to give up smoking, and I used to worry about whether or not he would actually break the habit. For a long while, I thought he really was breaking the habit, but in the end, he didn't! Instead, he broke our friendship. He was one who would rather lose a friend instead of face up to his shortcomings and correct them. On the other hand, he might have considered me too nosey, pesky, and persistent. Even though I wasn't that way, and my comments to him were out of my concern for him, he resented my concern instead of appreciating it.

For having eventually lost most of the friends I used to care and worry about, I have been caused to worry less. Also, I'm somewhat ashamed to admit that I have taken on a more callous attitude about it. Well, I'm not *that* bad about it, but I don't worry about what my friends do anymore. My not caring as much as I used to has eased the tension. Life is flowing more easily for me now. Yes, I still value my friendships, but I've removed myself from caring and worrying so much about their downfalls.

Let's get off on a little tangent here and do some cigarette bashing! I think that cigarettes are the curse of society. I've had more disputes and loss of friendships due to cigarettes than anything else. I've had to endure resentment – even inquisition – because of blasted cigarettes! I have found that many people prefer their cigarettes over their friends. I've tested people's loyalty by asking them to stomp their pack of cigarettes, and no one has ever done it. It seems that their cigarettes are better friends to them than their people friends. One "friend" just recently placed his cigarettes ahead of me. You better believe I resented it. I don't like being second rate to cigarettes!

One friend of mine from college once told me he believes smoking originated because someone tried to commit suicide. I believe he's right. Smoking has got to be the stupidest thing that people do. Smoke is not only harmful, but it is also terribly offensive and nauseating – worse than skunk odor! This is especially true for Aspergers, who are overly sensitive to odors. I don't know how anyone in his or her right mind can like smoking! Yet this world Earth has literally billions of smokers. Every time I pull up to an intersection while driving, there is always someone smoking in at least one of the other vehicles at the intersection. In this day and age of modern technology, when we know so much about the harmful effects of smoking, I am appalled that so many people are still doing it!

Some say that smoking is a great reliever of stress and/or depression, if used properly. Well, I am unable to condone such methods of stress relief. There are plenty of better ways. Smoking should have NO place among humans. I feel sure that there are other more advanced human societies out there in the galaxy where there is no such thing as smoking.

Over Appreciation, Forced Indifference

By now I'm sure it's obvious to the reader that I have always believed in wanting friendships and maintaining the friendships that I have. As I mentioned before, I have a high sense of loyalty to my friends. One of life's strange mysteries is that several of my "friends" think differently – not my true friends who are always glad to see me and enjoy my company, but others. They are bored with me and my conversations, even though I do *not* talk in monotones nor do I dwell on arcane subjects, such as talking about baseball statistics or boring train schedules, for example. Some say I repeat myself, but I've seen people without Asperger's repeat themselves more than I do. I can tell that some "friends" don't feel right around me, perhaps because they sense I'm a little different from them. A few of them even dislike me.

Even though I had wanted to continue a friendship with those people, I have had to learn the painful truth that they don't want me around. Since they are bored around me and are bothered by my presence, I have had to make myself be indifferent toward them. It feels very strange, like it's not right that I am forced to be indifferent to those people. I feel that it's not nice of me to do that, but then I've been forced to, because of their warped thinking and their lack of recognition of my genuine and sincere offer of friendship. My natural instinct is to speak to them if I see them. Instead I have had to learn to be indifferent. I have to remember and remind myself that they are on the "off" list. I also have to remember to turn my back to them. It makes me feel ashamed to treat people that way.

In trying to analyze this phenomenon, it seems to me that if I sincerely appreciate people – or might I say *overly* appreciate them – that is when they mysteriously shy away from me. So, I have to be more casual about things; that is, to (strangely) think less about them, and less about appreciating them, or it will strangely inhibit the friendship! So, I have had to become more discreet about expressing my appreciation. Some might think that I'm too intense or that I'm coming on too strong, but I don't think I'm that intense. While I consider it indifferent, even flippant to some degree, not to be able to openly express a lot of appreciation toward a friend, I have had to learn to express appreciation more sparingly, for fear of scaring off my friends. Strangely enough, that's what society dictates. One could make an analogy about my appreciation of being more discreet by comparing it to turning to the side, instead of facing it and appreciating head on.

I need to add that the above phenomenon occurs exclusively with those who, for a while, became good or close friends. With those who are my more casual friends, I almost never have the above-noted problem. Perhaps that is because I don't think about them as much, and as a result, it is more easy to communicate and do things with them.

I see life in the following way. I never, absolutely never intentionally do anything to others to lose a friendship. Nevertheless, it is absolutely appalling how many people mysteriously avoid me, develope dislikes and even hatred toward me. Are there nonphysical other-level "entities" behind a lot of that? Or do those people believe false truths about me? Have they come to false conclusions about me? I really wonder sometimes.

Friends, Genuine or by Destiny?

I sometimes wonder and feel like many people are *caused* by other-level "entities" or destiny, to be my friends for a temporary period of time; that is, destiny brings them into my life to serve a particular purpose – perhaps to help me learn a lesson in life, or to serve as a bridge to an opportunity. For the time they are my friends, they feel good around me, and they even enjoy my company. However, those feelings are not of their own accord, nor for genuine reasons. That is just how they are *caused* to feel. Just as soon as they serve their purpose, they suddenly exit, no longer wanting to be friends with me anymore! Even though I'm always nice to them, it's as if they suddenly come to some realization, and away they go! I guess it would be too much to ask to actually continue a good friendship with those types of friends, even though we likely met only for a temporary reason. While I believe it is true that we meet certain people in life that we need to learn from and that we, in a broader sense, create and set up those circumstances, what's the harm in continuing the friendship with them? None at all. Over the years, I've learned that there are very few genuine friends.

Friendships like those described above that have come to an end have caused me to feel quite sad – even depressed at times. To compensate, I usually go off hiking and camping in the mountains. Some people have recommended that I take medicine. There are a lot of people who take medicine to compensate for sadness and these types of losses. Well, I do not condone the use of medicine as treatment for sadness and depression, nor have I taken any medicine for that sort of thing. There are certainly better and more wholesome ways to compensate, for example, continuing to find new friends with whom to enjoy life. Therefore, I am always on the lookout for new friends, to keep replenishing the supply and make up for the losses. That is one of my most important quests in life, to continue making some really good friends. With the right people, you can feel really good, feel an inner sense of peace, and enjoy life.

In Memory of my Friend, Martin A. Enticknap
(1963 - 2003)

In June of 1994, I was walking the Pennine Way in the north of England, and when I walked into a remote mountain refuge hut, I had the good fortune of meeting a fellow by the name of Martin Enticknap. He related to me some exotic stories and various experiences, some of which I found very interesting. He told me he had written a book about dolphins. Plus, he related to me a story about a galactic salesman offering him a crystal ball in a dream, from which I derived and wrote my galactic salesman science fiction trilogy.

Martin and I swapped addresses, and we became good friends. We were in regular communication for nine years, being literary contacts. I appreciate the time he spent talking with me since that fateful day. We had many conversations by telephone, and he was a great friend and was very helpful with reading and reviewing my novels chapter by chapter as I was writing them. He gave me excellent suggestions, along with ideas and concepts to include in my stories. The various concepts he told me were like catalysts or seeds which spurred me on to deriving more good ideas to include in my books. He was amazing! It's like he said the right things at the right time. For future books I write, I regret that I will no longer be able to share them with him.

Martin and I theorized about other star systems, life on other worlds, the origins of the human race, dolphins, and even trees. We talked about many and various ideas, such as the origins of hieroglyphics, Atlantis, Earth crustal displacement theories, quantum energy systems, crystals, and so on.

Martin Enticknap was also a great friend for his uncanny ability to tune in and be able to understand a person's character. He was very perceptive. We theorized about views on human philosophy, and Martin was immensely helpful to me during many conversations when I related to him various problems I was having in friendships with certain other people. He was really there for me and didn't squirm to get off the telephone, like most other people do when being told about a problem. Martin was indeed a very special person. It will be difficult for one to realize all the good that he has done.

The extent of Martin's helpful ways can be realized in the following example. One morning in the autumn of 1998, Martin came forth and volunteered an offer by phone. I was just starting to write my third science fiction novel: *Heritage Findings from Atlantis*. He told me he had been thinking a lot about my new book and that he saw a vision and had some good ideas for it. Since I was somewhat at a loss for ideas at the time, I accepted Martin's offer, his ideas and suggestions with eagerness, and good ideas they were indeed! He suggested that I have my characters go to northern Alaska to assist in the building of a secret galactic station, and while they are there, they can find several frozen crates with Atlantean bodies. They revive them, and they become a major part of the project, including telling my characters where their hidden equipment exists, deep within a mountain. I took two pages of handwritten notes, and I stand amazed at Martin's ability to tune into a story's energy systems and capture the plot and theme of the story better than I could do it myself! I am grateful to Martin for all the help and ideas he provided me. In May of 2000, he pleasantly surprised me when he e-mailed me a fabulous wrap around cover image for my third novel, which he had done on his computer paint program.

Martin designed the front cover drawing for the *original* self-published version of this book. When he e-mailed it to me, he wrote the following message:

Hi Robert,
    Well, here is your cover.
    The idea behind the pic is that you are in your castle, calm waters around you. There is a barrier between the world, the city on the right and the forest on the left, but your light shines a way to overcome the barrier, like car lights as you drive out to meet the world on your terms. The light your perspective shines across the water is to invite the reader into your world and out back into theirs, changed and challenged by the journey. The subject of the book is not that easy to convey, but this is my interpretation of your journey. I like the colours, includes a calm mellow orange, which is your favorite colour if I remember correctly.
All the best.
Your friend,
Martin

Martin was very helpful in reading and reviewing the original edition of this book as I wrote it. Sometimes when talking with Martin, he would go into rant mode, and brilliant comments would come forth, almost as if he were chanelling the insight from some higher level. Perhaps he was. It was during one of those episodes that Martin up and commented that,

"Asperger's syndrome is not an illness. It is merely a different template for living. They have a different set of codes to work with. They are not to be loathed nor avoided." Thanks to brilliant comments such as those, this is a richer book with more insight than it otherwise would have been.

Martin, thank you for being such a genuine friend of mine. As you once wrote, our friendship was a "creative and thought provoking force in both our lives." Thank you for helping me to overcome so many personal obstacles in my life. To have had a friend like you was a blessing, a special gift. You will be missed.

*   *   *

Martin Enticknap on the day I met him, June 5, 1994

Robert Sanders and Fabian Flores, in Mexico, February 2003

Gilberto Hernandez, Robert Sanders, and Julian Amaro in the highland
forest up in the mountains, Mexico, September 1998

PART 5

ANECDOTES & BIZARRE STORIES

This next section consists of anecdotes mostly about various types of misunderstandings, of which I've had more than my share. Some of them have caused me to feel quite a bit of frustration, while others have been merely annoying. Of course there have been plenty of other incidents in addition to what I present here. Some of the incidents are bizarre and also illustrate the problems that people with Asperger's have in establishing and maintaining friendships. Even though some of these anecdotes might put me in a bad light, in the viewpoint of some of my readers, it is more important to *present* these stories than delete them so that you, the reader, can gain some awareness and insight into some of the difficulties that people with Asperger's have.

The Family Photo Albums Project

I took on the task of doing a major photo album project for my four sides of the family in 1993 and 1994. I had been interested in genealogy ever since I was age ten, and I made a point of tracing my ancestry as far back as I could on all lines. I had asked my grandparents, great uncles, great aunts, and other relatives for information. I secured quite a wealth of data, much of which would be impossible to obtain today, since most of the older relatives have long since died. After tracing my ancestry, I took on the project of compiling descendants information. This involved making a lot of telephone calls and dealing with people ranging from very helpful and nice to lackadaisical, hum-drum, and inhospitable.

It was in 1993 that I began to think how nice it would be to have complete compilations of all the available pertinent photos of all my family members, including ancestors, descendants, and relatives. I also planned to include photos from family reunions, and even photos of family homes. That way I would be able to look up all of my family relatives and see what they look like. My parents had lots of old photos, since I grew up in the same house where my great-grandparents raised their seven children over 100 years ago. We had tin types, glass types, and many old cardboard photographs. These were original, and for many of them, there were no copies anywhere else.

I began to investigate the best way to copy them into a book compilation, and I had positive halftone pictures made of all of them at a local printer. Then I cut the halftones and pasted them to each respective page as I typed the text that went with each picture. I did photo albums for all four sides of the family, and each of the four albums turned out to be over 100 pages. In addition to the pictures, I put genealogical compilations in the back, along with photo credits, and the names, addresses, and phone numbers of all the family members. The compiling process took me several hundred hours of work!

In addition to the compiling of information, I had to make trips to Georgia and North Carolina and to different areas in Tennessee, in search of pictures. In doing this, I visited *lots* of relatives.

(As a side note, before I made my trip to Atlanta in mid-March 1993, it began snowing and resulted in the worst blizzard I ever saw! We were snowbound for days, as there were snowdrifts that were impassable on the driveway. This sort of thing would likely occur in January or February, but *not* in March! It was unreal at that time of year in Tennessee. Something's changing in our environment, the Greenhouse Effect among other factors for our planetary use of fossil fuels and the millions of acres of equatorial rainforests continually being slashed down!)

Anyway, I was persistent, very thorough, and meticulous with my project. Most of my relatives were kind and accommodating and also complimentary, but there were some who weren't. I met with hostility several times and also ran into a few snags.

One major snag I ran into because of my persistence involved a cousin of my father's in North Carolina whose father was my great uncle. Since he was nearly ninety, I definitely wanted to see him. I drove more than 500 miles to that area of North Carolina, and I stayed with his grandsons. While I was there, they called their aunt (his daughter) to make arrangements about my going to see him, since he was partially under her care. She immediately declared, "Absolutely not! Tell him to go home!" and she hung up on them. That really irritated me! Immediately I picked up the phone and I called her. I told her there was no way that I was going home until I had seen her father, that he was my great uncle and a loved one too! The woman firmly told me that I had no right to see her father, that he gets upset with visitors, and she told me to just go home! When I told her how far I had driven, she told me she couldn't care less! I then proceeded to ask her to take me over there, and her answer was, "I will not!" Then she threatened me that if I went over there, she would call the police! She had recently written a couple of my relatives a very cold letter when they had requested to come over to North Carolina and see her father. I argued with her and firmly told her how hostile she was being to me, and that the letter she wrote our cousins very much upset them. She hung up on me. Later that day, I went to talk to her husband to "get permission." He also refused to accommodate me. So, because I was so upset and was so bent on seeing my great uncle, the wife of one of the grandsons took me over to the convalescent home anyway, where my great uncle was staying.

Why, he was glad to see me, and he *thanked* me for stopping by. No, he was not upset at all, and he didn't just thank me out of politeness either. He was sincere. That daughter of his had lied to me! I don't know why she was such a wall of ice and so mean to me, but what I do know is that she was over protective and very possessive of her father! Actually she was way out of line. I'm glad I went to see him anyway, because he died just a few years later.

I need to add that there is another cousin of the family who went to school with my great uncle's daughter, and they had been good friends. One day when he was in town, he called her and asked to see his uncle. She graciously took him right over there! Now is that double standard or what?! Anyway, there will always be some people who detest those of us who are persistent. Perhaps he is not as persistent as I am, but I must point out that she had laid down the law, telling me, "Absolutely not!" *before* I became conflictive and persistent with her.

Anyway, as I was compiling the albums, I typed up announcement letters and sent them to all family members offering them a chance to buy my compilation and pointing out that it would be a valuable and important book for all members of the family for generations to come.

When I had completed the compiling, I searched for the best type of copying machine to duplicate the many pages of halftone pictures. Another cousin of my father, (and this one is a nice man), supplied me, free of charge, twenty reams (10,000 sheets) of excellent 70-pound paper. He also referred me to Xerox Business Services in Nashville. I went to talk to them, and they introduced me to the Xerox 5090 and Xerox 5390 copying machines, which they had right there on site. They were excellent machines, and they copied the halftones perfectly. For the first book in 1993, I did the copying right there at Xerox Business Services. Next, I collated the pages, GBC bound them with plastic ring binding, and I sold the copies to family members at cost. I had a few of the copies hardbound, and some were done on acid free paper, as well.

The next year, 1994, Xerox Business Services no longer had their machines. So, I had to search for places of business that had that type of machine. I asked a lady at Xerox what places of business in the Nashville area had Xerox 5090 or 5390 machines. She called me back and gave me the name of a corner printer place of business in west Nashville, told me to call that place, and they'd be able to take care of my application. So, I called the owner of that corner printer to check on the price. I explained the type of job I needed done, the weight of the paper required, and how many sheets would be involved in the whole job. He told me that he would have to add it up and would call me back. I said that in case I wasn't home at the time he called to just leave the price quote on my answering machine. He suddenly got real huffy, said they're not in business to give the lowest price in town, told me to take my job somewhere else, and hung up! That angered me. I called him right back and told him I'd be glad to go somewhere else, because I didn't like the way he treated me, and if he wants customers, he needs to treat them nicely!

That wasn't the only place of business that had treated me rudely. The year before, a corner printer had gone strangely mad on me as soon as I asked if I could GBC bind some books myself. The woman snapped NO, told me to quit worrying them, that I never did anything worthwhile anyway, and she hung up! You can be sure I paid that place of business a visit later that day to tell her that she needed to be nicer to her customers!

I again called the lady at Xerox, told her what had happened, and I asked her if there were any more places of business that use Xerox 5090 and 5390 machines. She answered by saying that she had already done enough and therefore couldn't do anything else to help me. She also said that she had given me all the information she could. As a result, I got out the Nashville phone directory and called every printer in that city. I found AlphaGraphics. They had a Xerox 5390. In the same phone conversation, they immediately told me how much it would cost per page, and they were reasonably friendly and accommodating. I took the job to them, and they did fine work. At the end of the job, I paid them, and they thanked me for bringing them my business. Now, that's more like it.

What I want to know is, why didn't the lady at Xerox bother to tell me about AlphaGraphics? After all, Xerox has a record of all the places of business to whom they rent their Xerox copying machines, including the 5090 and 5390 models. She said she had given me all the information she could, but the truth was, she hadn't. Plus it's not convenient to Xerox when their employees don't tell potential customers where their machines are being rented, because Xerox makes money for every copy that is made, when *their* machines are the ones being used.

Why was I so bent on using Xerox 5090 or 5390 copying machines? In 1993, I was searching for the best copying machine to copy my halftones. I visited plenty of places of business and tried a total of some twenty different copying machines, both large and small, and all of them produced either blurred or grainy image copies. Therefore, I was pleasantly surprised when Xerox Business Services ran a sample copy of one of my halftones, with their 5090 model, and the result was a good and clear image. Excellent! I had found the right machine for my copying job.

All in all, most of the family members were really thrilled with my project and said that the books were a treasure to the family. They complimented me on my fine work and said that it was a very unselfish thing to do. Some of them told me that they hadn't have even dreamed of such a fine piece of work being produced. I was very glad to have accomplished a task that most of my relatives admitted was too monumental for anyone else to take on. I was also happy that my family was impressed by all the work that went into it.

Several of my relatives were kind enough to donate extra money to me for this project. I received enough donations to just barely break even on the project costs. One of my father's first cousins, the sister of the kind cousin who donated the twenty reams of paper, donated an extra $100. I appreciate very much the support of relatives like those.

My reward was in knowing that those photographic images – some of them priceless – were reproduced and distributed to all family members in an organized manner in book format. I was especially happy to have all the family organized, both in pictures and in genealogy, and also to see the satisfaction and appreciation of my family members.

The Child Picture Dispute

When I was rounding up pictures for Mother's side of the family, I visited one family in Atlanta who was not very accommodating. There was a picture of their niece who had died back in the 1950s of a mysterious illness at age two and a half. When I showed interest in including and reproducing that photo in the family album, the wife of my cousin suddenly became very protective, and in a mother-hen manner, told me that she would Not release that photo to me until she got permission from her sister-in-law, the mother of the child who had died. Well, I wanted to include everybody in my album. I didn't want to leave anybody out. Yes, I was persistent, and I asked her nicely several times, explaining the importance of including *everyone*. But she wouldn't consent, not until she got her sister-in-law's permission.

I later found out that instead of getting permission, she took that photo right over to her sister-in-law and gave it back to her! She never asked her if it could be put in the album. I had to call that sister-in-law myself, who then said she would think about it, as it was a very touchy emotional issue for her, having lost her child at two and a half and all. She had had her feelings hurt by the mother-in-law, who had blamed her for the child's death, that they didn't go to a doctor fast enough, etc.

A couple of weeks later, I finally found out through those non-accommodating cousins that the sister-in-law did Not want that photo in my family album! How ridiculous! That upset me, knowing that their behavior was unreasonable. I never ever saw that photo again! When I compiled the book, in place of the photo I had to put a blank rectangle, inside of which stated, "This photo exists, but is Not available for reproduction into this book."

My wishes must have struck a chord with the protective hen cousin, because she later told me that she was upset by my persistence, among other things. I was ready to deliver the photo album books to all of my relatives in Atlanta during Christmas of 1994, and I was having a terrible struggle finding some relatives to stay with over Christmas Eve! She certainly told me No and said it upset her that I was not with my family at Christmas. She made herself unavailable when I went to Atlanta to deliver the albums at that time. I left the book at their doorstep and wrote her a note saying that for me, Christmas was delivering the photo albums to my relatives with the hopes of pleasing them with such a fine piece of work. Was it too much to ask for them to have received their relative at Christmas? I finally did find some relatives to stay with in north Atlanta. They are Jewish, by the way.

As for the mother-hen cousin, and the sister-in-law, who my mother was good friends with back in high school and college, we have never ever heard from them again. What did I do?! It's amazing how some people are just too sensitive, and how they hold onto grudges as if they were jewelry! Couldn't they have stayed in touch like they had always done before?

Several months later, I spoke with my cousins' uncle, who is my great uncle. He was so complimentary of my family photo album and said, "Robert, I realize there were some of our relatives who didn't appreciate it, but I want you to know that I *really do* appreciate your fine book. You did a marvelous job." Never mind those certain negative cousins. At least my great uncle and his side of the family know the definition of appreciation, and I do feel satisfaction that at least I was able to please *them* with that book.

–commentary–

This topic really struck a chord with one of my readers of the earlier edition of this book. She told me that while she understood my desire to be authentic, this came down to a form over substance issue – that no matter what the circumstances, that picture had to be there, according to my perspective. That's the *form*. She went on to explain that neurotypicals deal with the surrounding circumstances, like the woman's *feelings*, and the fact that there were extenuating circumstances, like the child's death and the mother-in-law blaming the mother for it. That's the *substance*. She stated that regardless of whether or not we agree with their decision, they had the right to their opinion, and it must be respected. She also said that although I had brought it down to an issue of mere thoroughness, it's far more than that. Few people will understand why I fail to see that, because they don't understand the theory of mind problems and the lack of perspective-taking, which are Asperger's syndrome traits. She was concerned that I wouldn't be able to help them to understand those things by merely relating this incident. Therefore they will have no alternative than to put it into a frame of reference that they do understand – their own. That will put me in a negative light, from their perspective.

I wish to answer to that. I understand that there were extenuating circumstances, like the child's death, the feelings being hurt, among other emotional issues, but I personally cannot understand why they didn't want that photo in my book. I was doing a major favor for the family, and it should have been appreciated. Besides, my including that photo would not have been humiliating at all. On the contrary, it would have honored the dead child. I think it was kind of me to want to include her. I was quite upset at their unreasonable decision of NO, plus the fact that my cousin's wife took that photo directly over to her sister-in-law instead of getting her permission, like she said she was going to do! I was ready to cancel the whole project on that side of the family, because I was going to be "marching a hole" if you know what I mean. However, my parents talked me into putting in that blank rectangle and note in place of that photo, which I did. Thoroughness is important, and I wanted to do the job justice by including *everyone*.

Let's say for example that I have a 4-speed transmission that I need to have rebuilt. I take it to a mechanic and he tears it all down, replaces worn parts, and is ready to put it all back together. However, I tell him that I don't want one of the synchronizers put back because I have emotional attachment to it. I tell him to leave it out! He looks at me in a strange manner and tells me that won't work, but I won't reason with him. I've got *feelings*, and there is *substance* to deal with, don't you know. I have the right to my opinion, and he must respect it! Therefore he is forced to put it back together, *minus* that synchronizer. Do you know how well a transmission will work, missing a part like that?! One of the gears won't work, not to mention the end play caused by the missing part, likely resulting in the transmission's jumping out of all the gears when trying to drive! That's why it's important to be thorough. I know it's not quite the same way with the book. It can be missing a part and still be an entity, but it's not fair to the family, nor to the child who died, just the same way it's not fair to that transmission to leave that synchronizer out! This is a metaphor to try and point out the absurdity of leaving out that photo in a family album where the intent was to honor the *whole* family.

The March 1 Sleet Storm

I was in eighth grade, and on Saturday, March 1, 1980, a sleet storm arrived! I had made plans for a good friend of mine named Chris to come out to the farm and visit for the whole day, and of course the sudden weather change for the worse caused the plans to be cancelled. Chris and I were going to go hiking up in the Versailles Hills a few miles southwest of the farm. I was willing to go anyway, but the roads were so bad and icy that Chris' father said he wouldn't be able to bring him to the farm. Plus, it was too cold! Needless to say, I was disappointed.

Chris couldn't come, and I couldn't make that happen. (He finally came out April 5, as it turned out.) Although I had to accept that change in that day's plans, there was one thing that I refused to let be changed – that walk! Despite a strong north wind, falling sleet and snow, and 20° F temperature, I put on my snowsuit, wool hat and boots, and I walked over there and climbed that hill regardless! I made it just fine to the top, and it looked very different up there with sleet covering the ground. I walked back home without mishap, and the hike went well. A unique day it was indeed.

One can see that I was fixated on taking that hike, with or without Chris. I also did it as a protest against the change in plans due to the bad weather. So, the day was not a total loss, because I stubbornly made that part of the day right.

The Typewriter Incident

In my senior year of high school, I was taking typing so I could learn to type with all fingers instead of just hunt and peck. My parents had two typewriters at home, and both of them were manual typewriters. The high school had a modern fleet of IBM electric typewriters, all of them with the rapid rotating ball instead of proper keys, and they all had a return button instead of the lever. I was somewhat disappointed that *all* of the typewriters were electric. The keys were so super sensitive. If you even so much as *thought* about touching a key, that ball would suddenly slam a letter on the piece of paper. At home at nights, I would practice the same typing lessons on the manual typewriter so that I would be sure to know how to type properly on it, as well.

One Sunday night, a few weeks into the typing course, I was watching the *Disney Sunday Movie*. There happened to be a scene of a high school typing class, and every one of the typewriters were Royal manual typewriters with normal return levers. That made me envious and made me wish that the high school I attended had also offered the use of manual typewriters. Not a single one of the typewriters was manual.

Well, I decided to fix that situation, at least for me, that is. My typing class was sixth period, so right after fifth period, I walked to my car, and I with some difficulty carried my parents' heavy Royal manual typewriter to that class. I managed to get it in there without the teacher noticing. I set the IBM typewriter on the floor beside me, placed the Royal manual typewriter in its place, and I started typing like everyone else.

Around twenty minutes into the class, the teacher noticed and commented with quite a bit of interest, "Well, what have we here? Where did *that* come from?" She had a smile on her face. I couldn't help but laugh, and I explained to her that I brought it because I wanted to use a manual typewriter at least one day in that class. Many of my classmates remembered the unique typewriter incident for years to come.

The No Bread on the Table Incident

Back in late February 1986, I stayed with a recently married couple named Jeff and Mary in the South Island of New Zealand. My parents and I had met them the previous autumn while they were staying in Tennessee, and one afternoon and evening, we had them over and fed them a good supper. Later I went to Australia and New Zealand to travel around and enjoy the scenery. Anyway, while staying with them, things went fine, and I hitch hiked over to Milford Sound, hiked the Routeburn Track, and then returned to Jeff and Mary to stay a couple more nights before going north. I arrived a day earlier than anticipated, but they still kindly received me.

That evening, Jeff and Mary suddenly decided to take a shower together, and they ran into the bathroom. A few minutes later, while they were showering – and I did not open the door – I asked them where something was in the house because I couldn't find what I was looking for. I heard some grunting sounds. Then Jeff answered my question and told me where to find whatever it was that I was looking for. I said thanks and went into the kitchen.

The next day, we went over to Jeff's parents' farm, and I helped him gather up debris from road grading, and then I helped him chop up old dead sheep to feed to the dogs. He also burned old dead sheep carcasses and heads in a big fire. This work I did for free. They didn't pay me.

After that, we had lunch inside his parents' house – a good lunch consisting of lamb, carrots and potatoes, with apricots and vanilla pudding for dessert. Jeff and his father were watching a cricket match on TV. Before dessert was served, I noticed there was no bread on the table, and I innocently asked Jeff for some bread.

He quickly answered, "Not for lunch there isn't."

Again, I asked, "Could I have some bread please?"

Jeff replied, "I don't think you need any bread for lunch!"

I said, "I just wanted to make a sandwich." I didn't specifically tell him I wanted to make a sandwich with the potatoes.

Jeff said in a cross manner, "Look, when I was at *yore* house, I ate what was put before me! I didn't ask for more!!"

Quite taken aback, I said, "Well . . . okay, but if you had asked, you would have been welcome to have it."

Jeff now ignored me and continued watching intently the cricket match that was on the TV. He had no compassion. Meanwhile, I was appalled and quite irritated at his apparent inhospitality. That didn't seem like Jeff at all. He had previously been friendly and hospitable, and I was baffled at his sudden turn against me. After all, I had been asking for bread in other houses, and my hosts gladly served it to me. I didn't see anything wrong with it.

I left Jeff and Mary the next morning. I couldn't bring myself to get onto Jeff about his rudeness, but the next day, I wrote Jeff and Mary a thank you letter, and in the letter I told him how rude he was to me and how uncalled for it was!

That was nearly twenty years ago, and I have never heard from him since, not even a Christmas card or anything. Why didn't he have the decency to write me back and apologize? My parents and I later talked to a mutual friend of his, here in Tennessee, and he too was baffled. He said, "That doesn't sound like Jeff at all."

So, I wondered for a long time, *What did I do? What got into Jeff?* Then – and it was years later – I realized that it likely stemmed from the fact that I had talked to Jeff through the closed bathroom door, while he and Mary were showering together, and even though I never opened the door, he must have resented me considerably. As it turned out, I invaded their privacy, even though it was with no bad intent, and that "invasion" therefore likely interrupted his moment of *ecstasy* with his wife!

I must state that a lot of people are very intolerant, and it is appalling to me how they sever a friendship over very small things. While it turned out to be a mistake that I talked to Jeff while he and Mary were showering together, why would he resent me for that? After all, I didn't open the door, and I didn't see them *doing* the act. I thought I behaved myself pretty well there, not to mention how I kept my cool at his sudden outburst of inhospitality the next day at lunch.

The Midnight Bus Station Police Incident

In May of 1983 when I was seventeen, I was on the way to Monterrey, Nuevo León, Mexico to visit and stay with the family of an exchange student who had gone to my school the year before. He had been in some of my classes with me. My high school Spanish teacher had made arrangements for this homestay, and she was sending me down there. I was looking forward to my stay. This would be a great opportunity to practice my Spanish and make some friends in Mexico.

It was a two-day trip by bus, and I arrived in Dallas near midnight the first night. One of my cousins would come and pick me up at the bus station, as I would be staying with him and his family in Dallas for two nights. Once the bus pulled in to the terminal and I got off the bus, I went to the bus side to claim my baggage. The suitcases were just being unloaded, and I found my suitcase quickly enough. I began to grab it, when suddenly the baggage man told me not to touch that! I told him that it was my suitcase. He got real haughty with me, so I pulled out my baggage claim ticket with the matching numbers, and I said, "This is my suitcase. Look, it's got matching numbers! I'm taking it with me!" I swiftly picked it up and began to enter the station. I was a bit angry about the way I did it, too! I thought it was bizarre that he tried to prevent me from claiming *my* suitcase! Soon, the man was screaming some threat at me about if I didn't put my suitcase down immediately, he would do something or other – but I kept on walking. Then I heard some woman yell, "Call the police!"

Joe Gray, my cousin, showed up right at that moment, and thank goodness! I walked right over to him, suitcase in hand, and I shook hands with him. Then I told him the police were on their way because I had claimed my baggage. He looked at me dumbfounded, and I responded with a similar gesture because I didn't know what the baggage man's problem was with me! I was apprehensive and scared about what the police might do to me. One minute later when the police arrived, Joe, who was 6' 3", stood up for me and talked turkey with that police officer! Joe was taller than that officer, too.

"Now look here, officer! All Robert was doing was claiming his baggage. Since when is that a violation?!"

"Is he a relative of yours?"

"Yes, he's our cousin."

"Well, they're supposed to claim their baggage inside at the counter," the officer explained.

"How was he supposed to know that? Besides, he has the matching claim numbers," Joe pointed out.

The police officer was kinder than most officers, and he calmly explained the procedure to Joe. Then he checked my matching claim numbers. When he saw that I did indeed have the matching claim numbers, he wished us well, walked back to his car, and drove away. Whew! I'm glad that was over with! Joe and I went to his car, and he took me to his house.

At all the bus stations I had ever been to, the standard procedure was to claim your baggage at the bus side. Never had it occurred to me to go *inside* and claim it at the counter! There might have been a sign posted somewhere, but then how am I supposed to know to look for that? The bus driver certainly didn't warn us. Thank goodness my cousin arrived on time to pick me up. I am very grateful to him for having rescued me from the police that night.

The Cross Country Bus Ride Inquisition

In the autumn of 1989, I took a cross country bus trip to California. I boarded in Nashville, and it turned out to be the worst bus ride I ever took! In those days, smoking was still permitted in the last three rows of seats, which was just as bad as if it were permitted on the whole bus, with closed windows and air conditioning. I was on the way to Los Angeles in October 1989 to catch a Qantas flight to Australia. (If I had known how bad it was going to be, I would simply have flown to Los Angeles, despite the fact that air fare was around four times more expensive in those days.) While smoking was permitted in the back of the bus, which made the ride miserable enough, it was a serious violation for the bus driver to smoke while driving. I sat in the front of the bus to be as far away from the smoke as possible.

When I reboarded the bus in El Paso, Texas, halfway through the trip, and presented the new driver my ticket, he ripped off both the El Paso-to-Phoenix and the Phoenix-to-Los Angeles pages. I asked him why he did that, and he said that was standard procedure. I thought that was strange. After all, he was only driving the bus to Phoenix, and the next driver to Los Angeles should have been the one to rip off that part of the ticket.

Once on the interstate outside of El Paso, the bus driver must have thought he was above the law, because he pulled out a cigarette (cancer stick)! As soon as I saw him do that, I asked him not to smoke. He said that he was going to smoke anyway. I reiterated my request – even used the word *please*. I was persistent with my request, which I had full right to be. After all, there was no smoking in the front of the bus. Finally, he pulled the bus over on the side of the interstate, and he finished his cigarette while standing on the shoulder. When he stepped back inside, he called me a vulgar name among other negative comments, and he threatened me that he would take me to the police if I kept bothering him. I told him that if he did that, I would have to report him for smoking on the bus. He then proceeded to smoke while driving, saying that he didn't care what I thought! What I found appalling was that no one else objected to his smoking!

We got to Phoenix in the wee hours of the morning, and I complained to customer service at the bus station about the driver's rudeness. They didn't show sufficient concern, and the whole time I talked to the ticket counter and customer service personnel, I felt as though they viewed me, and perhaps all other passengers, as incompetent and as second-class citizens!

We got a new bus driver in Phoenix, and he was an S.O.B. sure enough! He jumped onto the bus and took off abruptly, neither greeting us nor introducing himself, like courteous bus drivers would have done. A few blocks into the trip, I kindly introduced myself to him, and I was telling him where I was fro– and he immediately jumped down my throat saying that he had heard about me and that he wasn't going to mess with my %*&! With that rudeness realized, I told him to take me back to the bus station. He said he'd let me out in Blythe, 150 miles west of there. I again requested that he take me back to the station. He rudely told me to shut up or he would let me out right there on the street side, several blocks from the station! For a third time, I told him to take me back to the station, but he ignored me and took me to Blythe anyway.

He was such an ogre and he frightened me so, that I didn't confront him nor object to him when he lit up several cigarettes along the way! I didn't want to be let out on the side of Interstate 10 in the middle of the Arizona desert and fifty miles from the nearest town!

When we arrived in Blythe, I got off and requested my ticket. It took him a while to find it, and while searching, he accused me of trying to ride for free! I told him that I had paid for my ticket fair and square, and that the previous driver, when we boarded in El Paso, had also ripped off the Phoenix-to-Los Angeles portion. The driver called me an idiot, and I told him that I'm not an idiot! Finally he found the ticket and gave it back to me. That's the *only* thing he did right. I changed buses in Blythe, and this time I had a courteous driver who took me to Los Angeles.

I was so angry at those two previous horrible bus drivers and the discourteous manner in which they treated me that I complained about them as soon as I arrived in Los Angeles. In addition to filling out a complaint form, I also wrote a five-page heated letter to the bus company's headquarters. I reported every detail that I could remember, how scared I was, that I was trembling with fright, and that they broke the law with their smoking, their threats, and their scare tactics! I told the bus company that if they wanted to avoid some future class-action lawsuits, they had better ban smoking entirely on their buses. I also told them to hire some truly safe and polite drivers, which is what the sign in front of the bus and above the driver conveys.

Even though my trip to Australia and New Zealand had gotten off to a really bad start, the several months I spent there went just fine. I had a great trip. Around a month after I had written the bus company's headquarters, I received a letter of apology from the one of the company's executives. He said that he was going to instigate an intensive investigation immediately! He didn't refund me for the ticket, but he did give me a $20 coupon and said that he hoped I would give the company a second chance, as they wanted to restore my faith in them.

While $20 was something, it wasn't all that much compensation, especially considering all the anguish that I had suffered. I made up my mind that while smoking was permitted on buses, I was never going to ride another one – that is, except in Oregon, because it had a state law against smoking on buses. So, when I got back to Los Angeles from Australia, I *flew* home to Tennessee.

I wrote another letter to the bus company executive and thanked him for the apology and the coupon. I also wrote letters to my congressmen requesting that smoking be banned on all parts of passenger buses. After all, Oregon had a state law against it, and California had recently banned it in 1988. So had Australia and New Zealand. Why couldn't the United States move on up to modern times and join them? To my surprise, the same bus company whose two drivers had caused me such anguish, suddenly banned smoking on all their buses according to their new company policy, and the United States soon followed with a federal law that same year in December.

I believe my letters must have really made a difference. Most people, as I observed on that bus trip, don't bother to object, but I did! I think that bus company must have taken my letter seriously. They didn't want any lawsuit problems from passengers in the future, not to mention the smoke contamination all their bus drivers were receiving.

Bus Ride Compensation

In July 1990, soon after my awful bus trip experience, I did give that bus company another chance, but only in the state of Oregon. The driver was great. I told him the story about what had happened to me in October. When I presented him my $20 coupon, he handed it back to me and said, "Use it next time. You can have this ride on us. Sorry about what happened to you last year." Now that was truly kind of him.

A few days later, I dug up some tree seedlings – mostly evergreens from the Cascade Mountains of Oregon, and I carefully packaged them in a box. Instead of using the $20 coupon for passenger service in the future, I used it to send my tree seedlings home via bus. The trees arrived home in good condition, and several of those trees lived and have grown very well.

I want to tell you that not all of my experiences on buses were negative. When I was in Australia, I rode Deluxe Coach Lines and took a fifteen-day trip out to Western Australia and also to the central portion where Alice Springs and Ayer's Rock are located. I found all of the bus drivers to be courteous, and each one had a good sense of humor.

In addition to that, while I was in Tasmania and hitchhiking back to my car after making a hike, a kind bus driver for Morses' Coaches out of Devonport stopped for me and offered me a lift. He was taking twenty other hikers to the same trailhead that I was returning to. That's where I had my car. As I boarded, he said, "Couldn't see you walking all that way." He put the lever in first gear, engaged the clutch, and proceeded, with me on board. I was very grateful that he was kind enough to stop for me, and I was relieved to be on that bus.

The climb into Tasmania's highlands caused the engine to overheat, and the driver had to pull over. He needed to add water to the radiator, but the mouth of the radiator was difficult to reach, and he didn't have a funnel. No one else did either. Meanwhile, many of us stepped outside, and I began to think about a way to get water funneled into that radiator. While looking at the Eucalyptus trees and forests in the area, a solution suddenly came to me. I picked up a curved piece of tree bark and handed it to the driver. A smile came across his face, and he told me, "You're a genius!" What a nice comment and good compensation that was indeed. That piece of tree bark made the perfect trough to direct the water right into the radiator, and in short order, the radiator was filled.

Robert Sanders helping the bus driver fill the radiator

We reboarded the bus, and the driver took us to our destination. When we all stepped down, he told me my ride was free. He also thanked me very much for my original solution which got us out of strife. I told him I was glad I could do it, and I thanked him for the lift. As you can see, some of my bus trips have had better outcomes.

The Professor who Smoked in the Classroom

As I'm sure the reader realizes, I am a person who will speak out and object to things that I don't like and/or aren't right, usually where others won't. I don't object frequently, but I certainly do, if objection is due. As you also likely know, I find smoking particularly noxious.

I remember an incident involving smoking in the winter of 1988, more than a year before that bus ride inquisition! I had a clash with one of my engineering professors, who on the first day of class came into the classroom smoking a cigarette. I refrained from saying anything the first day. The second morning he did the same thing! This time I asked him not to smoke in the classroom. He told me in a flippant manner that he *was* going to smoke in the classroom, and he proceeded right on with his lecture, cigarette in one hand and chalk in the other!

I interrupted him, and I objected by saying, "It is in violation of state law to smoke in the classroom."

He suddenly got real angry and shouted, "If you don't like it, there's the door!" The glare in his eyes made me think he was going to pick up something and throw it at me!

I got up and left the room immediately and I *never* returned to his class again. I also wrote a letter to the department head, and I explained what had happened. I requested another teacher for the same course. The department head said that while he could accommodate my request, he would not do so, because if he did, he would then owe several people some favors. The lazy bum! As a result, I dropped the course and took something else. The next quarter, I took the engineering course that I had dropped, and this time I had a different and much kinder teacher.

Many of the students remembered that event for a long time, and they were impressed by my bravery. Even three years later, a student happened to refer to that incident while talking with me. He had only heard about it from others, and he was unaware that I was part of it. He was telling me about how some student had spoken out and told a professor that there was a state regulation prohibiting smoking in the classroom. I smiled and told him, "I was that person who spoke out that day. You're talking to him."

125

The Three Month Job

After graduating from Tennessee Technological University in May 1991, with a degree in electrical engineering, I began to look for an engineering job. The job market was tight with a hiring freeze, and it took me two and a half years to finally find a job. While I was searching, I began to work for myself, doing carpentry and painting. I also managed to take several trips during which I enjoyed some backpacking, hiking, and camping.

Finally, in January 1994, an engineering firm, a company with seventy employees in Nashville, hired me. Things went well for a couple of months. One day, however, the executive of the company told me that he expected me "to wear a shirt and tie from now on," and I didn't like that at all. Wearing a tie felt like a hangman's noose around my neck, and there was just no way I could bring myself to put one on – the shirt and pants, yes, but not the tie. For a while, I thought that no one really minded, since there were numerous other employees there without ties. After all, why be more concerned about whether or not people have ties on than their performance at work?

One day, exactly three months into the job, I had a major automobile accident while driving down narrow two-lane State Highway 96, the highway to Franklin. I suddenly saw a car stopped to make a left turn directly in front of me. There was no way I could stop on the rain slick road, and I rear-ended the car at a speed of what must have been 45 mph. No one was injured, but the rear-ended car was totaled. The front of my white 1980 Ford LTD station wagon was badly damaged in the front.

I managed to drive my car home, called the office, and said that I would not be able to come to work that day. Immediately, I went to a salvage yard and bought $250 worth of car parts: a fender, a hood, grill parts, and a radiator. When I got back home, I called my friend Roger Schultz, and he came and helped me repair my car. By 2 AM, we had the car completely fixed. We had even spray painted the replaced hood and fender white.

When I went to work the next day with my already fixed car, my boss must have thought that I lied about the wreck in the first place, because the next day, the company let me go. The ninety-day probationary period was up anyway, and while they never said anything about the wreck having been the reason, I instinctively sensed that it might have been one of the underlying causes for my being let go. On the dismissal papers, the reason for letting me go was listed as: "unsuitable for position." Well, I will somewhat admit that I was unsuitable, what with my idiosyncrasies, but I believe a more appropriate term would have been: "*unsuited* for position," as in *suit*, seeing how the company thought it was more important that their employees dress sharp than the work they performed.

To mention car status, in the three months that I had worked there, I noticed that several of the employees had upgraded their cars. One employee had replaced his nine-year-old Honda CRX with a new black Nissan 300 ZX with $1,200 tires. Another one had replaced his Pontiac Bonneville with a brand new sleek, shiny, blue coupe, a Lincoln Continental Mark VIII. Another employee who carried a cowboy image replaced his vehicle with a new, sleek, black stepside Chevrolet pickup truck. The executive of the company must not have been satisfied with his new black, luxurious Toyota Lexus, so he bought another new black, luxurious Toyota Lexus, this time with *gold trim*. I used to watch from the upper office window as the executive would drive away to meetings in his new car. He would unconsciously touch his tie on his neck to check and make sure that it was properly tight and fitted. Though the executive didn't realize it, he only had three more years to live, before a heart attack would suddenly get him.

With the above upgrading of the employees' cars, and with my car being an old station wagon needing a paint job, how could the company have tolerated having me on their work force any longer? They just could not have the appearance of that old car in their parking lot!

I thought I had made some friends at work during those three months. I used to walk around the place on breaks and talk to the other employees. One of the fellows near my age took a liking to me right away, and he realized in a positive way that I was not like the others. He had a wife and kids, and he used to give me pointers on how to fit in better. After I left, I never ever heard from any of those employees again, not even the one who I thought had become my friend.

Throughout my life, it has almost always been a case of my having to look up my friends to keep up with any of them at all. Very rarely have I heard from a friend of mine out of the clear blue. I have come to learn that in general, friends just don't make a practice of keeping up with each other. In fact, many of them don't even answer, that is, respond.

At first, I was not pleased to have been let go. I had feelings of rejection, but then I was overjoyed at having been given three entire months of severance pay, the amount being $4,400. I already knew what I was going to do with that money: take a trip to England and Scotland with my bicycle and backpack. I would travel around there during the summer and then return to Tennessee to begin another engineering job.

After all, there was a friend of mine, Chris, who I had met in Australia four years earlier, who was living in England, and he had repeatedly invited me to come over. So, I was really looking forward to it. (Little did I know the future of that friendship.) I immediately bought a plane ticket from British Airways, and I flew over there the next month.

(As a side note, in those days, 1994, there were very few international flights that were entirely non-smoking. I was determined to fly over there and back *without* that awful cigarette smoke, and I called all the airlines. The only non-smoking flights from the USA to Great Britain were British Airways flights between Los Angeles and London, and between San Francisco and London, *none* from New York whatsoever! So, I loaded my Ford LTD station wagon, and I drove from Tennessee to Los Angeles. I flew from there. At the end of my trip, I flew back to Los Angeles and drove back home to Tennessee. By golly, I got it in right for a change. Finally, an entirely non-smoking international flight, for me!)

I enjoyed my trip to Great Britain and Ireland. While I was there, I hiked for six days on the West Highland Way from Glasgow to Ft. William, Scotland, hiked to the top of Ben Nevis, the highest point in Britain at 4,406 feet, and hiked for another six days on the northern section of the Pennine Way in northern England and Scotland.

In the months that followed my dismissal, I thought a lot about my three-month engineering job, and I realized how much I had disliked it. Never was I able to go through a single day at work without hearing numerous employees uttering foul language! I had detested foul language ever since I was twelve. It was absolutely *appalling* to me how often the employees of that company used it! I knew that was very unprofessional behavior, and since they were indeed *professionals* at an engineering firm, I felt that they should have acted like professionals!

I also remembered receiving my severance paycheck from the accountant on the last day. The chief executive of the company happened to be in the room, and I was going to say good-bye to him and thank him for having hired me. I was not able to do this, however, because he quickly turned away and left without saying a word! I was somewhat taken aback that he did not have the decency to wish me well on my last day at work. As a result, I never spoke to him. However, I did thank the accountant for the check. He wished me well and for me to have a great trip.

While walking through the town of Bellingham on the Pennine Way, I bought a postcard of the Lake District with a beautiful small lake lined by trees along its shore with mountains seen in the distance. I wrote that chief executive an anonymous short note, which I thoroughly enjoyed writing. The note said, "Glad I'm here, not there!" I laughed as I mailed it and wondered what the other employees would think of that one!

Granted the work wasn't all bad. I was grateful for the money. There were several days that certain company representatives came to promote their products, including lighting designs, and they used to give us free lunch while they gave their talk and demonstration. Most of the time they served marinated chicken, which I always took into the bathroom where I washed off the hot sauce under the faucet so I could have it plain.

There were also some things that bothered me, and I'm going to relate them now.

While smoking was prohibited in the office, it was permitted in the stairwell on cold days, or outside on warm sunny days. Every time someone smoked in the stairway, I had to get up from my cubicle and close the door to the stairway, which always happened to be open. If that wasn't enough, every time someone smoked outside, the window on the second floor (the floor I worked on) happened to be open, and I had to go close it. One of the employees commented that I had a NOSE.

The main secretary was also a smoker, and to make matters worse, she always wore strong perfume. The odor was putrid enough to make me nauseated! I had to keep my distance from her, except for those times when I had to talk to her. My clothes would get permeated, and I had to wash them before wearing them again.

If that wasn't bothersome enough, they had the radio softly playing every day. Worse yet, it was almost always playing country music, which I don't like, except for a few songs. When I work, I like it quiet, and the imposing radio was quite distracting and annoying! I had to wear earplugs to do my work. One day, when no one was looking, I managed to reach through the drop tile, and I disconnected the speaker wire to the speaker above my cubicle. Oh, what a relief! There was also a vacant office room, and I used to go in there to do my work at times. That room also had an imposing speaker, and it wasn't long before I also disconnected *that* speaker wire!

The real dispute occurred around two weeks before I stopped working there, when they moved most of the employees to different cubicles. Some of the cubicles had normal fluorescent lights, and some of them had gridded fluorescent lights, which didn't project as much light but also didn't glare over to the cubicles nearby. Well, they put me right by a draftsman named Tony, and they wanted me to install a grid. I needed more light than a grid would allow me to have, and I objected. Tony got angry and went to our boss to complain. I overheard the boss saying something about firing his you-know-what, saying it in a vulgar way! I sensed that the boss was referring to firing me. As it turned out, the boss took a vacation for a week.

During his absence, I came up with a unique solution. I insisted on not having the grid over the lights, and the next day, I cut and installed a hanging piece of cardboard on the left side of the light above my cubicle, blocking any possible glare from reaching Tony. He was impressed by my solution, and he was satisfied and thanked me. However, the following week when the boss returned from his vacation trip, he was *far* from impressed! He was quite irritated, and he said that what I had done carried a bad image for the company. My cardboard solution to the problem was taken down immediately, and I was not pleased. There was a vacant cubicle two spaces over, with normal lights, and I moved over to it, which they somehow let me do. Apart from that, I saw my boss as an unyielding man who didn't have appreciation for unique ideas, even though I was an engineer working for an engineering firm, where unique ideas are supposed to be the norm.

There was another incident that took place that also likely contributed to my dismissal. Sometimes, other employees would send me on errands that involved using my car. There was a petty cash box that the accountant used for reimbursing employees for the miles they drove on company business. The reimbursements were supposed to have been given on a monthly basis, but the accountant was rather lax about this. Sometimes as much as six weeks would go by before employees were reimbursed. One day, when my reimbursement was a week overdue, I approached the accountant about it, and I kindly explained that I would like to be reimbursed for my travelling expenses on the errands that I had done for the company. He got irritated and told me more than once that he didn't give a #%&!! I wrote a letter to the chief executive, who got the reimbursement discrepancy straightened out. I now realize, however, that being a new employee and writing a letter like that to correct a petty issue was "not kosher" on my part. It seems that my being precise was upsetting to the company, and I was not appreciated for standing up for myself. That's likely why the chief executive turned his back to me a week later and suddenly walked out of the room as the accountant was in the process of printing me the severance paycheck.

130

When the accountant handed me my severance paycheck, I thanked him and said to him, "Sorry about our little disagreement last week."

"That's okay. Just go on over to England and bicycle. Have a good trip."

There were likely other factors that also led to my dismissal, for example, taking marinated chicken into the bathroom to wash off the hot sauce. They probably thought that was abnormal.

After being away from that place a few days, I realized how glad I was to be out of there, what with all their cussing and their imposing country music from the radio on all of us! I felt free again, almost as if I had gotten out of a prison.

All of this goes to show how a person with mild Asperger's has trouble holding down a job. It also shows the intolerance and lack of compassion of engineering firms, even though engineers are known to think more literally and have more idiosyncrasies than the norm.

The Frustrating "Friendship" with Chip

The following is an anecdote that portrays how sometimes frustrating it has been for me to keep a friendship.

In 1996, I was introduced to Chip Collins, age twenty-four, by my long time friend, Roger Schultz. I was glad to meet a new friend, and I welcomed the opportunity. I was quite surprised to find out that Chip was Roger's next-door neighbor! He was easy to relate to and was an energetic person with plenty of spark and enthusiasm. His name Chip was appropriate because he was indeed chipper. A week later, I went to the office supply store where he worked to talk to him about a certain car part. Chip decided to take a break, went out into the parking lot and chatted with me for twenty minutes. I realized I had made a new friend, and I had genuinely good feelings about it.

One bizarre part of this story is that there were several surprising coincidences that occurred between me and Chip, right down to his phone number bearing significance with several bizarre things, such as dialling a wrong number for a friend and its being Chip's number instead, and this was before I ever knew him! His phone number also matched our age difference, which quite surprised me. Those coincidences were interesting to me as I analyzed them, and I wondered why? Perhaps the coincidences gave some validity for our being meant to meet and more importantly for our being friends.

Later that autumn, the Schultz family hired me for several weeks of work to be done around their house. At around 4 PM each day, Chip would arrive home next door from his work, and I used to walk over there to casually chat and visit with him. Chip used to tell some tall tales about his wild experiences, and we had some good laughs. I had a great time visiting. To me, it seemed like destiny was working in my favor. I was enjoying the opportunity, and I realized that the reason I had the several weeks of work to do at the Schultz was so that I would have the chance to become friends with Chip.

Three months after we had become seemingly good friends, Chip began to brush me off. There seemed no real reason. I made efforts to talk with him to find out why he had changed. Each time I went to talk with him, he made himself appear very busy like he didn't have time to talk. I began to feel frustrated by what had happened. Who knows? Maybe Chip had a dream that scared him off.

Why had so many coincidences occurred between me and Chip, if our friendship was only a temporary one? Plus, my friendship had been preceded by others, as Chip already had two other friends with whom he did things regularly. I was feeling somewhat lonely, having had some trouble in making new friends over the past several years. Many people were having trouble understanding my personality. There had been several other occurrences with other friends that had seemingly placed me in second position. I felt like I was never better than second place in anyone's mind, and that disturbed me. How was I to achieve first place?

Chip was sometimes of volatile nature, and because of that, perhaps it was best that we went our separate ways, but at the time, since I had achieved a decent friendship with him, I wanted it to continue. I kept being hopeful. After all, I was stubborn, and I had good reason. I had suffered several losses of friendships through the decade, and I didn't want to lose any more. Therefore, I made a declaration that I was going to keep my friends!

I couldn't figure out what had happened, nor why. One friend of the family told me that perhaps I was coming on too strong, and that I'd scared him off. I didn't think I had been that much out of order. Yes, I had gone to Chip several times over the past month in efforts to speak to him, but then how *else* was I supposed to do it? Still, I felt frustrated at the whole thing. How was I supposed to make and keep new friends? Where had I made my wrong turn with Chip?

Chip had expressed interest in working carpentry and painting jobs, said he enjoyed doing that sort of thing. Plus, he had told me he was stressed out and tired of his job at the office supply store and that he was looking for a new job. I wanted to and felt compelled to help him out. So, I decided to invite him to work with me on various self-employed carpentry and painting jobs. This happened to coincide with the time when he began to brush me off. Every time I went to talk to him at the office supply store he was brushing me off, which frustrated me considerably, because I was unable to make him the business partnership offer! Every time I would call or stop by his house, he was never home or had just left! Chip was frustratingly difficult to locate! So, resourceful as I am, I found out where one of his bosom buddies lived and attempted to look him up over there. He wasn't there either! That, I later found out, rubbed Chip the wrong way, when his friend told him about it.

Well, my stubborn persistence "paid off" because I finally did locate Chip at home in mid December, and we talked a brief few moments. While there wasn't enough time to talk about my business offer, I did ask him if I could feel free to come over and chat with him in the future. He said he didn't mind, and he told me, as best as I could tell, in a sincere manner.

Some readers might consider my actions as stalking, which never crossed my mind at the time. I didn't realize that what I did could be considered stalking. The above paragraphs point out how stubborn and persistent many Aspergers are. Actions like the above could have gotten me into serious trouble. On that point, I was lucky.

I was in Mexico during that winter, and while I was there, I talked it over with a friend of mine. We decided the best thing for me to do would be to write Chip a postcard where I would finally get to make the partnership offer. With high hopes, I mailed it to him at the first of the year. Maybe my friendship with Chip could be salvaged after all.

Five months later, in May 1997, I decided to stop by Roger Schultz's house and chat with him. We ended up chatting an hour and a half. I brought up Chip by asking if he had talked to Chip at all this year, and Roger answered that he sees him all the time. I had gotten no response from Chip whatsoever, and I asked Roger if Chip had ever talked about me and if he got that *postcard* I had sent him from Mexico at the beginning of the year.

"Yeah he got your postcard, Robert," Roger flatly told me. Roger leveled with me and told me everything. I was impressed at how Roger remembered all of the details. He and Chip must have had a detailed discussion, right down to the fact that I had somehow found out where one of Chip's friends lived and had attempted to look up Chip at that residence back in November. I admitted that I had done that. After all, I am remarkably resourceful, and I had been frustrated at not having found Chip at home in late November to make him that business offer.

Roger explained that Chip didn't want to work with me. He hadn't answered my postcard because he didn't want to face me and tell me no. Chip didn't want me coming over there either. Roger explained that Chip had a tight knit group of friends and that he didn't have any room for outsiders, nor for more friends. There were various reasons for that. As Roger continued talking, I realized the truth that Chip didn't want me to come over there and chat with him. It's just that when I had last seen Chip in December, he gave me an answer of consent that yes, I could continue coming over. However, the truth that Roger told me did not come as a surprise to me. I wasn't sure enough about Chip's consent, which is why I had not been over there in the past five months, anyway.

Regardless of my not being surprised, this was more severe than I had suspected, that Chip found me *that* objectionable! I thought about it, and it really bothered me.

So, I went to the office supply store to confront Chip and talk with him about it. When he first saw me, he made himself seem real busy just like he had done back in the fall, and he didn't want to talk to me. I insisted, and I told him I had talked to Roger recently, and that I didn't think it would hurt that I had come over and chatted with him back in the fall when I was working at the Schultz next door.

Chip entered the freight room, said for me to wait up a second, and returned to me. He leveled with me, admitted that he didn't want me coming over there, and that I had worn out my welcome! He told me he had his group of friends and that he didn't have room for any more. He had his own routine and said I'd thrown a wrench in it! I told him I didn't realize I'd done all that. We talked a few more minutes, and we actually worked out the differences. As I left the store, Chip said to me, "See you around, Robert."

Things had been cleared up, or so I thought. Roger was quite upset that I had gone over to the store to confront Chip! From that day forward, Roger was never the same good friend he used to be with me, even though he's a very intelligent and unique person who does some special projects with cars. We used to work on cars together, and he used to call me and chat with me sometimes. Never again has Roger called to chat with me nor come out to visit, since then. Still, I have chatted with Roger several times since that year, but it is always I who has to make that call, never Roger.

Plus, sometimes when I've arrived to visit, Roger has purposefully brushed me off. It's not a total loss, however, because Roger has a brother who is a good friend, and their parents are good friends with my family. Still, it's somewhat sad that Roger and I don't do anything together anymore, all because I innocently went about what I saw as normal maneuvers to become friends with and keep a friendship with his neighbor Chip, not to mention my efforts to help the guy by inviting him to work with me. I got no thanks whatsoever.

One can see that I was really encouraged initially by my new friendship with Chip. I welcomed it, and I enjoyed it. However I must admit that I feel like I had the rug pulled out from under me, and what is so frustrating is that I thought I had a good friendship and then it was suddenly over! This sort of example is what makes it difficult for me to figure who really are my friends in life.

There are many people who think that men who think and worry about friendships with other men are therefore gay. That is *not* always true. Friendships are important, and friendships are gold, whether between men or women. We are human beings with intelligence and reasoning faculties, and to be nice, we should place more importance on friendships also.

As a positive comment, I want to say that I always have high hopes for friendships and place high value on them. It's nice to know that there are indeed some people who are more sincere about being friends and who are also more grateful for the friendship I give them.

Let me point out how easy it is for others on a more normal scale to achieve friendships. A friend of mine whose name is Howard, who I've known since early childhood, recently told me about a good friend of his of eighteen years. He had met him through a mutual friend at the time. By coincidence, they happened to see each other at the Wal-Mart store three times the following week, and then when Howard was walking across a vacant lot to his home one afternoon, he was surprised to see his new friend. That wasn't as surprising as when his new friend told him that he lived on the other side of the vacant lot! Boy, destiny worked in their favor, and the case is impressively similar or parallel to how I met and knew Chip. We too were introduced by a mutual friend, Roger, and Chip was next door neighbors with Roger! Plus we had certain coincidences to strengthen our friendship. However, the main point here is that while the friendship grew and prospered for Howard and his new friend, it petered out between me and Chip. What knack did they have in their characteristics to so easily grow and prosper their friendship? How did they do it so easily? They laugh and have the best time being friends. Chip and I laughed and enjoyed our friendship too – but just for a moment, when compared with Howard's. How did resentment never get in the water between them? Why did it work out so well for them, but not for me? These are just some of many questions I have, pertaining to making new friends.

The Cereal Company Letter and BHT

Back in 1990, I collected and sent home a bunch of cereal boxes from a major American cereal company operating in Australia. Since the cereal was packaged there, unlike its counterpart in America, it did not contain the food additive BHT, as it had to conform to Australian food standards. In fact, *none* of the cereals sold in Australia contains BHT. So, I therefore wrote a detailed letter to the company in the United States expressing my disapproval of their continued incessant use of BHT in their cereals. I also sent photo copies of literature from food additive codebooks, as well as the flattened cereal boxes. The company didn't write me back, and when I called to follow up, they claimed they never received my package. I've always suspected that yes, they got my package, but slipped it into "file 13" because it must have struck a wrong chord with them. I'll bet they thought I was a "nut case" to have gone to all the trouble that I did to inform them of my disapproval. Well, I insisted on a reply, and I sent a copy of the same letter again, along with photo copies that I had previously made of the cereal boxes, plus more photo copies of the literature from the food additive codebooks. This time I got a reply.

I think my concerns were very reasonable. Cereals are dry, packaged well, and have a long shelf life. Why do companies put BHT in them?! It makes a person wonder, seeing that Australia does *not* use BHT in cereals at all. No one has successfully brought BHT use to a halt. I even personally gave my U.S. senator extra cereal boxes from Australia with an explanatory letter, and not even he could get the BHT stopped. I gave it my best, but to no avail, and I feel like I was placed on a list of psychotics because any further correspondence I have attempted to have with cereal companies has never been taken seriously.

One can see that I am straightforward and that I prepare my case very well. Despite this, it is not appreciated. In fact, it is resented! In that letter to the cereal company, even though I told them the truth and was very straightforward with them, they still didn't listen to me.

Some years later, I wrote another letter to the same company, this time to protest the adding of sugar to one of their cereal products. I got no reply whatsoever. So, I had some friends of mine write to the same company expressing the same concerns. My friends got nice and friendly reply letters of explanation. Even though I might be considered psychotic by the cereal company, they should have answered my letter too.

Here's the difference between me and the rest of the general public. When I tell friends, relatives, or other people about BHT in cereals, most of them hardly bat an eye. Others show concern and even make a point to buy only cereals without BHT . . . but only for a while. They soon forget and revert to buying all types of cereals again, with the excuse that they only eat those cereals every now and then. Well, I don't revert, never! Cereals with BHT don't come into my home, and I don't eat them elsewhere either . . . Never!

What I don't understand is why so many seemingly intelligent people have BHT-laden cereals in their homes? This has been my observation throughout life, pertaining to cereals. I know now that hardly anyone is ever going to speak up, and also that people think I'm from Mars because I'm always so aware of foods. It's true that I've always been a stickler for reading ingredients in foods ever since I was age ten. Plus, if everyone were like me, food additive manufacturers would soon be out of business, and what a great day that would be for all of us!

*   *   *

PART 6

MISCELLANEOUS CONCEPTS & INSIGHTS

This section contains somewhat controversial topics and insights, that is, topics that didn't fit in very well with the mostly chronological flow of this book. They are here for the reader to enjoy, and most of this is my viewpoint about certain things, how they are, and how they work.

Thoughts Outside the Brain

In early childhood, when I was age five, I had a strange experience of being pulled out of my body and being forcefully dragged feet first into the hall, where I heard some strange musical notes. I ran back to my bed, somewhat in fear. Perhaps it was a dream, but it seemed too real for that. So, yes, I believe in a detachable spirit with its own intelligence for each human alive on Earth, which leads me to the concept of thoughts outside the brain.

I believe in telepathy, despite the fact that a lot of Ph.D. clinicians and diagnosticians do not. I know this is a topic that a lot of people turn their backs to and ignore, but for the purposes of research, this topic needs to be seriously studied. As to the phenomenon of thoughts outside the brain. I've known what other people were thinking or doing in real life, though remote, through my intuition and also my dreams at times. On occasion, when drifting off to sleep, I've heard voices talk to me, and even tell me unique words.

Even feelings are, in a sense, thoughts outside the brain, and they are a form of telepathy.

As far as I'm concerned, while most people think all memories are stored inside the brain, most memories are actually stored outside the brain and body in the surrounding atmosphere, that is, in the ethereal energy field of each individual person. Very little of it is in the brain, which is merely a central processor of thoughts, a communication connector center for associating and recognizing the memories as they are thought and processed. Many memories are stored at physical locations, and when a person visits the same place again later in his or her life, he or she can remember more exact details of the place and can even remember what he or she was thinking about the last time he or she had been there.

The thoughts that a person thinks are literally recorded telepathically within the energy matrix of matter, that is, the material items of any location, such as rocks, soil, minerals, crystals, trees, or even buildings. The information of the thoughts are stored there indefinitely until the person returns to that site and triggers the appropriate recorded memories and thoughts to come forth and run through the mind of the visitor.

After all, one can realize that matter is mostly empty space, that is, bound up energy, and since it is mostly holographic in nature, there is literally a phenomenal amount of storage capacity within the energy matrix of matter itself of any location, and it can be tapped into later.

Reincarnation? Inexperienced Souls?

I'm going to use reincarnation as a metaphor to try and give some frame of reference for the general public to understand how life seems for a person with Asperger's. Considering the possibilities of reincarnation, it's as if the normal typical people have had plenty of Earth lifetimes (perhaps tens or hundreds) and therefore *plenty* of Earth experience. However for me, if I'm only living my *first* lifetime on Earth, then I've had no prior Earth past life experience.

This could explain why I behaved very strangely in early childhood but finally, by age nine or ten, became better adjusted and at least somewhat more normal. That is, I adapted. In other words, I would say that in my case of overcoming my autistic traits, I learned step by step, detail by detail (what others seem to know by instinct) the mannerisms of how to be a person, and how to grow up during childhood, that is, how to live my life here on planet Earth. Many of us who are Aspergers feel like we are from another planet, perhaps because all of our past lives, you might say, have been on a different planet in a different star system.

At present, autism in humans is on the uprise, with a higher number per capita than ever before. This could be due simply to better testing and awareness, but it could also be due to inexperienced souls.

To explain, all of us are aware that there are more people on the planet than there ever have been before, and it will increase in population to a, no doubt, crowded future, if it isn't curbed. Each person has a lifeforce or spirit, also called a soul, that animates his/her body. Now in the past, there has been a ready supply of souls for what was a more stable population on Earth, but with the recent population explosion during the past very few generations, where have all the extra souls been coming from? Granted, many of them can be considered to have come from past lives here on Earth, meaning that the people with those souls do have some Earth experience. Well, what about all the extra people alive today? I believe their lifeforces or souls are likely from somewhere else, some of them reincarnated from alien lifeforms, some more intelligent and some less intelligent. Some may be from humans that lived elsewhere in other star systems in the galaxy, and some may be from other lifeforms altogether. What these have in common is that they have no prior Earth experience. They have a unique way of thinking, and they will likely have a more difficult time becoming adjusted to life here in this world and culture. In other words, they have to adapt and learn. Some will do it successfully, and others won't, the ones who are institutionalized.

So, they have experience at living lives. That they do, but not any past lives on planet Earth. They operate by a different set of codes that is in accordance with that faraway planet, but not that of Earth's. So, for Earth, they are inexperienced souls. This could explain why those with Asperger's syndrome don't "read between the lines" so well, and also why they don't take hints.

When considering the concept of brain development and growth after birth, I want to speculate here that alien souls or spiritual beings from elsewhere can cause the brain and body of a person to react differently and grow differently throughout childhood, that is, in different proportions than what is normal. It's like a lifeforce that is not quite properly aligned or synchronized with the Earth human blueprint design, and this can result in interfering with the normal human growth pattern for those people on this planet with alien souls.

I have talked with some of my past teachers, and some of them have told me how a higher percentage of teenagers in this day and time are just not as lively and are just not with it, more now than in the past, like twenty or thirty years ago. Some of my teachers are quite concerned about it. I actually explained to one of my teachers my theory of alien souls for some of those teenagers, and he was quite intrigued. He said I might be right.

Another possible factor that might partially contribute to the recent increase in autism could have to do with repercussions of the many and terrible wars that have taken place on Earth over the past several centuries! In consideration of reincarnation, those souls were severely traumatized, and it could be that the souls of some of those casualties have come back to live another life on Earth. Having been shell-shocked from their past lives, it makes sense that they would have more trouble adjusting to living a normal life again.

I state the above speculations to point out that there is a lot out there

140

that we humans don't know. While my reasons for my abnormalities in early childhood likely stemmed from autism, perhaps they also stemmed from living my first life here on Earth.

Alternate Realities, Parallel Universes

For years, as I've thought more about it, I have come to believe in the existence of alternate realities or parallel universes. Not only have I read literature about it, but I have also had some experiences in my life that lend to the evidence of such a phenomenon. Parallel universes can be described as alternate realities, different grooves, different planes of existence, or other dimensions. While there exist plenty of higher and lower levels, for the purposes of this topic I am going to talk just about parallel universes equal in level to ours (not higher or lower) where most, but not all, of what exists here is duplicated there. Different scenarios are played out in what could be *many* parallel existences or grooves. In theory there exist an infinite number of parallel universes, but my own personal feeling is that there could be less than ten, or even less than five, that are as fully functional as ours.

As I mentioned that different scenarios are played out in each parallel universe, it is likely that people in parallel existences of planet Earth have a different set of codes to work with, a different template for living. Sound familiar? With the recent population explosion of people here in this reality of planet Earth, not only might souls be coming from faraway planets and star systems, souls might also be coming from parallel universes or different grooves of planet Earth. This could be yet another explanation as to where the extra souls are coming from to occupy the extra human bodies. Think about it. One or more of the parallel existences of Earth could have a surplus of souls and a shortage of people. Those souls would likely choose a different groove in which to live their lives, likely this reality of existence which has a surplus of people and a shortage of souls. Considering that souls from parallel existences of Earth likely have a different set of codes to work with and a different template for living, they would come across to us here in this reality as having autism or Asperger's syndrome. To me, this is one of the most logical explanations as to why there is more autism per capita than ever before.

I have always felt different from the norm in many ways, more so in childhood than now. I mentioned early on in this book that in my early childhood, I felt really alien to the culture here, like maybe I was from a faraway star system. I realized that I didn't like it here on Earth, because it was so different, hostile at times. I wasn't used to that, and at times I was in anguish. I felt like I wanted out; that is, I wanted to go back home . . . to my "planet of origin." I also mentioned that perhaps this is my very first lifetime on Earth, while other humans alive here today may be living their tenth, hundredth, or even higher-number lifetime, considering reincarnation.

There could be various reasons why I felt alien to this world in early childhood. My soul could have come from a planet in a faraway star system, and I am therefore living my first lifetime here on planet Earth. While I lean toward a different star system, my soul could also have come from a parallel existence or alternate reality of planet Earth. No matter what, during my early childhood, I felt like I had made a mistake, that I was born in the wrong groove here! I wanted to go back to where I came from. I felt trapped here and frustrated, but I finally got more used to it during my kindergarten years.

Now I am going to relate a few experiences that have caused me to believe in parallel universes.

In the summer of 1972, I remember waking up in the middle of the night. There was a terrible thunder and lightning storm taking place outside. I got up out of bed and for several minutes, I observed it through my bedroom window. When we got up and had breakfast several hours later, I commented on the severe storm that had taken place last night. My parents looked at me in a confused manner, and they informed me that there hadn't been any storm. I couldn't believe it, and I insisted that there had been a big storm last night! So, I went outside and checked. It was nice and sunny, which is certainly possible several hours later, but our driveway was perfectly *dry*, dusty actually. It had *not* rained! How was that possible? Had it been just a clear dream? For years I believed my parents that I had just dreamed it, but in more recent years, I don't think so. It was too clear to be just a dream. I believe what actually happened was that I slipped into a parallel universe, a different groove, for part of the night. In that groove of reality, a severe thunderstorm indeed took place, but in our groove of reality it didn't.

I'm going to relate another experience from August 2002, and this one was a dream, however it seemed more like an astral travel experience because it was more lucid and carried more truth to it than most dreams do.

I dreamed that I was in a town in western Georgia, and I was visiting some fellows I don't know in real life. I was behind their house in the backyard, and I was sitting at an outdoor table talking with one of them. I saw a car pull up in front of the house on the street, which was around 100 feet away. Three fellows stepped out of the car and walked down the paved driveway toward us. One of them was a fellow I had been told about, which is why I had come all the way down here to Georgia to meet him. He saw me, walked right over to me, smiled and introduced himself, and he told me his name was Brad Perryfield. We shook hands, and I told him my name. He looked around age thirty, was my height and size, had dark straight hair, was beginning to bald on top, and he looked genuine and friendly. Immediately I could sense that this was just the type of person I had been looking for, for travelling.

I woke up. The dream was already over. Where did he go? We were just about to have great conversation, but I already woke up! I really wanted to talk with him, to get to know him and become friends with him. During the course of the next several days, that dream was certainly on my mind. It had left quite an impression upon me. It was like a revelation to me and an answer to many questions. (Again I must remind the reader that my desire for a fellow travelling companion has nothing to do with marriage nor gay relationships either. It just has to do with finding a good fellow friend for travel.) In that dream, I had found who I was looking for, only to wake up and realize that it was a dream. But then perhaps it was a premonition of who I was later going to meet. The dream was so clear that no one could ever convince me that the fellow I met doesn't exist. Plus, it's very rare that I remember a first and last name out of a dream. His last name Perryfield sounded like an ordinary and common name. So, I went online and checked directory assistance for towns in western Georgia. There were no listings. So, I checked Atlanta, and there were no listings either. I began checking lots of big cities and even whole states, and there were No listings for that last name whatsoever! For a name that sounded so straightforward, I just couldn't believe it! I didn't invent that name. He told it to me when he introduced himself to me. When I first woke up from that dream, I thought it was a premonition, but when I checked directory and found no listings for that last name, I realized the unfortunate truth that Brad Perryfield exists in a parallel universe, in other words a different groove, and is therefore unreachable by ordinary means. Dreams like the above make me wonder if maybe that other groove is the existence where I was supposed to have been born.

One can see that different names exist in parallel universes. Names that are nonexistent or rare here are commonplace there, and vice versa. I find that very interesting. Most people have a duplicate there, but not everyone.

Plus, there are bound to exist people there who have no duplicate here, and vice versa. I wonder how many cases there are of people slipping back and forth between our groove and others without our even realizing it. Does it happen more often than we think?

In October 2003, I had an interesting dream of visiting a friend of mine who I don't know in real life, or at least in this groove. In the dream, it was 1986, and we were in our early twenties at the time. My friend still lived with his parents, and they had a sizeable yard with plenty of hardwood trees. We took his family car for a drive. It was a 1973 black 4-door Dodge Monaco, one of Dodge's full-size cars, and my friend let me drive it. Soon we were hesitating on the street in front of his house and yard, waiting to turn right on the four-lane boulevard. I hadn't paid attention until now, but I suddenly realized that my left foot was on a clutch pedal, and the column shift lever was in first gear. With an expression of surprise, I asked my friend if this car was a column shift? He answered yes. So, I engaged the clutch, made the right turn and proceeded down the boulevard, soon pushing in the clutch and shifting the column lever to second gear, and then to third gear a little while later. It was quite a thrill to be driving such a big family car with a standard shift. The engine ran so smoothly, and I really enjoyed driving it. I remember so many details from that dream. I even remember the distinct clanking sound the column shift lever and shift collar made when I shifted gears. I even remember how the clutch pedal felt on my foot. I drove the car for several minutes.

I woke up with a lasting impression of that dream on my mind, and I was very impressed with that car, though I don't know why. I don't even know why I had the dream. I hadn't thought about Dodge Monaco cars in years. I began to investigate to see if Chrysler ever made Dodge Monacos or Polaras that late in time with a standard shift. I knew they still made them in the late 1960s. It was several months later when I finally discovered that the answer is yes, because every Dodge Monaco through 1973 had a rectangle factory stamped in the firewall to allow the clutch linkage to pass through it. The 99.9% that were automatic had a plastic plug in that rectangular hole. So, there were indeed a very few of them that had standard shift, or Chrysler wouldn't have bothered to stamp that rectangle in every car that came off the production line.

I believe I astral travelled to a definite reality and perhaps visited a person who is a friend of my parallel counterpart. That standard shift 1973 Dodge Monaco exists there. It appears that for different parallel universes and different grooves, there are different options that exist and are commonplace there, while here in this reality they are either very scarce or nonexistent, and vice versa.

Although I have done many things and accomplished a lot in this world, there are still a few certain things that I have wanted but have been fundamentally unable to obtain, one being to find a fellow friend for travelling. There are a few certain goals that I have really wanted to achieve, all of which are reasonable expectations, but I have not been able to. I feel like they have been unattainable to me because I don't fit in so well here, that perhaps I was born in the wrong groove. To put it another way, what I want to obtain and achieve here, exists in the groove where I was supposed to have been born, and is easily obtainable there. That's where Brad Perryfield lives. That's where cars, like that 1973 Dodge Monaco, are commonplace with a 3-speed on the column. Perhaps I fit in better there than here. I have had several other dreams through the years to convince me of my viewpoint of having been born possibly in the wrong groove.

Nevertheless, I've done the best I can. I'm not despondent about it. It's not all wrong here. I have enjoyed a lot of travels in my lifetime, even though alone, however. I have indeed enjoyed a few short hikes on occasion with friends or relatives, but don't forget that to bring those hikes into reality, it took ridiculously excessive efforts on my part, strange as that might seem. No matter what, I have been lucky to have made some friends in this world, and in *this* groove, and to have been able to accomplish at least some of my goals.

Coincidences in General

In my life, I have experienced several coincidences. Another name for coincidence is synchronicity. I haven't experienced very many coincidences, but some of them are remarkable. I mention the topic in this book not knowing for sure if it has anything to do with being an Aspergers. There are some people who say there is no such thing as a coincidence. All coincidences are predestined, and there are no accidents. Others say that there are accidents. I say that coincidences are caused from higher levels of existence. I have lifted an excerpt from my 2nd science fiction novel: *Mission Beyond the Ice Cave: Atlantis-Mexico-Zotola*, where I explain my thoughts and viewpoints about coincidences. Below is the excerpt.

*   *   *

"While it is a known fact that some of the past ancient human civilizations arrived to Earth by teleporting themselves from their world existing in

145

alternate realities, it has been theorized that destiny originates from higher levels of thought in alternate realities. Quite often, humans have dreams, and though they don't always realize it, they are actually visiting those alternate realities in their mind and spirit, sometimes so clearly that they feel like they've actually been there. In truth, some of those alternate realities are where their long ago ancestors came from.

"In the true sense of reality, there are multiple levels of consciousness, and some of the higher levels are mentally out of reach or out of range. At these higher levels of thought in alternate realities, there are minds which operate and think and cause us on this level to experience coincidences and various synchronicities which cause us to think that many actions are predetermined or destined. Through the complex system of multiple levels of consciousness, there is truth to this. As those beings at higher levels of reality plan their lives and thoughts, we at lower levels are sometimes affected by their actions."

"Huh! That's really interesting," Steven remarked. "So, what is actually going on are higher levels of thought, and since they know more than we do, they therefore cause our destiny to occur on this level."

"Exactly," Fraxino agreed. "In truth, when you really look at all the levels, there is no destiny. Each being on whatever level plans his life and causes his own destiny as a result."

"I don't know," said Rinto. "I believe in destiny. I mean, we are affected by higher levels of thought and by their plans. By definition, that is destiny."

*   *   *

Mind Is All One

In a sense, mind is all one. All levels, including the subconscious level, merge into one free landscape. I have lifted an excerpt out of my 3rd science fiction novel: *Heritage Findings from Atlantis*, to give the reader an idea.

*   *   *

Fraxino translated Morris' comment to the Atlanteans, who shook hands with Morris and wished him well.

"You'll be seeing me from time to time," Morris went on. "However, I do feel it is my duty to make you aware of something, as this might ease this project's timely completion. It's been my increasing feeling that the existence of the subconscious mind is a myth. It's a learned response which gives human beings the excuse of committing unacceptable actions, like the mass dumping of those precious crystals and artifacts. While there are higher levels of consciousness and higher level beings, the human mind can become unified and be consciously aware of different levels, in addition to merging

146

the conscious and subconscious into one program. Let that movie be a lesson to you. Senseless actions would be far fewer if the humans would learn to do with their minds what I've just stated.

"With that said, I must leave you. All the best."

"Morris, what about . . .?" Rinto began to ask.

*　　　*　　　*

Mind is all one. It is a free landscape that is open and can be explored. It is not sectioned off, like many people have come to believe. That's just what human society has taught us through cultural influence and is what we have learned and taken for granted. The right mindset is all a matter of focus, awareness, and how we look at things. Granted there still is the subconscious "level" which is the most versatile and awake area of the mind. It may be considered like a broad beam of light, as it goes about picking up data and information and telepathically communicating with others outside of our conscious awareness. The important thing to realize is that not even the subconscious mind is sectioned off. We can merge the "sections" of our mind and be more aware of that subconscious mind of ours. For what human society has been taught, to think in certain ways, and that there are different levels or sections of the mind and consciousness, we have in essence been taught not to be natural explorers. Our mindset has been pigeonholed. We need to broaden our mindset and see it all. The conscious waking state may be considered like a beam of light focused on certain areas, compared to the broad beam of light of the subconscious. That conscious beam of light is capable of accessing and shining on the whole landscape, not just sections. Every frame of reference or mindset is flexible. It is not set in stone. We are capable of expanding our horizons, and we can add "programs" to our mindset, that is, change our own perspective to enable us to explore new ideas and concepts.

As stated earlier, it's all a matter of awareness. How well do we really understand our mental health? How adept are we about operating within our mindset? How adept are we in our abilities to create reality for ourselves, to achieve what we desire?

*　　　*　　　*

147

Robert Sanders on top of South Sister, elev. 10,358 feet,
in Oregon, August 1986

Robert Sanders on top of Mt. Whitney, elev. 14,494 feet,
in California, September 1992

CONCLUSION

I believe I have successfully overcome many traits and characteristics of being an Aspergers, but those traits that I retain, I value. I never considered myself as handicapped, which likely made the overcoming process a lot easier. Plus the reader has realized that I have made full use of my condition in many positive ways, having accomplished many projects in my life.

Like I stated at the beginning, I here reiterate that Aspergers are not to be loathed nor avoided, even though they might not have the best social skills and behavior. Most of them are good decent people with a lot to offer. Many of them are very thorough and exacting, and they have phenomenal memories. They are persistent and meticulous, which are advantageous for accomplishing tasks, plus other good traits. It has to do with a matter of focus in concentrating on projects at hand.

Aspergers find ways to expand their choices to make full use of their condition. They find a different way around something to get to the same point. As there is always more than one way to do something, it is not wrong to go about accomplishing something in a unique way. Sometimes it is the better way. Many Aspergers can see something that a lot of normal people cannot see, and as a result, they can improve a situation.

One example has to do with how I picked up that curved piece of Eucalyptus bark and handed it to the bus driver, so he could get water into the radiator. Another example has to do with the cattle troughs that Temple Grandin has ingeniously designed.

It's all a matter of how to cause the general public to look at the whole thing. People with Asperger's Syndrome deserve to be accepted and appreciated in society just like everyone else. They have their place in this world, and I give thanks to many of them for bringing into reality their inventions and creations, *most* of them with the goal of making this world a better place to live.

Anyone who puts himself in the right mindset and frame of reference can overcome barriers and be an achiever. Triumph is a process that we go through in our journey to explore new ideas and concepts.

Reading Between the Lines, an Afterword

In early July of 2004, my aunt and uncle in Nashville had loaned me a tall step ladder so I could use it to pick apples from some of the trees in my yard. A day or two later, I called my aunt to thank her for the use of it.

". . . and that ladder sure has come in handy for picking apples, plus other things I needed a tall ladder for," I said to her.

"Well, good."

"Plus, I was able to straighten out a crooked growth shoot on another one of my trees."

"Well, I'm glad you had some good uses for it – What do you think, Robert?"

For a brief moment, I thought she was asking me what I thought about the ladder, but then I suddenly realized that she had changed the subject, even though she didn't tell me that.

"Yes, isn't that great how Kerry picked Edwards for his running mate?" I responded.

"It's excellent news, isn't it."

"Yes indeed. I sure hope they win . . ."

*   *   *

I caught on. My perceptions worked, and I was reading between the lines. How did I do that? Back in high school days, I don't think I would have realized, and I probably would have asked her, "You mean, what do I think about the ladder?" It's just been within the last decade or so that my perceptions have been improving. Logically, she was asking me about the ladder, but somehow I knew and sensed that she was talking about Kerry's choice of Edwards for his running mate. Perhaps her tone of voice was slightly different, and maybe that's what gave me the idea. That or was it telepathy?

You know, I really have overcome this thing! Granted there are a few lingering traits, but this whole book is a story portraying my life of struggles but also my accomplishments, and the most important thing is that this book gives hope and encouragement to all of my readers that other Aspergers can also overcome their obstacles.

Reader comments for Robert Sanders' book:

"This book is a remarkable insight into the thoughts and personality, even the mind, of someone who looks at the world through a different set of lenses than most of us do. Robert, you have done a great service for others. Beyond whatever therapeutic value writing it had for you, think of how valuable the insights you provide, about living with Asperger's syndrome and ultimately overcoming it, will be to others with the condition, to family and care-givers, and to medical and psychological professionals."

Robert R. Reichenbach
Basking Ridge, New Jersey, March 2003

"Every now and then you may be lucky to come across a work such as this. It's a very honest, sometimes painfully honest account of one man's struggle to live in a world that is almost too alien to bear. The insights into the journey of overcoming Asperger's syndrome, sometimes sublime into the spiritual . . . to the very ordinary, are an inspiration. This is a must read! Whether your interest is professional or just understanding the human condition. You really do feel that you are walking with him every step of the way."

Martin A. Enticknap, (good friend and literary contact)
Isle of Sanday, Orkney Islands, Scotland, January 2003

"Temple Grandin gave us the poignant metaphor – *'an anthropologist on Mars.'* In this book, Robert Sanders brings us to the archeological dig!"

Diane Twachtman-Cullen, Ph.D.(executive director, ADDCON Center)
Higganum, Connecticut, October 2003

"Your new book is so fascinating! What a saga of self revelation and achievement it truly is."

Gertrude Little
Aiken, South Carolina, October 2002

"Your book is unique because your personal experiences and insights are most valuable in allowing families to have an intimate first person view of this condition. It departs from the common dry academic recitations that so many students of the subject review."

Paul J. Hletko, MD FAAP
Georgetown, South Carolina, October 2002

"This book should be an enormous source of information, comfort, reassurance, and inspriation to those with Asperger's syndrome and equally to their families. It should become part of every pediatrician's library because it is an invaluable source of information by one who has lived successfully with this condition."

Eric M. Chazen, MD (Robert's childhood pediatrician)
Nashville, Tennessee, January 2003

"Through this unusually fascinating and insightful look into how a person with Asperger's syndrome perceives his interactions with others, Robert shows – piece by hard-earned piece – how he continues to expand into, and make greater sense of the world around him. Anyone interested in learning more about life on the autism spectrum should read this book."

Stephen Shore (person with Asperger's syndrome)
Boston, Massachusetts, August 2004

"What a remarkable story and what good and clear writing! I get a clear picture of what it is like to be inside your thinking. Robert, you have done a wonderful thing recording your life's experiences. Your writing is so vivid, so honest and non withholding. It will mean so much to parents and others with similar patterns of thought."

Clifton Meador, MD
Brentwood, Tennessee, November 2002

"Robert Sanders is a gentleman with remarkable intelligence and insight. He uses these abilities to explain the world from his perspective. His experiences and wisdom will be of benefit to parents, professionals, and people with Asperger's syndrome."

Tony Attwood, Ph.D. (worldwide lecturer on autism)
Brisbane, Queensland, Australia, July 2004

"By reading your book, I was able to gain a better perspective on the inner workings of persons who live with traits of Asperger's syndrome. It is my hope that I will be a better school psychologist after reading your compilation of very personal and insightful experiences. I can say that your book was one of the most interesting autobiographical stories I have ever had the privilege to read."

Allison S. Gunne (licensed psychological examiner)
Normandy, Tennessee, April 2003

"Up to now, most of the materials I have read on this matter have been written from clinical, diagnostic perspectives. I think it is very hard for people, even highly trained professionals, to grasp the perspective of the affected person. However, your vivid descriptions have provided a most relatable experience. Your very own words are quite powerful and lead the reader to honestly feel the bittersweet reality of your struggle."

Jo VerMulm, (parent of an autistic child)
Murfreesboro, Tennessee, October 2002

"I read your book with great pleasure and interest. It is a marvelous book of which you should be justly proud."

Tony Badger (university professor)
Cambridge, England, April 2003

"Your book is a remarkable achievement for which you are to be congratulated. In your particular case, you are a loner. It is a complex book which requires the maximum level of concentration to appreciate the message."

Gordon W. Trinca MD, (paediatric surgeon and family friend)
Melbourne, Victoria, Australia, March 2003

"Sharing your insights and tremendous accomplishments are uplifting and can be a great source of encouragement to others."

Helen Alford, (RN and social worker)
Nashville, Tennessee, December 2002

"I found your detailed accounts of personal experiences most revealing and enlightening. I want you to know that I learned a great deal about autism and Asperger's syndrome from your book. Thank you for sharing some of your inner-most thoughts, opinions and feelings about people, social encounters, and interpersonal relationships."

Thomas F. Hartley Murfreesboro, Tennessee, October 2002

"I enjoyed reading your latest book. You certainly have a lot of interesting insights and you are to be complimented for your efforts to shed light on Asperger's. I enjoyed seeing the old bike-riding picture from so many years ago. It brought back some great memories!"

Lewis Collins (good friend since early childhood)
Wellesley, Massachusetts, April 2003

"It is very impressive that you have such insight into your own problems, and that you so generously and honestly share the difficulties you have experienced relating to Asperger's syndrome. Your willingness to face these problems has enabled you to work toward overcoming them."
Frances W. Dean
Murfreesboro, Tennessee, November 2002

"Your book challenges the reader to understand your struggle with Asperger's syndrome and to reflect upon how tolerant he or she is regarding differences in others. I believe that your intriguing, touching, and sometimes humorous tale will be an invaluable resource for students in a variety of academic settings, including psychology and ethics."
Christopher McCord, PhD, (Associate Professor of Philosophy)
Kirkwood Community College
Cedar Rapids, Iowa, March 2003

"Your efforts to share your life's experiences are very worthwhile. Friends will benefit from the clarity and openness in your book."
Carol & Bob Treen
New Hampshire, December 2002

"I found your book not just interesting and instructive, but positively riveting! I've learned so much!
Anne Marie Shellness, (child safety seat advocate)
Winston-Salem, North Carolina, December 2002

"Robert, you have overcome so much, and now with this book, you will be able to help others in similar situations, giving them inspiration and hope for their future. You have written something that can help others and enable them to live fuller lives."
Peggy O. Mason
Murfreesboro, Tennessee, October 2002

"Your latest book is so readable. It was hard to put down. I spent two nights reading, then I have read parts of it again and again. I truly feel that it is a good resource for people who have similar conditions. However, the greatest value is for people who need to realize that triumphs come for those who have the patience to keep following their dreams."
Sarah Malone   Murfreesboro, Tennessee, October 2002

APPENDIX

FOOD ADDITIVES AND HEAVY METALS

Though I'm not an expert on this subject, I think it is important to include this material in my book. I believe some of it is pertinent to autism, and perhaps some of my readers will likely find the following pages helpful to them. Besides, I have some excerpts from my science fiction novels.

Heavy Metal Poisoning

I think food additives and/or heavy metal poisoning cause a considerable number of cases of autism. Some behavior characteristics observed in autistics parallel that observed in people suffering from heavy metal toxicity. Brain chemistry is very important, and not only can an imbalance be caused by certain contaminants, it can also be caused by eating the wrong types of foods. I recommend that anyone who is autistic be checked for heavy metal poisoning and chemical imbalances. I have heard that more than 50% of hyperactive children with learning disabilities, who are on Ritalin® by the way, actually have heavy metal poisoning!

Chelation therapy, either oral or intravenous, can be administered to clear out excess heavy metal contaminants, such as lead, mercury, aluminum, arsenic, copper, cadmium, and other heavy metals.

Lead (Pb) is a soft malleable grey colored metal, and it causes significant health problems at relatively low exposures. It harms the human nervous system, reduces the production of red blood cells, harms the kidneys, the reproductive system, and alters behavior. It remains in the blood stream for short periods of time, and then it settles in the bones and teeth, taking the place of calcium. I believe lead also causes chronic diseases.

Lead poisoning is caused by a variety of sources. Lead was used in house paints for many years, but was banned in those products in the 1970s. Lead was used in regular gasoline in the United States until the summer of 1995, and in Mexico until the autumn of 1997. Even today, many nations still use leaded gasolines, including many nations in Europe! Burning leaded fuels in millions of automobiles spews literally millions of tons of exhaust, including lead into the atmosphere! Lead is still used in car batteries, ammunition, and lead solder. Lead poisoning is also caused by drinking water from houses where plumbing was installed using lead solder!

Mercury (Hg) is a heavy, silver/white liquid at room temperature. It is very toxic indeed, more so than lead. Mercury is used in thermometers, pesticides, pharmaceutical preparations, some dental fillings, and certain switches and lamps. Mercury poisoning and autism have remarkably similar symptoms, such as: self injurious behavior, social withdrawal, lack of eye contact and facial expressions, repetitive behaviors, and hyper-sensitivity to certain noises and touch.

One of the main sources of exposure (which causes poisoning) comes from mercury amalgam tooth fillings, which as far as I'm concerned should never be installed by dentists! There are other materials such as white composite that work very well and are NOT poisonous. While OSHA has classified dental amalgam as toxic waste, the American Dental Association thinks differently, that mercury amalgam is perfectly safe while it is in your mouth, and also in the mouths of children! This causes an on-going and constant source of exposure 24 hours a day, 365 days a year, due to chewing and the fact that mercury vapor leaks continually from the fillings. Recognizing how toxic mercury really is, the practice of installing mercury amalgam dental fillings is atrocious to say the least! Mercury has NO place in our mouths.

Mercury poisoning also comes, seriously, from pharmaceutical shots and vaccines! Thimerosal is a mercury containing preservative in many shots. That also is atrocious to say the least!

Aluminum (Al) is the third most abundant metal in the Earth's crust, and it is used in a surprisingly wide variety of products, such as cookware, aluminum foil, antacids, buffered aspirins, and some vaccines. Aluminum is even added to salt itself as an anticaking agent. Utility districts, in addition to adding Sodium Fluoride to the drinking water, also add aluminum.

These different exposures can cause aluminum poisoning, and let's not forget about Aluminum Chlorohydrate, which is used in anti-perspirant deodorants. Aluminum poisoning also comes from eating foods utilizing baking powder, such as Sodium Aluminum Phosphate, and Calcium Aluminum Phosphate! As a result, biscuits, pancakes, and waffles are excellent sources of aluminum. Read the ingredients on pancake mixes before buying them. Most of them are very faithful users of Sodium Aluminum Phosphate, instead of Monocalcium Phosphate. Please be aware that there are, thankfully, some brands with more natural ingredients and most importantly without aluminum!

Sodium Aluminium Phosphate is listed in *The New Additive Code Breaker*, a guidebook used in Australia and New Zealand and written in England by Maurice Hanssen and Jill Marsden. It states:

"Sodium aluminium phosphate has been considered by the toxicological committees on the basis of its aluminium rather than its phosphate component. Aluminium poses a problem because of the evidence that an accumulation of it in the cells of the nervous system could be potentially toxic, and responsible for Parkinson-type diseases and senile dementia."

Sodium Aluminium Phosphate is not permitted in foods in the countries of Australia and New Zealand.

(In British Commonwealth countries, aluminum is spelled aluminium.)

There are other toxic heavy metals that cause health problems. Among them are Arsenic (As), Antimony (Sb), Cadmium (Cd), Thallium (Tl), and even Copper (Cu) and Nickel (Ni). For further reading, please refer to an excellent article that came out in the May-June 2001 issue of *Autism Asperger's Digest Magazine*. There is also plenty of other literature about heavy metals, including Internet web sites.

A few years ago, while writing my 3rd science fiction novel: *Heritage Findings from Atlantis*, I decided to write some comments about lead in particular, from the perspective of the residents of the city of Zantaayer on a planet around the star Al Nitak. Below is the excerpt.

*   *   *

". . . scandal is only a moderate one compared to others."

"Such as what?" Fraxino asked.

"Such as nuclear power production and the high risk and dangers from that, not to mention possible harmful radiation exposure . . . and the element lead being added to Earth's fossil fuels for driving their automobiles and other vehicles . . . atrocious, that is. I tell you!"

"At least here on our world, we have hydrogen," said Rinto.

"And we can count our blessings on that one, sons," Glecko stated. "Earth's fuel companies *know* we can! Lead is extremely bad for living beings and is known for dulling intelligence, in addition to promoting chronic diseases because it accumulates within the body's tissues. It's a toxin which has no business *ever* being put into automobile fuels!"

"That really is appalling!" Tecoloteh declared. "We had no idea Earth's people would do anything so ridiculous!"

"They do," Rinto told Latorna and Tecoloteh.

"Special interest groups and other factions control a lot of Earth's scandals," Glecko went on, "and don't forget to consider that other star systems may be behind some of it, using Earth's people as test subjects for long term studies. Design your project crystals accordingly, and we'll make this galaxy a better place to live after all."

"Right on, Dad!" Fraxino declared.

"Dad, with the way we grow those crystals," said Rinto, "we'll have every one of those scandals squelched and abolished!"

"That's your intelligent genius at work, sons," their father commended them. "With your two friends from Atlantis, I'm sure you'll do fine work."

They continued talking and soon finished breakfast.

*   *   *

Even though some of what I wrote is speculation, it does make a statement and gets the message across to my readers the absurdity of the use of lead here on our world Earth!

Food Additives

In addition to heavy metals, there are many food additives that are bad for you, and food manufacturers are faithfully given free reign to put them in food products to their heart's content! Around 90% of all cereals have BHT: Butylated Hydroxytoluene, a seriously bad food additive and preservative known to cause sterility in lab animals!

Referring to *The New Additive Code Breaker*, BHT does not occur in nature and is derived synthetically from p-cresol and isobutylene. It was developed initially around 1947 as an antioxidant for use with petroleum and rubber products.

BHA: Butylated Hydroxyanisole, is another nasty chemical used mostly for preserving cooking oils. It also doesn't occur in nature, and it is derived from a mixture of 2- and 3-tert-butyl-4-methoxy-phenol, prepared from p-methoxyphenol and isobutene.

In a food additive book called *Eater's Digest*, it states that BHA and BHT "should be barred from food; safe alternatives are available."

TBHQ: tert-Butylhydroquinone has a worse report. It is derived from petroleum. Small amounts of TBHQ have caused vomiting, nausea, ringing in the ears, delirium, suffocating feelings, and collapse! TBHQ is used as a preservative in certain foods, such as pies, some types of crackers, and even some types of loaf bread!

MSG: Monosodium Glutamate is very bad indeed, with many people having severe adverse allergic reactions to foods that contain it. Among them are numbness in the neck, hands, and chest, tightness in the jaw, vice like headaches, and temporary paralysis. In laboratory animals, MSG has caused damage to brain cells. Some food companies are "ashamed" that they put MSG in their foods, so they hide the fact that they put it in, by calling it other names such as "Hydrolyzed Vegetable Protein," "Autolyzed Yeast," and "Natural Flavoring."

For further reading about food additives, check various food additive codebooks and handbooks.

As far as foods are concerned, read the ingredients on all food labels, and just because it's clear of preservatives does not guarantee that it will *still* be clear the next year. Companies are bad about slipping additives in without your realizing it. Be consistent about continually checking food labels and ingredients.

I also recommend buying organically grown foods and 100% natural foods whenever possible.

Basically, closely monitoring food intake in the right proportions can really help a person achieve a closer sense of stability.

Breads are very bad about having food additives and preservatives such as Calcium Propionate, TBHQ, and lots of dough conditioners and emulsifiers such as Ethoxylated Mono- and di-glycerides and Sodium Stearoyl-lactylate, Potassium Bromate, and more still. Some of these cause migraine headaches and tightness in the chest, anxiety, and other reactions!

Nearly all soft drinks have 1/1000 (0.1%) Sodium Benzoate, another preservative and headache causer, not to mention beer and wine containing that and/or Sodium Bisulfite, which certainly contribute to hangovers . . . not just the alcohol!

People think I'm crazy and that I'm from Mars because I'm always so aware of foods, and I've been a stickler for reading ingredients in foods ever since I was age ten. If everyone were like me, food additive manufacturers would soon be out of business, and what a great day that would be for all of us! Why don't they send their products and byproducts of production to toxic waste dumpsites, or better yet send them to the Sun, instead of slipping them in our foods!

I have also pulled an excerpt from my 3rd novel: *Heritage Findings from Atlantis*. This one is about MSG in particular.

*   *   *

"Excellent work, sons," their father complimented. "Were your Atlantean friends of help?"

"Oh yeah," Rinto answered. "They've got a better handle on this than we do."

"Really?" Glecko asked with surprise.

"They really are whizzes when it comes to growing crystals," Fraxino stated.

"Well, I suppose that would make sense," Glecko admitted. "After all, they are original Atlanteans, who certainly know the art."

After looking over the array, they walked back in the house again. They ate some breakfast. Glecko started reading Zantaayer's morning newspaper.

"Land sakes! Another scandal from planet Earth!" he declared.

"What's it about this time?" Rinto asked his father.

"This report has to do with Earth's use of MSG, known as Monosodium Glutamate, another byproduct of manufacturing. Instead of disposing of it properly by sending it to the Sun, food and drug companies across planet Earth have been paid under the table to approve the nasty chemical to enhance food flavor, to the point that they don't even list it on the ingredients of food products that contain it."

"How can they get away with that?" Fraxino wanted to know.

"They use clever cover-up names like: Natural Flavoring, Autolyzed Yeast, and Hydrolyzed Vegetable Protein, of which MSG is a considerable part of each one of those."

"Dad, how scandalous do they get, down there on planet Earth?!" Rinto declared.

"I'm telling you!" Glecko agreed. "The report goes on to say that the use of MSG is at an all-time high, as a result."

"How awful!" Fraxino exclaimed.

"The main driving force behind it is intelligence suppression. MSG is a nasty chemical and has no business ever being added to food products. It causes headaches, and for those more allergic to it, it causes paralysis for up to hours and disarms certain people of their senses and mental capacity."

"Golly! Why don't they ban the stupid chemical?" Fraxino asked his father.

"Because chief administrations have been paid under the table," Glecko simply stated. "It's just one more part of the intelligence suppression study driven by unscrupulous factions that need to be halted. Let's just hope the arrays you four have built and grown do the trick."

"Thanks, Dad. We'll hope for the best," said Rinto.

"Of course, here on our world, as you know," Glecko pointed out, "nasty chemical byproducts like MSG are flown *straight* to Al Nitak, a far superior incinerator than what this world has to offer."

"Right on, Dad!" said Fraxino.

"And why can't Earth capture that bright idea?" Rinto asked his father.

"I wish they would, sons."

*   *   *

Some of what I wrote about MSG is likely speculation, but it is true that for many people, it causes headaches, and for those more allergic to it, it causes paralysis for up to hours and disarms certain people of their senses and mental capacity. On a TV report/interview several years ago, I saw some people interviewed who complained of suffering from those symptoms. The same news story documentary also said that the use of MSG in food is at an all-time high! Personally I think MSG has no place in human foods, and it should be banned entirely, considering the severe adverse reactions it causes in many people.

*   *   *

Robert Sanders at Spectacle Lake, Alpine Lakes Wilderness in Washington, July 1985

Annotated References

If you wish to learn more about autism and Asperger's syndrome, the following publications and materials are recommended:

Asperger, Hans and Uta Frith, *Autism and Asperger's Syndrome*, Cambridge University Press, Cambridge, England, 1991

Increasing numbers of eccentric individuals intellectually gifted, but mentally handicapped, are being recognized as having Asperger's syndrome. They suffer from a form of autism, but they can compensate. Foremost experts in the field discuss diagnostic criteria. This book is richly illustrated with examples, including clinical and personal accounts.

Attwood, Anthony and Liane Holliday Willey (video); *Crossing the Bridge*; published by Starfish Specialty Press, Higganum, Connecticut (www.starfishpress.com)

Crossing the Bridge presents Asperger's syndrome through the eyes of Liane Holliday Willey. Tony interviews Liane as they discuss her struggles and triumphs. Aspergers are not defective, but are different thinkers who have wonderful traits for humanity.

Attwood, Tony, Ph.D., *Asperger's Syndrome: A Guide for Parents and Professionals*, Jessica Kingsley Publishers, London, England, 1998

This is a guidebook that will assist parents and professionals with the identification, treatment, and care of children and adults with Asperger's syndrome. It provides descriptions and analyses of unusual characteristics of the syndrome and practical strategies to reduce those that are most outstanding or debilitating. It brings together the most relevant and useful information on Asperger's syndrome, including some case studies.

Autism Asperger's Digest Magazine; Veronica Zysk, Editor-in-Chief; published by Future Horizons, Inc., Arlington, Texas (www.futurehorizons -autism.com)

This is a magazine that specializes in helpful and insightful articles pertaining to autism and Asperger's syndrome. Also included in each issue are several excerpts from other autism related books.

Autism Spectrum Quarterly (magazine); Diane Twachtman-Cullen, Ph.D., Editor-in-Chief and Liane Holliday Willey, Ed.D., Senior Editor; published by Starfish Specialty Press, Higganum, Connecticut; (www.ASQuarterly.com).

This "mega journal" combines the readibility and interest of a magazine with the substance and depth of a professional journal. You'll find articles by, for, and about individuals with ASD, as well as exciting, user-friendly information from the world of research.

Bashe, Patricia Romanowski and Barbara L. Kirby and Tony Attwood (Foreword), *The Oasis Guide to Asperger Syndrome: Advice, Support, Insight, and Inspiration*, Crown Publishers, New York, New York, 2001

This inspiring book offers sound advice, comforting support, and remarkable insights with such clarity of purpose, profound honesty, and depth of meaning. It is destined to become a classic in its genre.

Grandin, Temple Ph.D., *Thinking in Pictures and Other Reports from My Life with Autism*, Doubleday, New York, New York, 1995

Temple Grandin, Ph.D. is a gifted animal scientist who designs livestock handling facilities and lectures widely on autism. She thinks, feels, and experiences the world in ways different from most of us. This is a document of an extraordinary person who tells us how she breached the boundaries of autism to function in the outside world.

Ledgin, Norm, comments by Temple Grandin, Ph.D., *Diagnosing Jefferson: Evidence of a Condition that Guided His Beliefs, Behavior, and Personal Associations*, Future Horizons, Inc., Arlington, Texas, 2000

This book was written by a historian who has a son with Asperger's syndrome. Ledgin examines one of the most brilliant U.S. presidents, Thomas Jefferson and his many behaviors that match traits and characteristics of Asperger's syndrome. This book gives fascinating insight into the multiple factors that contribute to this diagnosis.

Sacks, Oliver, *An Anthropologist on Mars, Seven Paradoxical Tales*, Alfred A. Knopf, New York, New York, 1995

In this book, Dr. Sacks presents seven case studies and stories of interesting people in the autism spectrum, including Temple Grandin.

Shore, Stephen, *Beyond the Wall, Personal Experiences with Autism and Asperger Syndrome*, 2nd edition, Autism Asperger Publishing Co., Shawnee Mission, Kansas, 2003

Much more than a typical autobiography, this book examines sensory issues and accommodating children in the public schools. Challenges faced by adolescents and adults, such as higher education, relationships, employment as well as self-advocacy and disclosure are also discussed.

Shore, Stephen (editor), *Ask and Tell, Self-advocacy and Disclosure for People on the Autism Spectrum*, Autism Asperger Publishing Co., Shawnee Mission, Kansas, 2004

Filling a gap in the literature of self-advocacy and disclosure for people with autism, all contributions from the cover art, foreword (by Temple Grandin), and the chapters are by people on the autism spectrum. Some of the areas include communicating and connecting with others, a graduated six-stage procedure for teaching self-advocacy and disclosure to others, using the IEP for developing these skills, dealing with social service agencies, building alliances and community identity, and numerous ways of disclosing and self-advocating to others.

Willey, Liane Holliday, Luke Jackson, *Asperger Syndrome in Adolescence: Living with the Ups, the Downs and Things in Between*, Jessica Kingsley Publishers, London, England, 2003

With ideas from parents, people on the ASD spectrum and professionals, this book examines real and tough issues affecting adolescents with Asperger's syndrome. Sexuality, depression, friendships, sensory integration issues, cognitive behavior therapy, and self-acceptance are among the topics discussed.

Willey, Liane Holliday, *Asperger Syndrome in the Family: Redefining Normal*, Jessica Kingsley Publishers, London, England, 2001

In *Asperger Syndrome in the Family*, Willey explores the effects of Asperger's syndrome on the family. Through her personal story, Willey frankly discusses the challenges a family faces, suggestions for how the family can work together, and how each member can support the other.

Willey, Liane Holliday, Tony Attwood, *Pretending to Be Normal*, Jessica Kingsley Publishers, London, England, 1999

Pretending to be Normal is an autobiographical story of a wife and mother of three who, after years of unanswered questions and misdiagnoses, learned that she had Asperger's syndrome. The book includes Willey's struggles, successes, intervention tips, and a series of substantial appendices, which provide helpful ideas that are based on Willey's own experiences, for a range of situations.

Additional References

The following listings refer to selected books, magazine articles, and newspaper articles, even TV documentaries, that were brought to my attention as I wrote this book. Of course, there are plenty of other books and articles pertaining to autism and Asperger's syndrome, which can be found in libraries or through search engines of various web sites on the *Internet*.

"A Neurologist's Notebook: An Anthropologist on Mars," by Oliver Sacks, *The New Yorker Magazine*, New York, New York, 27 December, 1993, pages 106-125

Beers, Clifford Whittingham, *A Mind That Found Itself: an Autobiography*, Doubleday, New York, New York, 1953, first published in 1908

"Brain Chemicals May Point Toward Cause of Autism," *The Tennessean*, Nashville, Tennesseee, 4 May, 2000, Section A, page 8

Extreme Health, *Oral Chelation and Age-Less Formula*, Alamo, California
Extreme Health, *Heavy Metal Toxicity*, Alamo, California
(For more information, see http://www.extremehealthus.com)

Hanssen, Maurice with Jill Marsden, *The New Additive Code Breaker*, Lothian Publishing Company Pty Ltd., Melbourne, Victoria, Australia, 1989

"Heavy Metals," *Autism Asperger's Digest Magazine*, Future Horizons, Inc., Arlington, Texas, May-June 2002, pages 12-18

Jacobsen, Michael F., *Eater's Digest, The Consumer's Factbook of Food Additives*, Doubleday Anchor Books, Garden City, New Jersey, 1972

Mindell, Earl, *Unsafe at Any Meal*, Warner Books, New York, New York, 1987

Murphy, Dr. Joseph, *The Power of Your Subconscious Mind*, Prentice Hall, Englewood Cliffs, New Jersey, 1963

"Number of Kids, Teens with Disabilities Rises," by D'Vera Cohn, *The Washington Post*; printed in *The Tennessean*, 6 July, 2002, section A, page 13

Talbot, Michael, *The Holographic Universe*, Harper Collins Publishers, New York, New York, 1992

"The Secrets of Autism," *Time Magazine*, Time, Inc. New York, New York, 6 May, 2002, pages 46-56

"Understanding Autism," (re: toxic metals, biochemical imbalances in the brain), by William Walsh, Pfeiffer Institute, *McNeil Lehrer News Hour*, PBS TV, 24 August, 2001.

Other books by Armstrong Valley Publishing Co.

These books are print-on-demand titles available for order through Ingram Book Company or also through http://www.Amazon.com.

Mission of the Galactic Salesman
ISBN: 1-886371-35-0, (published 1996, subsidiary of Eggman Publishing) (to be placed back in print with ISBN: 1-928798-04-7)
written by Robert S. Sanders, Jr.

   A galactic salesman has a mission to link Earth's telephone network with other star systems. The people of his home planet in the Sirius B star system have lost contact with their fellow Sirians now residing on Earth as human beings. To re-establish contact, he makes a deal with eight teenagers, who are juniors in high school, and together they build a galactic communications device. The teenagers benefit from the deal by receiving the gift of transport by thought, and they have adventures to different places on Earth and also to other star systems. They enjoy travelling and exploring and learn a considerable amount about life on other planets and also learn about some of Earth's past history and how it came to be. Readers interested in technical matters, travelling, flora and fauna, and speculation about the origin of modern humans will find this book of interest. Suggested target audience: teen/young adult.

Mission Beyond the Ice Cave: Atlantis-Mexico-Zotola
ISBN: 1-928798-00-4, published 1999
written by Robert S. Sanders, Jr.

   In this sequel to *Mission of the Galactic Salesman*, a group of teenagers visit an ice cave in Antarctica, where they meet two young lively fellows, Rinto and Fraxino, having arrived in their Velosa cruiser craft from a planet around the star Al Nitak in the Orion star system. Descendants of the people of Atlantis, they are visiting Antarctica to research their Atlantean heritage. They travel home with them in their vehicle-craft to a land they call Zotola. Rinto and Fraxino live in a city called Zantaayer, Zotola, a beautiful clean city nestled within the Ciruclar Mountains. Their society is on the same level of technological advancement as their cousins on Earth.

   While visiting Zotola, they discover a buried crate of holographic metal plates in an ancient galactic dumpsite. Tom, the galactic salesman comes forth and offers another mission. The Orion star system needs to be added to their telephone system, and communication is mysteriously blocked from Earth. He sends them to the mountains of northern Mexico. Can the teenagers with the help of their new friends from Zotola pinpoint the problem and clear the mysterious block?

Discover with them what the walls of the ice cave in Antarctica contain. Find out what information the holographic plates reveal when they examine them. Venture with them as they investigate some ancient cliff paintings in Mexico, left by the people of Atlantis, and what significant coincidences they reveal.

Heritage Findings from Atlantis
ISBN: 1-928798-01-2, published 2000
written by Robert S. Sanders, Jr.

This novel is the continuation of *Mission Beyond the Ice Cave: Atlantis-Mexico-Zotola*, and is the third novel of the Galactic Salesman trilogy. Having completed their mission in Mexico by eliminating the mysterious communications block, the teenagers return to Al Nitak in the Orion star system with their lively friends, Rinto, Fraxino, and Chispo in their Velosa cruiser craft. They examine more holographic plates, revisit the ancient galactic dump site, and find another bronze crate filled with . . .

Tom the galactic salesman comes forth with yet another mission, this one the grandest of them all. He sends the characters to the high mountain reaches of remote northern Alaska, where the Galactic Federation is overseeing a hugh galactic station project connecting literally millions of Earth's telephone numbers. By chance, they find 5 frozen crates of time-frozen bodies . . . from Atlantis! Can they revive them?

Find out the true reasons for the galactic dump site and why the holographic plates were dumped there. Discover more revelations about trees and plants, from sacred stories, holographic plates, and the Atlanteans. Venture with them as they help Tom and his crew in building the galactic station in Alaska, what it features, from adventures, to time travel, and how it . . .

GALACTIC SALESMAN TRILOGY SYNOPSIS
a Summary and Synopsis of the 3 Science Fiction Novels:
1) Mission of the Galactic Salesman, 2) Mission Beyond the Ice Cave: Atlantis-Mexico-Zotola, and 3) Heritage Findings from Atlantis
ISBN: 1-928798-10-1, published 2003
written by Robert S. Sanders, Jr.

Welcome to the galactic salesman science fiction trilogy, a great set of novels with fun and wholesome adventure, which promote peace, travel, friendship and communication, NOT galactic wars and battles, like so many other science fiction novels.

It all begins when a galactic salesman has a mission to link Earth's telephone network with his home star system and other star systems, as well. His real name is Tomarius (Tom), and he makes a deal with a group of teenagers, Robert Joslin and his friends, grants them the gift of transport by thought, and together they build a galactic communications device in the corner of the Joslin's woods on their farm in Tennessee.

Robert and his friends enjoy numerous adventures. With their gift of transport, they travel far and wide to many places, including other star systems.

In the sequel, they meet some lively young fellows: Rinto, Fraxino, and Chispo. They are descendants from Atlantis and are living in the Orion star system. Robert and his friends go home with them and spend a lot of time there, and together they help Tom, the galactic salesman with another mission, to go to the mountains of northern Mexico and clear a mysterious communications block between Earth and the Orion system.

All of this is just a practice run for the grandest project of them all, a major galactic station involving millions of Earth's telephone numbers, to be built high up in the mountains of northern Alaska. During the project, they unearth five bronze crates, each containing a time frozen body . . . from Atlantis!

They revive them. Discover what information and insights the Atlanteans have to offer.

Join Robert and his friends on their travels, and venture with them as they help Tom and his crew in building the galactic station in Alaska, what it features, from adventures, to time travel, and how it . . .

Note: This is a Summary and Synopsis, which is approximately 10% the size of the full length novels.

Walking Between Worlds: a novel of an American in Mexico
ISBN: 1-928798-02-0, published 2001
written by pen name: Robert Alquzok

In this fiction novel based on a true story, an American fellow from Tennessee has an interest in Mexico, learning the language and culture, investigating ancient cliff paintings, exploring, and travelling. Roland

Jocelyn makes repeated trips over a period of several years to a small quaint town in northern Mexico called Bustamante, Nuevo León, situated at the foot of a beautiful mountain range, which includes the Lion's Head Mountain.

It is very rare for an American, with no Mexican roots, to visit and spend considerable time in a small town in Mexico. Roland enjoys numerous adventures, both in town and in the mountains, and he enjoys making friends, some of them becoming so special that they influence him to visit Bustamante more frequently.

However, Roland also makes some enemies, even though he never does anything intentionally wrong, and he gets himself into some danger at times. Read about the surprises, adventures, and malicious gossip that a small town can offer, from having a great time enjoying friends to being viciously run off, including shrewd tactics involving the police!

Join Roland in his adventures as he battles rumors, gossip, and the subtle forces of evil in efforts to continue his favorite friendships in that town. Read about misunderstandings and weird experiences . . . for his romantic interests in a young woman. Can he overcome the obstacles? Can he successfully establish a good reputation among the locals?

With the recent influx of Mexicans into American society, this important novel portrays an example of Mexican-American relations and culture.

EXODUS: the Dolph/in Saga
ISBN: 1-928798-35-7, published July 1999
written by Martin A. Enticknap, © 1990-1999

This is a highly original, enchanting story designed to capture the reader's imagination. In the long ago past, dolphins and man could likely have had a shared existence. Mr. Enticknap has brilliantly captured an essense of truth about the dolphins' long ago past, their way of life (including family life and love stories), and he has brought their stories to reality in this novel he has written. You will find yourself enchanted by something magically different, and you will never look at dolphins and whales in quite the same way again. An outstanding work of genius, this novel is an excellent resource for helping people gain a broader under- standing of their fellow beings. As we enter the new millennium and a new era, it's very important for the human race to realize the importance that there are other sentient beings here on Earth and what they have to offer us.

A LEGEND IS BORN.........

A NEW VISION IN THE BIRTH OF A RACE
BEYOND EVEN HISTORY -
35 MILLION YEARS AGO THE FUTURE WAS CREATED.
THEIR STORY IS OURS - THEIR HOPE IS A GIFT WHICH WE
IGNORE AT OUR PERIL.
THEY SPEAK - WE DO NOT HEAR
BECAUSE WE DARE NOT LISTEN.
THE ANCIENT GREEKS HONOURED THEM;
KILLING THEM WAS PUNISHABLE BY DEATH.
THE IROQUOIS PEOPLE ALSO SAW THEM DIFFERENTLY AND
SPOKE OF THEIR WAY.
THEY WITNESSED OUR BIRTH AS A RACE, BUT NOW WE NO
LONGER SEE THEM AND THEY DIE IN THEIR THOUSANDS.
AS OUR NEW AGE BEGINS
IT'S TIME FOR THEIR LEGACY TO BE REALISED.
YOU'VE BEEN INVITED AND WATER-TIME IS OPEN TO
ALL............

THIS IS THEIR BEGINNING............

Arc of the Ancients and Other Poetry, a Collection
ISBN: 1-928798-34-9, published March 2003
written by Martin A. Enticknap, © 1994-2003
This is a compilation of many insightful and soul stirring poems, written by Martin A. Enticknap. The book contains a myriad of poems and other writings, which you can dip into whenever you want to touch your soul with their evocative magic, with something special and very different. Listen to their harmonies and their wisdom with your spirit and share some moments in time with the poet. Sometimes you'll find your perceptions challenged, sometimes you'll feel inspired, sometimes you'll be enchanted, sometimes you'll be uplifted, sometimes you'll feel the wisdom, sometimes you'll share a precious moment, sometimes you'll feel spiritual, sometimes you'll be moved to tears, and sometimes you'll laugh, but you'll not remain untouched. These poems are unique and of original ideas. There are also some short stories and compositions containing Mr. Enticknap's brilliant philosophy on various subjects.

The following books are available directly from Robert S. Sanders, Jr. They may also be ordered at retail price directly from Ingram Book Company of LaVergne, Tennessee, or from www.Amazon.com and www.Amazon.co.uk .

ORDER FORM

Please send me:		quantity	amount
On My Own Terms: My Journey with Asperger's	@$19.95	_____	$_____
En Mis Propios Términos: Mi Jornada con Asperger's	@$19.95	_____	$_____
Overcoming Asperger's: Personal Experience & Insight	@$17.95	_____	$_____
Mission of the Galactic Salesman *special reduced price*	@$12.00	_____	$_____
Mission Beyond the Ice Cave: Atlantis-Mexico-Zotola	@$15.95	_____	$_____
Heritage Findings from Atlantis	@$15.95	_____	$_____
Galactic Salesman Trilogy Synopsis	@$ 9.95	_____	$_____
Walking Between Worlds:			
a novel of an American in Mexico	@$19.95	_____	$_____
EXODUS: the Dolph/in Saga (by Martin Enticknap)	@$16.50	_____	$_____
Arc of the Ancients and other Poetry (by Martin Enticknap)	@$14.95	_____	$_____
Tennessee residents add 9.25% sales tax to subtotal			$_____
– Out of state orders, NO sales tax –			$ 0000
Plus shipping and handling for one book			
(surface rates: $3.00 within USA, $6.00 foreign)			$_____
Plus shipping and handling for each additional book			
(surface rates: $2.00 within USA, $4.00 foreign)		_____	$_____

Please remit funds in US dollars.   Total enclosed $_____

Make checks or money orders payable to: **Robert S. Sanders, Jr.**

Discounts:
10 to 99 books: 10% off
100 or more books: 20% off

Books make great gifts and/or Christmas presents for your friends and relatives.

Send order to:
          Name_____
          Address_____
          City_____State_____Postal Code_____
Phone number _____

Send orders and checks payable to:
Robert S. Sanders, Jr.
P.O. Box 1275
Murfreesboro, TN 37133 USA
FAX: 615-893-2688

www.ingramcontent.com/pod-product-compliance
Lightning Source LLC
Chambersburg PA
CBHW030528020726
47494CB00004B/1271